Jayne-Marie was born in 1981 in Suffolk; but currently lives in Hertfordshire. She has a Diploma in Administrative & Secretarial Procedures, and works as a Personal Assistant for the UK's leading tyre retailer.

Aside from writing, her other passion in life is dance, belongs to a local school, and is an amateur member of the IDTA.

She knows she is a writer because she wakes each day knowing she must write. The magical effect of stringing words into one sequence or another never ceases to thrill her. Literary success of hers is thanks to a constant desire to write and her family's support.

THE DANCER'S GHOST

For my little sisters and best friends, Claire & Sarah xxxx

Acknowledgments

As always, thank you to my family and friends for their on-going support.

Thank you to Alexia Allman AdvDip THP(SHAP)MCRAh NLP Prac GQHP who helped me to understand hidden memories and the secrets and fascination of the world we enter when we fall asleep. Thanks to Martin Cutler and Lyndon Wainwright for their expertise on dance competitions of the fifties and sixties. The skating system of judges has been used only as far as suits the plot, but is based on the system of the day.

Extra special thanks to my highly talented and lovely dance teachers:

Trudina Youngs Fellow Hon's IDTA, who runs the superb Mirrors Dance School, and Marcia Magliari Dip DMT, authentic expert in Brazilian Carnival Samba . Thank you both, for helping me with the accuracy of the technique in my text. Dancing it in real life is quite different to writing it down; if I've made any mistakes then they are certainly not theirs! www.mirrorsdance.com www.edunara.com

Thank you to Ann Macreadie and Trudina Youngs for their much valued assistance with the final round of proof reading.

Jayne-Marie Barker

THE DANCER'S GHOST

AUSTIN MACAULEY
PUBLISHERS LTD.

ISBN 9781849633291

www.austinmacauley.com

First Published (2013)
Austin Macauley Publishers Ltd.
25 Canada Square
Canary Wharf
London
E14 5LB

Printed & Bound in Great Britain

By the same author:

Beneath The Daisies
ISBN 978 1 84963 073 3

Distant Shadows
ISBN 978 1 84963 176 1

For further information go to:
www.jaynemariebarker.com

twitter: @jaynemariebarke

Facebook author page

FOREWORD

Written by
Lyndon Wainwright

"Jayne-Marie Barker is a keen dancer, a successful author and in "The Dancer's Ghost" she has produced a fast moving, attention grabbing story of the lives of a couple of World Champion dancers, Joyce Capelli and Michael Sutton and their daughter, who was abducted shortly after birth. The story has two main themes nearly half a century apart. One follows the career in dance of Joyce and Michael, the domination of Joyce by her father, and Joyce's continuing efforts to find her missing daughter. She is haunted by the fear that her father might have had something to do with the abduction, all of which is compounded by the activities of a mysterious stranger.

The narrative moves along at a brisk pace revealing the tensions in Joyce and Michael's relationship and their dance training, as well as their success in the World's Championships. Joyce's life is dominated by her efforts to find her baby, and Michael's disinterest, resulting in disharmony between the couple. Joyce's own life seems threatened by the actions of a mysterious stranger.

The second section deals with Rebecca's life in the modern day, and the fact that she is subject to a murderous attack for motives known only by the assassin, but despite the horrendous ups and downs of the characters, the end, as in all good stories, is a happy one."

Lyndon Wainwright, Ballroom-Dance Expert, Teacher & Author.

http://lyndon-wainwright.co.uk/

PROLOGUE – 1959

It was the dead of night. The hospital was eerily quiet with a tranquillity that seemed to aid her mission. Wisps of cleaning fluid were assaulting her nostrils, making her feel edgy and reckless. A fleeting glance in all directions told her all she needed to know. It had to be now. She inhaled deeply and slipped through the ward doors, leaving them swinging soundlessly.

Cautiously she approached the selected cot and peered in over the sleeping baby. For the thousandth time she questioned her own madness, and for the thousandth time she told herself it was the only way. Nothing else had worked.

Francis looked into the melting darkness of the child's eyes as they fluttered into wakefulness. Did the child sense her presence? An instant connection, a bond...perhaps this time it was the right child...finally.

Her fingers began to tremble as she wrapped the pink blanket tighter around the sleeping baby, and lifted her clean from the warmth of the cot. Pressing her close she felt the warmth transcend into her own bosom; the texture soft and creamy, the fleecy material so easily warmed by the innocence it encapsulated.

In her heart she knew it was wrong, but it was too late now. She had done it again. Far too late to stop...a small cry pierced her conscience as she looked down at the baby, a splutter of sound, only just fathoming out how to echo effectively.

'Shh...' Francis whispered, snuggling the baby closer still, to stifle the impending doom of a single squawk. What was she going to do now? She had to leave, run away, and quickly.

Deftly she tip toed across the tiled ward, into the chilliness of the corridor, hugging the child and praying for her to doze safely back into the land of dreams. The land where she had spent most of her life, praying, hoping, wishing…

Her soft flat shoes were noiseless on the tiles, her long dark coat masking her against the shadows of the twilight hour. By now she knew how to blend.

The faint hum of activity drifted from a distance. Staff. She held her breath and closed her eyes momentarily, listening to the watery voices dissipate into silence. Sprinting the last stretch in blind abandon, she felt her heart flutter at the sight of the main doors. The home straight…

As she leant her back heavily against them, the hospital spanning out before her, she closed her eyes and prayed for forgiveness. Then, she slipped away into the night. A moment later, guilt followed her.

Chapter One – Modern Day; March

10th

'I'm very sorry Mrs Houseman,' the Police Inspector coughed and looked carefully at his highly polished black shoes. The coolness outside drifted uninvited through the slightly open window, its flimsy voile fluttering in the breeze. Rebecca held the duster in her hand as she watched him, a statue of ambivalence, the cleaning chores only partially completed at his unexpected knock.

Rebecca gestured towards the settee but the young Inspector shook his head determinedly and remained solid by the mantelpiece. He was young, new to the position, she surmised. Perhaps this was the first time he had had to deliver bad tidings. She froze. He was going to tell her something terrible. She gasped, put her hand to her mouth, her eyes wide, and sank into a chair. She waited, held her breath, her anxiety swelling inside her until she felt as if she were choking. Was it one of her children, Eliza, Samuel or Katherine, one of their partners, surely not the grandchildren…? She found herself looking up at him, pleading silently that he wouldn't give her further heartache.

'I'm sorry,' the Inspector looked at her quickly, his courage mounted, his lips set grimly into a thin line. 'I have to tell you that your husband was murdered.'

20TH MARCH

On the turn of the last card he sucked in his breath, his face pale with trepidation, his dark pupils dilating with certain knowledge of the price yet to pay. The green velvet cloth shimmered in the languid light as his palms pressed into its slinky depth, his fingertips white with pressure.

The air was musty with dried sweat; fear, washed up hope swiftly drowned in whisky. A rumble of voices carried by wisps of smoke and illegal substances drifted across their heads. It was the moment he had been dreading, staving off for months with snippets of chance here and there.

'Game's up,' the man opposite him drawled, his tongue rolled around a cigar as he lounged in his chair, the creases of his evening attire beginning to reflect the dawn that was insistent on breaking through the gap in the long heavy drapes. 'You're all out,' Fisher whispered, his face poking through his cloud of cigar smoke with an unpleasant creasing around his mouth. He didn't reply. Instead he got up, his chair scratching across the floor.

Suddenly everyone was watching him, the condemned man, the guilty…the dead. He cast them a sweeping glance, a wide smile of defiance and sauntered over to the roulette table. He swung his jacket over his shoulder as casually as his shaking fingers could muster. So the cards had failed him, he thought gloomily, but there were always other avenues to risk. He wasn't done for just yet.

With measured care he placed his chips on the table, his face drawn and translucent; his eyes darting from one to another of the crowd surrounding him, the onlookers eager for his downfall with increasing cruelty.

The roll of the ball echoed around the roulette table, tauntingly hovering over his desired numbers, fleetingly flashing him a glimpse of victory before slipping either side as the wheel crawled to an agonising stop. Silence reigned, a sea of washed faces grey with gloomy thoughts stood around him, pretending they didn't know what was coming to him. He had lost – again – only this time it was worse, far more than ever before with absolutely no way of breaking even.

Something in the pit of his stomach told him that they all knew; they avoided his gaze, ignored his involuntary shudder. If he wasn't mistaken he had now used up all his chances, appeal fought and lost, there was nothing left but to face the firing squad.

It took moments for the hands to press onto his biceps, his white shirt creasing at their touch, the sweat lining the seams, breaking through like a bust dam. He found himself treading air as they whisked him away, the brightness of the dawn now striking him in the eyes as they left the hidden den of sin.

The office was dingy, paperwork strewn about in the struggle whilst the thugs hauled him, effortlessly, into the lair. The door slammed loudly and they stood by it, blocking the only path of escape. He found himself dumped in a chair, as the man behind the desk spoke, his face hidden by the broadsheet newspaper he was studying with premeditated vigilance.

'You pay me,' his voice as smooth as silk, 'or I'll pay you' the newspaper suddenly crushing beneath his fists. It shrivelled into a mess, the words slipping into a mess of confusion. 'Your choice,' he said with a masked smile. 'Clear?' he asked; his voice perfectly even, his face scarlet and his eyes indicating the hired thugs who stood menacingly by the door.

He nodded, swallowed hard, focused his gaze on the shock of white hair that framed the man's face, and watched him iron out the newspaper on his desk with calculated movement.

'Clear,' he said quietly. 'I have an idea,' he ventured. The white-haired man paused in his repair of the newspaper, looked up sceptically.

'Everyone says that,' he sneered, proceeding to refold the broadsheets.

'You'll like this,' he replied, his confidence growing. 'I'll pay, big time, far more than you're owed.'

'I'm listening,' the man cast the newspaper aside, leant over the desk. 'Tell me.'

It took him less than twenty minutes to convince the white-haired man that the plan would work. Everything was now set and all parties agreed, some voluntarily, others not so. Now all that remained was for him to provide the documents as proof of his claim, then he would be free of his gambling debts. He left the room jauntily, a cocky smile in place to disguise his shaking hands, and went straight home to shower and change. On his way back he would make his search.

The darkness was deep and thick, punctuated only with lamps softly lit up around the room. His white evening gloves were stretched over his hands tightly, as his fingers nimbly leafed through the pages encased in the desk. The rustling of the paper sounded loud in the silent room.

On the far side of the house his father lay dead, signalling absolute safety for him to continue his frantic search. The death had been quick and painless, according to the nurse. A sheet now covered the body, a silhouette crisply cutting a shape beneath the creamy cloak. The nurse had fled an hour ago and the house was empty. At first opportunity the ambulance would take the body away. Until then, the domain was his to explore.

With annoyance he tossed the pages back into the folder and crammed it into its supposed secret hiding place in the writing desk. If Henry found him it would all be over. Fairly sure Henry would not come around until the ambulance crew arrived, he opened another draw, emptied it carelessly onto the floor and rifled through the contents hastily, his fingers coldly sifting through the family history.

The room itself was quite large, the furniture wooden, creaking its age with every breath. He had always hated it, the status that clung to it; a smug superiority that seemed to reign over him, jesting him, sneering. He looked around the room in malice, his dark hair suspended in the beam of light from one of the lamps. In an instant he flicked the switch to reduce himself to darkness. It was where he belonged.

Maybe it was at the solicitor's office. It would be just like Henry to have advised their father to keep it there, away from his devious grasp. A shadow slithered up the wall before him and he froze, the papers scattered around him guiltily. Just as quickly as he glanced up it had gone, vanished into the ether like a spy. An inward sigh racked him and his blood ran cold in a flash, a shiver of fear seeping through his veins. Hurriedly he scanned the papers. He had to get out of there, had to find it quickly, before the ghosts in the house found him.

Yes, his damned brother must have advised father to keep it at the old codger's office. Still, no matter, he could easily…Ah, but no, it was not the original, merely a copy but it told him all he needed to know. He unfolded it from its envelope and spread it out across the floor, his white-gloved fingers pressing out the creases as he read. The paper was thick, a flourish of signature at the bottom and a stamp embedded into the grain.

Yes, it gave a name. He hadn't known his father had ever found out even that much. Perhaps he had traced her himself, after all. Probably not, he noticed, his dark eyes narrowing meanly as he read on. No, he hadn't actually found her, only her existence, thanks to an expensive specialist in the field. Damn him, already some of the precious family wealth had been spent on her, with provisions to spend far greater sums still, not to mention a share of the inheritance waiting for her now that father was dead.

This was scandalous; he felt the colour rising in his face, his eyes tunnelling until they lost all focus, staring grimly at the document on the floor. It had to be stopped. He needed it all, every penny of the inheritance. It was bad enough that his brother Henry should get a share. Henry in his wealthy self-made black and white palace; he didn't need it.

A noise from somewhere caught his attention. He flinched, held his breath and listened. A cry from the garden convinced him it was a cat. Hastily he collected the remaining papers up and crushed them back into the writing desk. With a slight clunk he pulled the heavy wooden lid closed and turned the key, a plan already developing in his mind. He left the house, the document slipped into his inside jacket pocket, smoothing out his evening attire and hailed a cab.

The night was clear and crisp, a steady dusk beginning to close in. He stood back as the taxi drew towards the kerb, its engine ticking reassuringly, willing to hurry him away. Thanking his lucky stars there was only Henry and he, he climbed into the taxi and sat quietly back in the seat, his mind racing.

'Belvadere Club, driver,' he snapped.

No more could be spared; it would have to be stopped, he thought as the taxi began to pull away. If he wanted to keep his legs attached to the rest of him there was no other option. The agreed plan had to proceed. He needed it all. It was no big deal; he had done it all before, almost. She couldn't have any of it. She would have to be stopped, and there was only one way for him to do that. She would have to die.

APRIL

Panic hit her immediately as she pressed the brake pedal to the floor, the steely clonk of metal against nothing. The hill was steep. She was heading south, quickly, the junction at the bottom roaring with traffic…she couldn't stop the car. Rebecca thumped her foot on the brake pedal repeatedly, willing it to work. Her own screaming was frightening her. By her sides the houses swirled past in a daze, the traffic looming large before her.

Lines of sweat were beginning to crease her brow. Frantically she careered the steering wheel towards the kerb, the lampposts looking dangerous, the other way, the oncoming traffic looked gigantic. She was almost at the bottom of the hill. Her hands were sweaty, her body rigid with fright.

A flicker of sanity scuttled across her mind. Rebecca wrenched the hand brake up. The car spun a full circle, skidded over the road perilously close to the middle. She cupped her face in her hands. The oncoming traffic slowed as she felt herself thrust towards the window, bang her head on the glass, and bounce back into her seat. Then there was nothing. Silence. Stillness. She breathed out. She had survived.

It was a bright Wednesday morning as Rebecca Houseman pulled into her driveway. Since Craig's death she had sat in the house feeling lost, as if she were misplaced in her own life. The market always came to Atwood on Wednesday mornings and a sudden urge for fresh air had driven her outdoors. Now, as she collected her purchases from the boot, she was keen to hide away back in the safety of her rose pink lounge, where she could cry if she felt like it, without inquisitive eyes of strangers on the brink of indecision. It was a bizarre feeling, being of such fascination and wonder to people she didn't know. The thoughts flickered through their eyes, she could see them wrestling with hesitation to ask her if she was ok.

As usual the market had been packed, especially so given the bright sunny day and the warm air. It had been something she had always done by herself and she felt better for having done something normal, since…she couldn't even bring herself to think about it.

'Mrs Houseman?' a voice distracted her as she fiddled with her keys to the front door.

'Yes?' she turned around, hoping it wouldn't be even more flowers.

'I'm DCI Allen,' a tall man told her, presenting a rather ragged looking warrant card in a plastic case smudged with dirt. 'I wanted to have a word with you about a recent accident,' he said, a cigarette dangerously close to burning his lips. He flicked it out with practised ease and crushed it between his nicotine-stained fingertips with a wide boyish grin.

'Sergeant, where are you?' he bellowed suddenly, making her jump. 'Sorry,' he tipped his brown checked hat at her with his free hand, as a considerably shorter man of stout build trotted up behind him.

'Here Sir,' he mumbled, 'just locking the car, Sir.' The Inspector held out his cigarette butt and the Sergeant took it; stared at it for a moment with glum resignation and slid it into his pocket quickly.

'Mrs Houseman,' the Inspector began again, his thinning grey hair catching the sun's rays, 'may I come inside for a moment?' He spun on his Sergeant with a rapidity that would rival the most athletic of men, 'you can wait in the car son,' he said. 'I'll just be a minute.'

'Right Sir, yes,' the shorter man trundled off.

Rebecca nodded at the Inspector's poignant gaze at the house, dumbfounded by the double act with slight amusement and opened the front door. She busied herself with releasing the shopping bags on the floor and wiping her feet

'This way,' she said, proffering the lounge to her right. DCI Allen wiped his feet dutifully and sauntered through into the room, its sunny disposition making it bright and airy. 'I'll be with you in just a minute,' she said, removing her coat and shoes. 'Would you like a cup of tea?' she offered, hovering expectantly in the doorway.

'Oh that's very nice of you Madam, but no thanks, bit pushed for time today,' the Inspector told her, his hat now spinning on his fingers. She smiled faintly at his worn grey suit hiding behind a stained mackintosh that looked ideally placed to match his warrant card, and indicated a chair. 'Thank you,' he half nodded at her and slumped gracelessly into the chair with a sigh. 'Nice place you have here,' he commented, tweaking his fingers at a grey moustache.

'Thank you,' she smiled, this time with genuine amusement. He didn't look like any police Inspector she had ever seen, not that she had any comparison to make. 'How can I help you?'

'Oh it's a simple matter,' the Inspector assured her, glancing around the room and noticing the lack of ashtrays he removed a pencil from his pocket and chewed happily on the end of it. 'Just a couple of routine questions.'

'About the accident?' she queried, deciding not to comment on the pencil, 'it was nothing really. A silly mistake.'

'No, no, Mrs Houseman, it could have been very serious,' he insisted, removing his blue scarf and stuffing it inside his hat with great enthusiasm. 'The brakes failed you as you approached the T-junction at the bottom of Stubbs Hill?' he asked.

'Yes, but as I said; the garage had just fixed them and it was probably a mistake.'

'I don't think so Mrs Houseman,' the Inspector said gravely, 'you see I've had a word with the mechanic in question and it seems,' he paused, 'you'll forgive me Madam, you're a widow?'

Rebecca nodded tearfully, trying in vain to blink the tears away without having to reach for yet another tissue.

'I'm sorry Mrs Houseman, I didn't know,' he said gazing at the various bunches of flowers and sympathy cards that lined the mantle and windowsill.

'That's alright Inspector,' she choked on the words, which came out in a mumble of sound. 'Your station are handling it,' she whispered. 'My Craig was,' she sobbed quietly, 'murdered.' DCI Allen allowed her a moment of peace. He hadn't heard of a recent murder enquiry being resolved.

'I don't think they've got any suspects,' Rebecca's words were lost to tears as she tried to compose herself.

'How...?' Inspector Allen lowered his voice in sympathy.

'Something in his medicine, made it look like a heart attack,' Rebecca held back her sobs but her voice wobbled revealingly. 'I don't remember the name of the drug...' she whispered, waving her hand dismissively. It hardly mattered what it was, all that mattered was what it had done to him, her lovely husband. The man she had shared her entire life with.

'That may have a bearing on the situation,' the Inspector spoke almost to himself but she found herself jolted back to the present in a flash, swiping away her tears with her own frustration. 'I'll make enquiries for you Mrs Houseman,' he decided instantly, 'see what I can do.' A wide beam threatened to split his face. 'As I was saying,' he continued, 'the mechanic took a back-hander I'm afraid, to err, tamper with the brakes on your car.'

'You mean like a...' she stared at the odd looking man who sat comfortably in her lounge. He must be mad.

'I'm afraid so Madam yes, a bribe of sorts. Now, he says the man who paid him this bribe was a short fat guy, about thirty-five with ginger hair.' The Inspector grinned wickedly. Rebecca fought the urge to laugh at his expression. She hid a slight smile. 'Don't suppose there's anyone you know fitting that description?' Rebecca shook her head quickly. 'I didn't think so Madam,' Inspector Allen beamed, 'highly suspicious description in my opinion, probably doesn't exist. Funny thing though,' he toyed with his moustache again speaking quietly, more to himself. Despite what he was telling her she couldn't help but be amused by the Detective Chief Inspector; his thin face in concentration and his nose crooked as if it had been broken in prior years. 'Can't quite see why the mechanic would shield the culprit.' His voice was lost to her, trailing away in his own little maze of thought. 'No matter,' he bellowed cheerfully, 'don't you worry Madam, I'll get to the bottom of it,' he assured her, plopping his pencil back into his pocket and springing to his feet.

'Thank you,' she said, rising also and smoothing out her skirt with her palms.

'And you've used that particular garage before?' he suddenly asked, his voice high with intrigue, ducking to avoid hitting his head on the low light fitting.

'Oh yes Inspector,' she almost sang, 'for years. My husband...' she stammered, 'he...'Rebecca struggled with a deep breath, noticing the Inspector's patience and gratefully tried to continue without drama. 'He always took our car there, since the children were little,' she told him softly.

Inspector Allen paced the room quietly, his gaze flicking over the various photos of the couple's long married life together, a kindly face smiling out of a silver frame next to his wife, the woman standing nervously in front of him now. Several photographs of children with the same couple in their younger years adorned the walls and shelves around the room; happy snapshots of family life. He cast his eye over more recent photographs on the mantelpiece, Mrs Houseman with babies in her arms, new faces next to the children now grown up.

'You've had no further threats of any kind?' Inspector Allen asked, keeping his gaze on the photographs. He spun on his heels to see her shake her head. 'Good, good. Well, call me at the station Madam, if you do. Sergeant Wellington will take a message if I'm out and about,' he cast a friendly smile, admired her cleavage unashamedly as he unwound his scarf from inside his hat.

'Yes, of course,' she blushed and led him back into the hallway. DCI Allen followed her, his usual strides shortened by her slower pace over the beige carpet. 'Thank you for coming Inspector,' she said, opening the door to the sunshine that flooded them instantly.

'I'll be in touch Madam,' he grinned, flinging his scarf around his neck loosely and flicking his hat haphazardly onto his head with skill. He bent towards her, 'be careful,' he almost whispered and sauntered off down the driveway towards a waiting deep blue police-owned Saab.

***

Rebecca fingered the delicate black lace veil with care, drawing it slowly over her face. The hat had belonged to Neil's mother, a nice woman, such a shame she had been ruthlessly taken so young. Neil had insisted she have the collection of hats. She had hoped to wear one of the more colourful ones first, at her youngest daughter Katherine's wedding to Neil, before the black sombre one. Life could be so cruel.

The hearse would be with them shortly. She surveyed herself in the mirror once more, thought about the times Craig had laughed at her vanity, teased her mercilessly. She smiled. He had been a wonderful husband and she already missed him more than she could configure into words. It was true that nobody knew what tomorrow would bring, and she was glad suddenly, that she hadn't seen the fatal heart attack coming.

Now though, the police had told her that his blood pressure tablets had been tampered with, some poisonous substance she couldn't pronounce, or understand. What had appeared to be a natural death, had in fact been murder. His death had been completely unexpected and the doctor in attendance had insisted on a post-mortem. Horrified at the thought she had had no option but to agree. Now she half wished she had fought against the move. It would be easier to think God had taken him willingly, rather than an unknown hand. It was madness to even suggest that someone wanted Craig dead. He had been everybody's friend…she inhaled deeply and closed her eyes.

She really did have no idea what tomorrow would mean for her anymore, and she wasn't sure she liked it. She had never been a woman to seek adventure. There was a kind of reassurance in knowing that at least the new day would have Craig in it. Suddenly it didn't, and the thought of life without him frightened her.

Fleetingly she wondered if there was any real threat to her, as the police Inspector seemed to think. Craig had gone to that garage forever, surely not. She pushed it from her mind and twisted the hat slightly.

The sun was bright, slicing the room in two as it spread itself through the window intrusively. Rebecca wiped a stray tear away, feeling the sun's warmth on her cheek. For a moment she stood in her bedroom; the room she had shared so many years with him, and wondered why she kept expecting him to appear through the door. His clothes hung neatly in the wardrobe next to hers, the last book he had been reading on his nightstand with his glasses. Whatever was she going to do now?

'Mum?' a call up the stairs, her daughter's voice, kind and soft, just like her father's.

'I'm just coming,' she called with a last glance in the mirror. 'Well my love,' she said to herself, 'it seems it's time to say goodbye,' she whispered.

Rebecca took the carpeted stairs cautiously in her new black court shoes, her fingers brushing the handrail lightly. It had been several years since the carpet had been laid, seen a wide variety of spills and stains, the pattern of family life depicted beneath her feet. Perhaps she would get the house redecorated, she thought, instantly dismissing the notion. No, not yet, it was too soon.

The scent was strong, fresh and powerful. Rebecca inhaled the aroma and tried to smile as her daughter came towards her. The lounge looked like a florists shop. Always having loved flowers she realised she would be glad when some of them went with the hearse today.

'Dad would have been proud of you,' her daughter said softly, trying to smile but failing. Rebecca took her daughter in her arms, squeezed her briefly and withdrew. Too much affection would set her tears free.

'He'd have laughed at me spending all that time changing and staring in the mirror,' she said. Katherine's smile found its way forward and Rebecca was pleased. All she had to do was get through the service, try to be brave for the sake of her children, and then she could be alone, with her grief. 'Are Eliza and Sam here?' she asked.

'Samuel and Tina are on their way,' Katherine told her mother, 'they've dropped George off at Tina's parents. Apparently they don't want him to come.'

Rebecca nodded; it would be too hard for George. He was so fond of his grandfather and five-year-olds' never really grasp what death means. Why should they? There's time enough for sadness as an adult.

'And Eliza?'

'Oh she and Chris are in the kitchen,' Katherine said, her voice clipping her father's again. Rebecca blinked, trying not to cry. It was odd how she hadn't noticed it so often before. 'The girls are at Chris's sister's house I think.' Katherine touched her mother's arm lightly. 'You do look lovely,' she whispered.

'Thank you dear, so do you,' she attempted a half smile. 'How is little Craig today?' she asked, delighted she and Neil had opted to name their new-born baby son after his grandfather, even before his untimely death.

As if on cue, a cry from the far side of the lounge led Katherine away. Such an excellent mother, she thought, the years of watching her elder sister must have helped too. Rebecca hadn't been at all surprised when her eldest daughter Eliza had had children so young; it was all she had ever wanted. Samuel, on the other hand, had been a little more reluctant to relinquish his freedom but he and Tina seemed happier than even they had imagined, and George was a delight. Any doubts of fatherhood Samuel had ever held vanished on sight of him.

Rebecca wandered towards the kitchen, anxious to leave Katherine some freedom to feed her son without too many interruptions from the others. Neil stood by the sink, his dark suit tailored and smart. He and Katherine would make a perfect picture together on their wedding day. Baby Craig had delayed the date but it was fixed again for the summer and Rebecca was looking forward to it. Her only concern was who would give Katherine away now. She knew Katherine herself would have thought of this but neither of them had ventured to speak about it yet.

Neil was a tall man with clean-cut ebony hair and deep blue eyes. She could see why Katherine had fallen for him. She had so often seen him on his return from the office, his tie loosened and his white shirt freer about the neck, his jacket slung casually over his shoulder. Such an attractive man, with a smile that could enrapture any room. Today he looked different, his suit tightly in place, no visible hint of the casual relaxed man they were so used to.

They had talked recently about Neil's decision to set up a financial advisory business on his own, ditching his secure if slightly dull position with a large corporation. It was a risky move, but a calculated risk and she knew, deep down, that he would make a success of it. Despite their concerns she knew Craig had believed in him too. She wondered now what Craig had done with the funds they had set aside to contribute to the wedding. She supposed she would have to visit the bank, another task she wasn't looking forward to.

Rebecca stood in the doorway to her kitchen, Eliza and Chris with their backs to her. Neil afforded her a moment's peace, acknowledging her presence with a wink that made her smile, the first genuine one of the day. For this simple act alone she would always welcome her soon-to-be son-in-law into her home. Craig had liked him immensely. Rebecca remembered the day he had come to the house alone, to ask Craig's permission for Katherine's hand in marriage. She remembered every minute detail of Craig's face, his smile always more of a beam, lighting up the room with limitless laughter and joy.

'Mum,' Eliza turned, her blue eyes sparkling, and came towards her quickly. Rebecca touched her daughter's arm, anxious to keep her sadness at bay as she hugged her, Eliza's dark blonde hair, so like her father's, splayed out over her shoulders.

'Hello my dear,' she said, kissing her eldest daughter lightly on the cheek. 'Chris,' Rebecca accepted a brief hug from her son-in-law. 'Christine and Charlotte are...'

'At Ellen's,' Chris finished for her. 'I didn't think they were old enough...' his hazel eyes lowering to the floor with discomfort. He was a man of stature, a giant next to his wife's petite frame, but a gentle man and Rebecca felt for him. Never one to push himself forward, he would struggle more than most with grief, she thought. Peculiarly it would probably be Eliza doing most of the comforting in their household after today.

Craig had got along so well with both Chris and Neil that she knew they would miss him just as much as her daughters.

'No, no, of course,' Rebecca nodded at Chris understandably, a gentle pat on his arm to comfort him. It was strange to think the only grandchild to be at Craig's funeral would be the youngest of them all, his little namesake he had barely had the chance to know.

'Mum,' Eliza whispered, her slim frame elegantly dressed in a long black dress that draped her ankles, the lace overskirt skittering about her prettily. 'Do you want a cup of tea?'

'No thanks dear,' Rebecca said quietly, 'the car will be…' she felt the words drying up in her throat.

'Perhaps some water,' Chris offered quickly, finding a glass from the cupboard behind him and handing it to Neil who stood by the sink. Rebecca watched Neil fill the glass and accepted it gratefully. They had been fortunate that their children had all found such nice kind partners to share their lives.

'Thank you,' she said taking a sip.

'I'll tidy up,' Eliza offered, removing the cups and teapot and heading towards the sink. A clatter of distraction filled the room, pierced by baby Craig's announcement that his mid-morning snack was concluded. At the sound Neil patted her lightly on the shoulder as he left the room to join his fiancé in the lounge with their son.

'I suppose we had better get ready,' Chris mumbled. 'Where are Sam and Tina?'

'On their way,' his wife told him. 'I hope they're here soon though…' the front door opening made her pause and voices from the hallway called out. 'Here,' she half smiled as her brother and his wife greeted them.

'Hello dear,' Rebecca greeted her son, their second child who had inherited her piercing blue eyes and jet-black hair. Now though, she mused sadly, hers was a dark blonde shade from a bottle.

'Hi mum,' Samuel gave his mother a kiss on the cheek. 'How are you?' he asked, his hold of her firm and reassuring. 'How are you bearing up?'

'I'll be all right my love,' she whispered, taking his hand and patting it with more conviction than she felt. 'Tina dear,' she hugged her daughter-in-law tightly. Tina was a small woman, platinum blonde hair that shone like the sun and eyes the colour of lavender. Rebecca found her bubbly character a delight and she hoped the day's proceedings wouldn't drive her cheerfulness away completely; it may be just what they all needed later on.

'I think the car is here,' Tina told them, as Rebecca released her from her embrace. 'Do you need me to do anything?' she offered.

'No, no, thank you,' Rebecca tried again to smile at Tina. 'Just be yourself dear,' she whispered. 'We'll all need a little bit of your cheerfulness later on.'

'I'll try,' Tina promised with a bright smile that reached her eyes with a gleam. 'Shall we?' she indicated the door.

'You all go ahead,' Rebecca said, quickly hugging Chris and Eliza as they followed Tina and Samuel out to the car. Neil had baby Craig in his arms as he took up the rear of the party, dragging the folded pushchair over the step with him.

Rebecca watched her family busying themselves as they climbed into the procession of black cars that now sat outside her house. She felt the tears sting her eyes, hot and instant. This was the moment then, the moment she had been dreading.

'Oh mum,' Katherine came towards her, hugging her tightly. The soft chenille of her daughter's black cardigan felt nice against her cheek as she closed her eyes, realising she could no longer keep the tears under control. 'Shss…' her daughter's voice sang to her as if it were really Craig's. 'It'll be all right,' she whispered.

Rebecca wiped her tears away quickly, pulling at her hat with its veil to straighten it. Katherine took up command of it easily and she let her, grateful she had stayed behind. It had always been one of the things she loved most about her husband, his ability to know what she would need even before she needed it. Katherine had inherited that same second sight, the thoughtfulness that would make her such a superb mother herself, and wife.

'You look lovely,' Katherine assured her, taking her hand as they left the house together.

Inspector Allen sat in his chair, his feet up on the desk creasing the files carelessly. He blew out a large smoke ring satisfyingly and watched it drift towards the filing cabinet, fizzle into nothing and collapse into many white wisps. A loud knock at the door made him flinch. Quickly he thumped his feet on the floor and stubbed his cigarette out in a brimming ashtray in the second draw of his desk.

'Come in,' he barked, frantically waving his hands about the draws as he slammed it closed with a bang.

'That information you wanted Sir,' the desk sergeant offered a blue folder.

'Ah, thank you son, thank you,' he took it greedily as the man left the room. He opened it out and spread it over the paper littered desk. The file on Craig Houseman's murder was slim, no leads, no clues, no suspects. It was all but closed. There had to be a link with the recent vandalism on his widow's car. He turned to the fresh evidence; the statement from the mechanic, now typed up onto police headed paper and signed. What a farce, he thought to himself; instinctively he knew that this guy didn't exist. It was as plain as the face now entering his office.

'Sir?' Wells came in and settled his rounder frame on the edge of his own desk, crossing his ankles and arms.

'Yes Wells?' the Inspector piped up chirpily. Wells was a nickname. The good Sergeant Wellington was used to it by now.

'I reckon we ought to go back there,' he said wagging a chubby finger at the paper in the Inspectors grasp. He shoved a stack of multi-coloured files aside; they sailed perilously close to the edge of his desk, threatening to waterfall to the floor.

'Yes I reckon you're right son,' Inspector Allen mused, flicking the cigarette from behind his ear up into the air and catching it on its spiral back south. 'Come on, let's get some fresh air,' he said leaping to his feet with renewed energy. 'There's something strange going on here son,' he said as the two left the office companionably. 'I don't like it,' he confessed in a whisper. 'Why attempt to tamper with that nice woman's car hey?' he questioned his Sergeant who shrugged his shoulders, fiddling for the car keys as they swung out through the double doors towards the car park.

'Don't know Sir,' Wells said, 'where we going?'

'Just drive son,' Inspector Allen told him, 'I'll let you know in a minute when I've figured it out,' he grinned, slipping into the passenger seat. 'Nice woman,' he mused as Wells started the engine.

The second Wells indicated to turn out of the car park and onto the main road Inspector Allen opened a window and lit up his cigarette, his gaze deep in his own mind. 'Head back to that garage and park up on the other side of the road,' he instructed Wells. 'Let's just watch them, see what they get up to,' he waved his cigarette at the windscreen, 'we need more than that flimsy bribe to go on,' he said, his voice a hiss of irritation.

'You mean the ginger haired guy that mechanic told us about, there's something fishy there Sir, if you ask me.' Sergeant Wellington was staring out the window towards the oncoming traffic with diligence. The Inspector grinned at the back of his head boyishly. 'Of course, if you wanted to deflect attention away from yourself...'

'That's it son,' he exclaimed. 'He made him up!'

'Made him up, Sir, but why?' Wells glanced at the Inspector quickly as he pulled the car out of the junction and into the road where the garage was hiding behind a trading estate.

'If you were up to no good son, and I came poking my great big nose in, what'd you do, hey?' the Inspector grinned, puffed out a smoke ring and waited, his toothy smile hazy through the white wisps between them. 'You'd lie son,' he continued, 'you'd tell me it was someone else and,' he jabbed his cigarette at the windscreen again, 'you'd tell me it was someone we were not likely to find.'

'You mean with the ginger hair and all,' Wells smiled, 'I guess so Sir, yes. Whatcha gonna do though, to catch him out I mean?' he asked, drawing to a slow crawl beside the kerb opposite the garage where a silver Mercedes was navigating its way between the posts of the vehicle lift.

'Well, for one thing we'll have the git down the station looking at mug shots for a few hours, that'll waste his time, hey.' Inspector Allen let out a hollow laugh, 'make him sweat a bit too, with any luck. Hmmm,' he was musing, his cigarette burning close to his fingertips. 'Let him think we're really after this ginger sod.'

'We could send in a decoy, Sir,' Wells suggested, 'see what they have to say, another brake job.'

'Nay, I don't reckon it has anything to do with the brakes son; or the car. It's about her, the pretty widow. Who killed her husband? There are lots of family,' he mused; his cigarette extinguished and out the window in a single fling. 'We'll get onto them all. Question them about the deceased, the accident, anything we can think of. We're missing something son, I just don't know what.'

'The motive you mean Sir?' Wells asked; his pink face expectant and his mousy brown hair curling behind his ears.

'Yes son, the motive, exactly; if only we knew why…'

'Sir, look,' Wells cried. The silver Mercedes was now parked safely on the car ramp and its owner, an older man with a tidal wave of white hair had stepped out carrying a white envelope. The mechanic was wiping his greasy hands down his overall in anticipation, his eyes eager, moving towards the white haired guy at pace. They shook hands, the white haired man limply bringing a tissue from his pocket and surreptitiously cleaning his fingers as the mechanic peeked inside the envelope with a greedy grin. A silent exchange and the man slid effortlessly back into his car, proceeded to reverse out the garage and drive away.

'Get his reg son,' Inspector Allen barked. Wells squinted at the car registration plate, calling into the radio. They waited as the station clicked over a few keys, the tapping from the other end echoing around the car.

'John Francis,' it spat out at them, '45 Broadbent Gardens, Keyes.'

'You want to follow him Sir?' Wells asked, his fingers poised over the ignition keys, but the Inspector was still, his gaze fixed on the garage.

'Nay, we know where to find him son, let's stop on here a bit. See what else he does now. Payment, that's what that was son.'

'You think so Sir?' he spoke quietly into the radio signalling the end of the call. 'I guess it was a rather quick job,' Wells agreed. 'How'd you know Sir?'

'Just a feeling son,' the Inspector said, a sly smile spreading over his face as he lit up another cigarette. 'Just a feeling.'

Rebecca woke with a start, jolted up in bed. She felt around the bed sheets, remembering Craig would not be beside her and feeling the grief wash over her for the hundredth time.

The dream, it was so vivid, so real. A cold sweat was making her skin chilly as she shivered, slid out of the covers and reached for her dressing gown. Softly she padded downstairs to make a cup of tea, the dream whirling around her mind in misshapen images.

A girl, a young girl with long hair, could have been Katherine, or Eliza. A park. A bench. A woman. Soft dove-grey gloves and a long coat.

Rebecca flicked the kettle on and sat down at the table, closed her eyes and sighed. In an instant the dream was gone and she realised she was glad. When they had started, the same images playing in her hours of darkness, Craig had been around to hold her. It had happened the first time after a news bulletin that a man had died, aged seventy-two, of natural causes. He was famous, so the BBC news broadcast had informed her. She barely knew of him, his success being when she was very young, but the news had affected her strangely, an uncomfortable feeling that refused to leave her.

That night when she closed her eyes all she saw was his face, something about it oddly familiar, the look of her own son Samuel in the stranger's eyes. She had woken, distressed and unable to figure out why. The next night the dream had started. Now it was a regular thing, triggered mostly by something unsettling and the funeral was bound to be at fault this time. If anything in her life was unsettling then her husband's funeral had to take the first spot.

It had gone well, she supposed, but she had been glad when it was over. Glad to be able to put it behind her, despite being reluctant to move on. Blankness stretched out ahead of her. She closed her eyes again briefly, wishing Craig were there to hold her now, as he had done before.

They weren't unpleasant, the dreams, they were nice in a way. She was probably remembering taking her own children to the park; probably nothing. Craig had told her it didn't matter; they would no doubt fizzle away in time. Except they hadn't, if anything they had grown more persistent, as if someone were trying to tell her something important.

It still bothered her. Whatever was he trying to say to her at that horrible moment? She shuddered, not wanting to remember the look of pain in his eyes, his insistence in trying to reach her, to make her understand his mumbled words in his last moments of life.

Rebecca poured the hot water over her tea bag and tipped in a fraction of milk. It was too late for caffeine but she knew sleep would evade her, again, as it had most nights recently, especially so since Craig's death. She sat back down at the table and sipped at her mug, wincing slightly at the heat.

If only she could have understood. There was something, she would never forget, something important he was trying to tell her as he died in her arms. Too struck with grief she hadn't mentioned his undelivered message to anyone else. It was soon forgotten anyway, after his passing. Only the Inspector's visit had planted it firmly back into her mind. Could somebody really have wanted her car to fail her? Whatever for? Who would want such a dreadful thing? Was that what Craig wanted to tell her?

It occurred to her she should tell the Inspector about Craig's attempt to speak, but what could she say, her husband was dead, she had no idea what he was trying to tell her, possibly it was simply that he loved her, that he wanted her to tell the children how much they meant to him. No, there was nothing she could actually tell the Inspector. It was the last moment she had with her husband and despite its pain, and Craig's obvious distress at trying to speak, it was deeply personal and she didn't feel like sharing it, not with anyone.

'Oh my love, whatever will I do now without you?' she spoke into the darkness. Only a silence greeted her, the ticking of the clock in the lounge, marking time until the dawn broke.

CHAPTER TWO – LATE AUGUST 1959

As I look into his brown eyes they narrow like slits and I know for certain that he is responsible. My fingers are clenching into fists by my sides, the anger rising up my body, unstoppable, gathering strength, flickering viciously like a fire, its heat burning me like a torment. I feel wretched, out of control. I lash out at him in an instant. There isn't room for reason any more.

'How could you,' my voice whips at him, 'my baby, how dare you take my...' I feel my words die on my tongue, exhaustion racking me, my tears hot and fast, relentless.

My father watches me in silence. The flecks of grey in his thinning hair pick up the gleam from the setting sun as he sits, unmoved, in his chair by the window. I gaze at him with hatred. How could he do this to me, my baby, his grandchild, my baby...He is staring at me coldly.

'Why?' I screech at him from the marble steps leading down into the lounge. I choke on my own tears as they continue to stain my face. 'Why?' flinging my arms wildly I narrowly miss sending a vase of flowers into flight. I hasten towards him, over the luxurious fur rugs and stamp past the glass tables. He is still sitting, silently, staring at me as if I am the mad one.

My mother's soft voice is lost in the background, I am not even sure she spoke but I feel it, her presence; her damned diplomatic presence. What good is that to me now?

As I near him he gets up in one easy movement, his full height towering over me. My mother has reached my side, she pulls me back gently and I let her take me into her arms fleetingly.

My father treats me to another cold glance and strides towards the vast drinks cabinet in the corner of the room. In my mother's embrace I hear him clinking bottles and glasses. The gurgle of the liquid slopping into the glass is muffled by my mother's cream knitted jumper with little sparkling pearls. He does not offer us a drink. With renewed strength I spin away from my mother, my blue eyes piercing his as he turns to face me once more. My mother attempts to speak again but whatever she is saying is lost in the atmosphere, swallowed up into the void.

'I'll find her,' I threaten, stabbing a finger at him. 'You'll be sorry, I'll find her.' My father does not speak; instead, he takes a perilous step closer to me. I wave my finger at him again. 'I swear it,' I shout. 'I know you did this, you see you gave yourself away far too early,' I cry, my voice high and thin, bordering on agitation, 'it was rather silly of you to insist on an abortion wasn't it,' I cast a mock expression at him, 'I thought you were smarter than that Father, you do disappoint me,' I flap my arms around, let them fall heavily to my sides. He is standing right in front of me, a growing anger shining from him like a beacon but still he says nothing. He stares at me. With resolve I begin again in a soft, dangerously quiet, voice, 'now you're the only suspect, the only one who didn't want her...' my words die suddenly on my lips at the building colour in his face.

'Don't you dare insult me, child.' My father's voice is loud and booming. The expansive room shakes with the volume but I stand firm. I am my father's daughter; in other circumstances he would be proud of me.

'Insult you!' I laugh hysterically, my tears blinding me, 'You wouldn't even notice. You're so thick skinned. All you ever care about is money,' I accuse him, my voice high and tired as I stumble towards him, almost tripping over the rug. My strength has vanished. I feel weak, exhausted, all energy spent on tears but, I am still standing, still fighting, still against him.

'Now, come on, just calm down...' My mother's voice is soft. My father strides towards us, shoves her to one side as if she is a feather. She falters and resigns.

'Money. You think that's what this is about?' he swings his hand suddenly; the glass with it. The liquid flies through the air and clings to the table where it lands with a slight splash.

My mother sits in the white leather armchair with a sigh, beaten, and rests her face in her hands, her perfectly manicured pink nails sinking into the fringes of her blonde hair.

'Isn't it always?' I cry, taking the glass from his hand quickly. He tries to retrieve it but I shove it behind my back playfully. 'Isn't very nice is it?' I shout. My face, normally a warm olive complexion, is flushed with emotion. 'It isn't nice when someone takes something of yours.' I throw the glass to the ground suddenly. It shatters, the fragments spread out, crunching beneath our feet on the marble tiles. My mother cringes, begins to sob pathetically in the chair. I look at my father.

'You've gone too far this time,' he says, his voice bubbling beneath a roar, 'get out, get out, get out,' he erupts, 'GET OUT!' His face is flushed a nasty shade of red and his eyes are bursting out of his head. I glance at my mother, crestfallen in the chair. She looks even paler than usual against my father's Italian colouring, deepened with rage.

'Gladly,' I cry. I leap up the steps towards the hallway. At the base of the wide curved staircase I can still see them, the open plan downstairs spread out like a panoramic view. 'You'll see,' I insist, my voice low but I know he can hear me, 'you'll see.' I am standing on the bottom stair. My father is watching me. He takes a step closer, a crunch over the broken glass. My mother's sobs are getting louder. He goes to speak but there are no words. Instead he stares at me with his face red and his eyes burning with fury.

'You'll see,' I mumble through my veil of tears. With a swish of long dark hair I sprint up the stairs.

The pillow is not absorbent and I turn it over, my tears dampening the other side with equal speed. The hospital must be held to blame too. How could they let a perfect stranger walk out with my child? How did this happen?

I know he arranged it. He must have done. Michael looked stunned when my mother told him. I will never forget the moment; Michael standing limply by my bed; my mother whispering to him, her face a little puffy with grief and her eyes fluttering.

'I'm so sorry,' she said. Sorry. As if that were enough. She must have known what my father was up to…she must have…what difference does it make anyway, I think. She wouldn't have stopped him.

I reach for a clean handkerchief and attempt to dry my eyes, uselessly. There is no point. I never knew it was possible to cry so much. I feel empty. It hurts so much that I ache.

How is it possible that I love her this much after only fifteen minutes of holding her, ten tiny fingers, ten tiny toes, her little body pressed close to mine, snuggled in a warm cosy sleep. I watched her sleep in my arms, her beautiful little squashed up nose, her eyes tightly closed, her breathing… the most beautiful sound I have ever heard. Her little body rose and fell gently as she breathed contentedly; wrapped in a large pink blanket. That first moment she curled her little finger around mine.

My heart feels like a lead weight. I want my baby. I curl up into a ball on the bed, my energy drained and my spilt tears drowning me, rocking endlessly. I want my baby back… Eventually; when I am beyond exhaustion, I fall asleep.

It is a new day but I feel worse, if that's possible, than before. I struggle to get out of bed, to shower and dress. It is a normal day; I must tell myself it is a normal day. The shower is horrible, battering down over me. I would rather a bath but there isn't time. I feel weak from the birth. I am drained of blood and tears. The mirror is misted up. I swipe at it as if it is to blame, and stare blankly at my reflection. I am looking pale. My usual warm sunny complexion has faded distinctly but I do not care. I care only about my baby. I must act as if it is a normal day. I will find her; I will find her, I chant inside my head as I brush my teeth, renewed energy at my thoughts. How am I going to set about tracking her down?

The thought of squeezing into my dance underwear makes me sick with dread. I cast it aside. Even my usual rehearsal clothes are tight. With pain I force myself into the only looser fitting garments I can find in my wardrobe. My abdomen feels swollen, empty and hollow. Probably I should be resting. Instead I gather my dance shoes and a towel and toss them into my bag, open on the bed.

This is my life I remind myself, the constant rehearsal, practice session after practise session. Yet another tournament, another title to be won, spotlights, glitter, competition…It is endless. All I want is to sink back into oblivion but that is not my fate. He would not allow that.

'Best to just get back to normal,' my mother said. Back to normal, is that what she would have done if somebody had stolen me from her arms after half an hour? Perhaps she would. Where was her spirit, her gumption? It has been eroded by father over the years, I decide, well that won't work with me.

I sweep a selection of toiletries from my en-suite bathroom into my bag with one movement. Suddenly a shooting pain takes me savagely and I lean on the bed for support.

Surely this is wrong, I can barely walk. The surgeon had said it was quite bad, would take a day or two to heal. I would be sore. What did he know? Agony was more accurate. I bite down on my teeth hard and try not to cry, blink away the threatening tears as best I can. After a couple of heavy breaths I inhale deeply. Ok, time to face the music.

The thought of breakfast makes me feel nauseous. There is a heavy silence hovering over the table like a fog. My father does not look at me. He is seated at the head of the table scoffing eggs and sausages, washed down with gulps of orange juice. My mother eyes me constantly, her blue eyes, like mine, avoid my father completely. I wonder if I should voice my plan to her, maybe she would help? No, no, what am I thinking? She would never defy him.

I sip at my coffee quietly, contemplating my next move. I will go to the police. They have already been called, of course, but I will go all the same. It is a crime, to snatch a baby. They must act.

Rosa gestures the coffee pot at me. I accept with a nod and she pours, offers my mother some, who declines. Deftly she glides back into the kitchen, her canvas covered feet silent as a grave over the marble tiles. Rosa, she must know the truth, or have they concealed it from her too?

It would have been obvious to Rosa, she would have heard my morning sickness, seen me looking pale, watched me gain weight despite the seven hours of dance a day. She would have known...they may have fooled the media and the world at large, to a point, but they couldn't have fooled Rosa, she had been right here in the house, attending to her duties as housekeeper faithfully.

'How are you today, Miss Capelli?' she had soothed as she made my bed in the mornings. When I emerged from my bathroom wrapped in a towel and looking a little pale, she would have known. Surely, she would have known. She is a woman after all. Perhaps she will help me now? Is it fair to ask her? Maybe.

I have not stepped foot in the dance hall in five months, hidden away in my grandmother's house on the coast. Ridiculously I feel nervous.

The dance hall is mine, as is the house where I live with my parents. It is my success, my earnings that have given us both properties; in fact it is my success that pays Rosa's wages. Why then, do I feel that I cannot ask her to help me? Why can I not easily overturn my father's rules? Why does he sit at the head of the table? I have heard it a thousand and one times before.

'When you are of age you can do as you please, until then my child, I am the head of this family and I will look after the money,' he has always grinned like a Cheshire cat at this situation. Soon; just you wait father, I think to myself now. Just one more year and you will have to release part control on my eighteenth. Then at twenty-one I gain full control. Whatever will he do then I wonder, briefly smug.

'Ah, my favourite beauty, how was your vacation on the English Riviera, 'eh?' Vivanti, our dance coach, springs towards me as I emerge through the swing doors into the dance hall. Michael is already here, I see him stretching in the far corner.

'Hello Vivanti,' I hear my own voice quietly, completely crushed by Vivanti's insistent kisses of air either side of my face. He is wearing skin-tight white leggings that leave no part of his slim frame to the imagination. His bright multi-coloured top hangs loose with exception of a few gestures of reining in around the sides. 'So, to work eh?' he grins, 'we have much to do. Oh la la…' he prods me in the stomach and I step back, try with all my determination not to double over in pain. 'You too much enjoy the ice cream, eh!' he laughs, a booming sound that echo's around the room like a foghorn. 'We soon have you back in shape,' he smiles quickly and spins away from me on his toes, prancing across the floor, 'now, to work, come, come my darlings. There is much to do…' his voice trails over his shoulder to me as he gravitates towards Michael. 'You are fit, no?' he drags Michael to his feet and onto the dance floor to begin.

I sink into the chair and unzip my bag. Another shooting pain creases me in two and I close my eyes for a moment. My shoes feel strange as I squeeze into them. I have not worn them since father demanded I be confined to my grandmother's. Heaven forbid anyone should see me with child. With reluctance I am now grateful for that, at least no one will ask me about her. Maybe that was part of his plan, to discredit me should I shout and rave about her being kidnapped. I can picture it.

'Oh but what baby my darling,' I can hear Vivanti now, 'you have no baby, have you been dreaming again my beauty? Come now, to work eh?'

The sprung wooden floor is highly polished. I can see my reflection stretched out like a silhouette before me. The windows are tall and narrow, high with long white spidery fine drapes that barely conceal the sunshine streaming through and lighting up the floor. In the intervening months since my imprisonment at my grandmother's, someone has slotted large green plants in the corners of the room, their gigantic leaves bursting out of the ceramic pots with wild abandon, marking out the edges like guards.

Vivanti and Michael are practising the opening steps to the new title piece in the centre of the floor. I watch them, my expression vacant. The light is bouncing off Michael's dark hair as he marks out a series of strong athletic steps across the floor like a path for me to follow.

Michael's character lives in the music and the movement, when the music stops he reverts to the calm, the collected, the English gentleman. I have never known anyone who can switch passion on and off as he does, or at least make it appear so. He possesses such great control of temperament. His excitement when we dance, his energy, it stirs me into another being, another world. Yet when it is all over he will calmly walk away from the floor, carefully pack his belongings into his purpose bought bag, neatly folding everything into precision fitment. He will make studious notes, watch archived films of couples that have trodden the pretentious path to stardom before us, configure their sequences and analyse their success.

I, well I cannot be bothered with other people's careers and precision of sequences of bygone days. I used to live only to dance, the act itself far outweighing any financial gain in my mind. There has never been any need for me to study anyway, except my footwork. Michael and Vivanti have always soaked up the ludicrous demands of society's current whims like sponges. Now, I live only to find my daughter and in order to do that I must continue to dance, to earn the glittering prize money to fund my quest.

The walls are white, the ceiling high; the music from the corner spanning out like a fan. I look around at it all blankly. How can I do this? The tears are ever there, one careless thought away. I close my eyes and sigh deeply.

'Come now my beauty,' Vivanti is calling me from his stance opposite Michael. 'There is much to do. We must get shape back, work off all those ice creams, eh?' He laughs casually and I attempt a half smile, utterly lost in my own world that is suddenly singularly about finding my beautiful baby.

Dancing has been my entire life, my passion, my desire, everything, until now. Right at this moment I would happily sacrifice it all, just to have one more moment with my daughter. Vivanti is calling me again, his arms swaying wildly in encouragement for me to join them, or is it instruction? I can never be sure which.

I stand, feel a little faint, and walk towards them slowly. I try to catch Michael's eye but he will not look at me.

'Like this darling, like this,' Vivanti is saying, spinning on his toes like a man possessed. 'I want you to feel the music, listen,' he halts his spinning, taps his chest to the beat of the music, his eyes closed, his dark hair sleek, creamed back onto his head like a swim cap.

Michael has a more English look than I. His mother's Italian roots are there, hidden, masked by his father's English gentlemanly manner that he has inherited utterly and completely. His true spirit only emerges when the music starts, or the curtains are drawn. Sometimes he frustrates me, like now. I look at him but he is afraid to return my glance. It was his child too, how can he just get on as if nothing has happened? I watch him in despair mimicking Vivanti's demonstration with the tapping.

'Come now my beauty,' Vivanti is alert again. He drags me by the hand towards Michael. He looks at me for the first time since it happened, his dark eyes penetrating me with ease. I realise there is no need for words; he is hurting too. 'Now,' Vivanti swirls away, his arms flying passionately; 'we dance!' he sings, falling to the sides as the music starts.

Michael leads me into a waltz, around the room one, two three, one, two three, one, two three…I wonder if it is Michael who has asked Vivanti if we can start with a waltz. It is easiest for me to hold my body upright, no sudden abdominal twists of the Latin steps, to let him glide me around the floor lightly. I am afraid to speak to him.

In the spirit of the dance he does not look at me, or I him. The hall flashes past me in spurges of shape, the light flickering in stabs of stark contrast, the plants the only indication of speed or location.

I feel weaker than I imagined, faint, my vision a little hazy. I stumble but Michael carries me through it, whizzes me quickly away from Vivanti's studious eye as the music picks up pace. He leads me into a natural turn followed by a change step, a reverse turn, and we whisk into promenade position and chasse across the floor.

He has always been a gallant man, a gentle man. Father claims he is pathetic, only tolerates him for the sheer brilliance of his dancing ability and the fact that he and I have already made a name for ourselves in the eyes of the industry press as the number one dancing couple. It would be utter madness for him to suggest that I find another partner at this point. He may as well kiss goodbye to his precious income.

Vivanti has failed to notice my slip and suddenly I am grateful to Michael, ashamed of feeling frustrated at him. How does he manage to cope so much better than I? I try to catch his eye but the movement is too awkward and I am too unbalanced to focus properly. It is Michael who is supporting me, utterly and completely, and he knows it, is masking it, and moving me deftly away from Vivanti's watch at every conceivable opportunity.

The room is still passing me by at a speed I have lately become unaccustomed to, as my thoughts skate through my mind like a slide show. Even in grief and mourning for my lost child, dance still has the ability to sweep me up, to capture me. Perhaps my mother was right, for once, this is easier than I imagined, the music, the floating in Michael's arms; it releases me onto another plane where I can be myself, alone with my own private thoughts.

Michael takes me into another natural turn but instead of completing it he leads us into a spin turn. I pivot on my right foot, step backwards on my left toe still turning and brush my right foot up against my left. We are diagonally facing now as I step forwards on my right into Michael's space. I close my eyes and let him lead me around the floor, anti-clockwise of course, into half a reverse turn and the weave...

It is considered scandalous to have a love affair outside the bounds of marriage. You would think, I decide, given that already this century two World Wars have threatened complete destruction, people would be more open-minded to love, in whatever guise you can obtain it. After all, isn't that all that matters in the end?

Michael's tender age of nineteen may have been excusable, the passionate virile young man sowing his wild oats; he may even have been cast as a reluctant hero in his circle of friends and social acquaintances; but my seventeen years would never have been accepted. It would definitely have been me to be cast as the tramp, the villain of the piece, the damaged goods.

If we had not conceived our daughter no one would ever have known that our passion continued long after the music had stopped. My father had been predictably furious at the news of my pregnancy. He had roared the house down. Rosa must surely have heard. In fact, the entire estate must have heard including the grounds-men. Oddly, I had been amused by his reaction. It was so predictably raucous; his disgust at my behaviour, his complete lack of understanding in my choice of lover, this topic had lasted some considerable time, his utter disbelief at our foolishness, what were we thinking and so on...Finally we came to the real crux of the problem for my father, what was I going to do about it, why not have it aborted, how gracious of him to suggest that no-one need ever know. Another family row was inevitable when I simply refused to kill my own child, wouldn't even consider it as an option.

Despite being frightened at the prospect I had been happy, I had felt her grow inside me, her feet kick out in momentary reminders of her presence. I had been afraid, but in a good way. I knew the moment my father had suggested the abortion that I wanted my baby, more than anything I had wanted before. That sealed my fate, and hers, I think to myself with a sadness that suddenly threatens to engulf me. I swallow hard and try to focus on the dance.

Michael spins me towards the centre of the floor building the crescendo towards the final flourish of movement. As the music is drawing to a close I remember being banished to the coast to stay in confinement at my grandmother's house, with strict instruction not to be seen.

I remember Michael's face at the news that we wouldn't see each other for at least five months. As I look at him now, knowingly disobeying the rules of not facing my partner in ballroom, I see his relief at my return. There is a sparkle in his eye. As the music fades into nothing there is a silence and we are still, stationary, locked in the finishing position of the dance, as if in respectful recognition for the invisible orchestra.

Michael half smiles at me now and his eyes reflect the sunlight. It is a curious smile that leaves nothing open to misunderstanding. He releases me from his hold, wipes a stray tear gently from my cheek. I feel the vibration of his touch tingle through me, stretching right down to my toes. Despite the longing for my baby I realise with some shock that I have missed Michael, a lot. There is just a split second but it is enough. A look passes between us, an acknowledgment, a simple understanding of shared grief and entrapment; can I risk asking his help in tracking her down? It is his daughter too...

Vivanti's loud clapping pierces the moment with precision as he prises us apart in one easy movement.

'Lovely my darlings, lovely,' he applauses, 'now let me see, what dance shall we venture for the medals next month? I think a rumba, yes?' He does not wait for an answer; instead he flounces towards the stereo sound system, dragging me forcefully behind him by the hand. As I swing out at his command shooting pains dart through my abdomen and I grimace in silence, masked by a sigh. Michael hurries to keep up behind us, takes my free hand fleetingly, caressing my fingertips.

'Let's take it easy today Viv,' he suggests as Vivanti releases me and fiddles through his music collection for an appropriate rumba tune.

'Eh?' he utters with a quick glance over his shoulder, still flicking frantically through the records. 'Now you know the rumba, it is the most difficult Latin, but you do it so well,' he is saying, lost in his collection. 'I want you to…' he gestures, his fingers fleetingly leaving the records as he springs up like a cat. '…make sharp your sense of rhythm. You Michael,' he points at him savagely, turning back to bend over his music instantly, 'I want you concentrate on timing. The rumba, muscle control and timing, it will help you.' His voice is dulled by the flicking of his fingers through the records.

'I said,' Michael strokes my hand and lets it go, 'let's take it easy today. We have plenty of time before the medals,' he flashes me a glance as Vivanti spins on us like a puma.

'Ah, my beauties, you two make a lovely rumba, see, we try this,' his voice a hoarse excitable hiss as he slides the chosen shiny black record onto the player. 'You can do this, you can do anything, anything!' he sings.

With gratitude I allow Michael to take me to the floor as the music floats over our heads. We are starting with the forward and back basics in hold. Two three, hip placement on four. I can sense Vivanti wanting us to progress into more complex steps. We can feel his pressure but there is something romantic in the movement, my body obeying Michael's lead without question, and it's strong enough to blot Vivanti out.

Michael takes us into New Yorks' both left and right, a spot turn followed by hand to hands', a forward basic into a Fan and Alemana.

As Vivanti relaxes into his favourite chair, his legs crossed girlishly and his bright top creasing into the poise, I let myself be swept into the dance. We are back in closed position now and I look into Michael's eyes, our passion smouldering as we swing our hips into the cucaracha. Even my pain seems to have subsided slightly. The magic of the dance of love with Michael soothes me.

Perhaps dance will save me from my anguish, even if it can only last for a moment. When the music ends I realise I have tears on my face. Michael pulls me close, absorbing my pain.

CHAPTER THREE – MODERN DAY; APRIL

Rebecca sat primly behind the large reception desk. As yet Neil hadn't interviewed for a receptionist, and today he and Katherine had taken baby Craig for his first set of injections at the doctors' surgery. Glad of any distraction, she had been happy to sit in and hold the fort. It was only for an hour anyway. With a sigh she realised she half wished it were longer.

The phone had rung several times and she had duly noted down a list of neat messages on the notepad for Neil, but now a lull stretched across the morning and she found herself at a loose end.

Glancing out she thought about the new office space. It was the latest in technology and design, neatly curved desks to mould to the user, friendly prints on the walls. There was an infinite glass frontage and she felt a little as if she were in a gold fish bowl. Idly she supposed the new receptionist, whoever that turned out to be, would no doubt be used to such surroundings.

The spring sunshine was illuminating, radiating beams across the office space, its rays deflecting off the walls like a glitter ball. It was unusually warm for April. Part of her wished the woman in the red jacket who had spoken to her from the confines of her television screen would be right, that the forecast would stay this way, warmer than usual for spring. It suited her that summer may start earlier than normal, stretching the distance in time between Craig's winter death and the present. It was daft; she knew exactly how many days it had been since he had been so suddenly stolen from her. Yet, the warm weather made it all feel so much further away, and just the tiniest drop of rain could plummet her back into that awful depressive gloom. Attempting to lie to herself she was pretending he was simply at work, would be home in a few weeks but even she didn't believe it. Having been a long distance truck driver she had been used to two or three weeks absence at a time. The physical pain at missing him now surprised her. Deep down she knew he wouldn't be coming home soon. With a wash of sadness she wiped her eyes dry and rose to make more coffee, anxious not to be found crying in the office.

She massaged her tired eyes, vowing to have an early night. It didn't make much difference but she would try. Her grief kept her awake until all hours, then when she finally did drift into the blessed relief of sleep her dreams had her waking in fits of sweat and anxiety, leaving her with a nagging feeling of something unpleasant. Something she just couldn't shake off.

Drumming her fingers on the desk she watched the towns' occupants zipping by the windows, their shopping bags a trail of their adventures so far that morning. Boots, Waterstones, New Look, the plain bags that everybody knew meant the cheap pound shop, Burtons and WH Smiths. Several had bags from Marks and Spencer's the newest store in town, having finally taken the enormous empty space that was once Woolworths.

She sipped at her coffee. At a loss she flicked on the computer and stared blankly at the screen. The business logo filled the display, a neat tidy corporate image. What could she do to pass the time? She had never been a fan of games. Perhaps she could look up something on the Internet… Without conscious thought she found herself typing "dreams and insomnia" into the search engine.

She blinked twice. Several hundred entries appeared in the Google findings. Clinical psychology, cognitive behavioural treatments, stimulus-control therapy, relaxation training, simple lifestyle changes to make a world of difference to the quality of your sleep, positions of sleep and what they say about you, hypnotherapy… the list was endless.

She began to read, exhausted by the sheer number of entries and desperate for a simple answer.

Katherine smiled as little Craig slept peacefully in her arms, painfully aware that his sleep would be interrupted sharply by the needle at any moment.

'I'm worried about mum.' She spoke quietly to Neil who was flicking through an ancient copy of a fishing magazine, his pages the only sound in the hushed waiting room. Half smiling and half afraid of her reaction she tried not to look at the magazine. Dad had loved fishing.

'She'll be ok sweetheart,' Neil said, tossing the magazine on the empty seat next to him. 'She just needs time.' There was a smell of disinfectant in the air, pierced with coughing and people unwrapping packets of soothing lozenges.

'I know,' Katherine sighed, fingering a stray strand of her dark hair. 'It's just that she keeps having these odd dreams.' Neil watched his son sleeping, stroked his rosy cheek with a light finger. 'Do you think it's just grief?' his wife's voice was even quieter, 'or something else?'

'Are the dreams about your dad?' Neil asked, looking up from baby Craig and into his wife's beautiful dark eyes. She shook her head. 'What then?'

'She doesn't really know,' Katherine said. For the first time she noticed a man sitting across from them, a pair of probing eyes in the half-full waiting room that seemed to be scrutinizing them from behind the camouflage of an issue of *Men's Health*. She treated the man to a cold stare and leant in closer to Neil, her voice barely clear. 'They're odd,' she whispered, 'a little girl in a park.'

'Not nightmares then?' Neil spoke equally quietly, keeping his glance on his wife and child as the doors opened and a new stream of patients bustled in with prams and shopping bags.

'No, but she wakes up feeling sort of weird, not happy.' Katherine nestled Craig closer to her chest as he fidgeted slightly.

'Craig Carter,' the plump receptionist called from behind the desk, barely registering that she had been heard as she attended to the newcomers.

'Come on,' Katherine said, rising carefully, pointedly staring at the intrusive man as she walked past him towards the nurse's room. Neil followed her, conscious that they were not going to be too popular with their son when the nurse carried out the injection.

Five mugs sat gathering mould on the windowsill as Inspector Allen added a sixth to the bunch and collapsed into his chair, its protest at receiving him by squeaking loudly.

'Where'd that lot come from son?' he jabbed a nicotine-stained finger at the large pile of buff coloured files on the edge of his desk.

'Stolen cars, Sir,' Wells told him. His round face was shining in the sun beam through the narrow window that split the wall high above their heads. 'Been a bit of a boom lately so I heard in the canteen.'

'Well park them over there, son,' the Inspector gestured wildly around the hazy office, anywhere but on his desk, chuckling lightly at his own joke. Sergeant Wellington shuffled them onto his own desk in an instant and took his own seat; his bulky frame squashed between the armrests. He lifted some statistics from underneath a stack of papers on his desk and extended them to the Inspector, who waved them away dismissively with a loud sigh. 'Later son, later,' he plonked his feet up on the now-free space on his desk. 'What we getting involved for, shouldn't uniform be dealing with it?' he protested. 'We've got other things to think about...' his voice fading as his fingers narrowed the ends of his moustache into fine points.

'No Sir, the Super wants you to handle it,' Wells said, reading from a fresh memo pinned to his desk with a large yellow post-it that claimed it was urgent. 'Says it's becoming an epidemic and he wants CID to put a stop to it,' he read; his eyes studious over the memo. 'Sir?' he lifted the memo but Inspector Allen waved this away too.

'File it son,' he sighed, taking his cigarette from behind his ear and replacing it instantly as the door opened.

'Don't you knock kid?' he boomed irritably as a newly recruited Police constable stood wobbling in the doorway. 'Sorry son, sorry, what's that?' he coughed guiltily and gestured vaguely at the report in the young constable's hand. With relief the new recruit handed it to Inspector Allen and left the room hurriedly.

'What is it Sir?' Sergeant Wellington asked abandoning the statistics and hoping it would take them both out from the office.

'It's another damned memo from the Super, son,' Inspector Allen told him, folding the paper into an aeroplane as he clicked his tongue restlessly. 'Stolen cars hey, here,' he set the plane alight and it floated towards Wells. 'File that with the other one. We'll see to them later,' he announced.

'Shall I tell the Super, Sir?' Wells asked tentatively. 'That we're onto it, I mean?' Inspector Allen didn't answer. He sat thoughtfully, his fingers narrowing his moustache until the ends resembled a waxed point better suited to the 1930s.

'Come on,' he sprang to his feet decidedly, 'let's go and harass Mr big-bucks, what's his name son?'

'Who Sir?' Wells asked; his body now moulded to his chair comfortably.

'The old sod we saw at the garage,' Inspector Allen grinned. 'You know the one with the silver sleeker,' he insisted, reaching for his coat and blue scarf despite the clement weather. 'Quick son, quick,' he grinned.

'John Francis Sir,' Wells said, pushing his chair from his body with some difficulty and hurrying to follow Inspector Allen who was already striding for the door, his hat on his head at the last second as he slipped out of sight.

'That's the one,' he shouted over his shoulder from half way down the corridor, his long legs taking him away at speed. 'Come on son, let's go,' he was calling as Wells trotted after him towards the car park.

Sergeant Wellington drove the short distance towards Keyes. A rickety old sign swung lightly in the mild breeze, welcoming them to the village. Inspector Allen watched the village green float past him as they drove peacefully towards

Broadbent Gardens. One of the three daily buses let out its airbrakes at the bus shelter as it pulled to a noisy stop in front of the pubs, where a line of elderly ladies stood leaning on walking sticks.

Sergeant Wellington parked the car further down the road, out of sight from number 45 and looked at the Inspector who was busy puffing smoke rings out the window with quiet amusement, watching the silent road with interest.

Broadbent Gardens was a mere lane, an almost private road with a blanket of dainty pink blossom fluttering casually south from the trees. The houses were large, set back from the lane with luxurious curved driveways and double garages hiding ridiculously expensive Porsches and Aston Martin's. Inspector Allen surveyed the road with distaste, blew out a long trail of white smoke and frowned. From their vantage point they could make out number 45; just, half hidden as it was with a large willow tree and another smaller tree that was adding to the blossom carpet as they watched.

'You want to go inside, Sir?' Wells asked; turning off the ignition and unbuckling his seat belt, ever keen to outsmart the Inspector's rapid movements that caught him off guard at every turn.

'No son, let's sit here for a minute. It's almost two, he's bound to go out soon…' his voice trailed into a whistle. 'See what'd I tell ya,' he grinned, jabbing a finger at the windscreen. Wells followed his gaze. The man with the shock of white hair was at his entrance gate, peering through the tall black iron bars as if on the inside of a prison cell. 'What's he up to?' Inspector Allen mused. 'I reckon he's a wrong-un son,' he said, crushing his spent cigarette between his fingers tightly and tossing it out the window where it rolled into the blossom, unseen.

'John Francis, aged 69 Sir,' Wells was reading from a file he had managed to pick up on his way out the door. 'Widower, used to own Forbes Sir,' Wells said, flicking his glance at the man again. Inspector Allen listened intently, his eyes never leaving the man at the gate.

'Forbes you say,' he mumbled.

'Yeah Sir, you know, the department store. It closed down a few years back…' Wells picked the papers apart and read on. 'Closed ten years ago, he sold the assets separately Sir, broke the whole company down and made a mint.'

'Did he indeed,' Inspector Allen's gaze turned to Wells as the man drifted from the gate and went back to his house, now standing by the front door expectantly. 'He's waiting for someone,' the Inspector said.

As they watched the man checked his wristwatch, the gold blinking in the sun, began pacing his driveway, checking his watch a second time.

'Do you want to go and ask him Sir?'

'No son,' the Inspector's hand lifted, halting Well's questions, as a midnight blue car glided past them soundlessly. 'Shss…'

The man with the white hair bounced towards the gates and let the car in.

'Sir,' Wells exclaimed, 'it's the mechanic.' They watched the greasy mechanic remove himself from the car, a seat cover clinging stubbornly to his overalls as he stepped out into the sun. Another envelope passed hands, a set of keys too, a handshake; the work of a moment sealing the deal. The man reached for his tissues again, wiped his hands and watched the mechanic stroll away, ripping the seat cover from his body in one swipe and discarding it lazily on the pavement behind him.

'Let's go son,' Inspector Allen announced, 'radio in that reg, it'll be stolen, then join me over there,' he stabbed a finger at the gates, swung his legs out the car and strode towards number 45.

Wells mumbled into the radio, unsure how the Inspector seemed to know these things. The newly arrived car had been reported stolen the previous week. He hurried after him and reached the Inspector who was now at the iron gates, the older white-haired man trying to close them, a look of insolence on his face.

'Yes?' he snapped, 'who are you?' his gates wedged open a fraction by the Inspector's foot. 'This is private property,' the man hissed. Sergeant Wellington watched the Inspector produce his smudgy warrant card and fiddled for his to wave at the white-haired man.

'Mr Francis?' the Inspector asked, taking a wide step and pushing the gates open to allow he and Wells in. 'A word Sir,' he grinned. 'May we come in? Oh thank you very much Sir,' he rattled on, closing the gates behind them. 'Nice place you have here,' he beamed. 'Shall we go inside?'

The man had piercing blue eyes, a blaze of anger narrowing them unpleasantly as he surveyed the Inspector with a look of scorn.

'I don't think so,' he decided, 'what do you want?'

'We're investigating some car thefts Sir,' the Inspector began, circling the man, his feet planting heavily on the blossom-covered driveway. Sergeant Wellington looked at the Inspector in amazement. Weren't they supposed to be investigating the accident of Mrs Houseman?

'Car thefts? Nothing to do with me, now, if you'll excuse me I'm a busy man,' John Francis announced, making towards the gates to show them out.

'Oh but they are everything to do with you,' Inspector Allen grinned roguishly. 'This one for instance,' he spun on his heels towards the new midnight blue vehicle. It was stolen...' he glanced towards Wells.

'Only last week Sir,' Wells chipped in.

'You see Mr Francis, just last week this lovely car was stolen and today it is here, on your driveway.'

'I've just bought it you fool,' John Francis snapped. 'I didn't know it was stolen.'

'Really Sir?' the Inspector smiled craftily. 'That is a shame. Where'd you buy it?'

'At auction, two days ago. Now look here Inspector,' the man's voice hardened. 'I've paid good money for this car...'

'Oh yes Sir, no doubt you have. And you've got another business haven't you?' Inspector Allen pulled out a cigarette and lit it whilst the man started at him incredulously.

'I sold my business several years ago Inspector,' he sighed petulantly. 'Just what is all this about?' Inspector Allen circled him patiently, silently smoking. 'I'm a busy man Inspector,' John Francis repeated.

'Oh yes, I know you are,' the Inspector agreed amiably, spinning his glare at the man suddenly. 'Who was that man who left here with an envelope stuffed with cash a few moments ago?'

'You're the detective,' he snapped. The Inspector let out a hollow chuckle. 'It was the garage, if you must know, delivering the car. The envelope was payment,' Mr Francis exasperated. 'Honestly, so it's illegal to buy a car now is it?' he flapped his arms around him, turning to keep up with the Inspector's narrowing circle.

'It is to buy a stolen car, yes Sir,' the Inspector stopped, glared at Francis quickly and walked on. 'So we'll be taking this one back now Sir; you'll get a receipt. I'll have someone come to pick it up later.'

'What? No, I refuse,' his face bright crimson and his chest puffed out in defiance.

'Oh he refuses,' Inspector Allen grinned in mockery, smiled at Wells. 'Did you hear that Sergeant? Well in that case, son, arrest this man...'

'All right, all right,' John Francis shouted. 'Take the damn thing. Here,' he slammed the keys into the Inspector's hand, his face darkening with rage.

'Thank you Sir, the Constable will take your particulars later on, the papers, log book and so forth,' he wagged his cigarette at the car, 'when he comes to collect it. Say about four o'clock tomorrow Sir? Does that suit you?'

'No it bloody well doesn't, I'll be out,' he shouted, stamping his way toward the front door. 'Call and make an appointment,' he demanded grumpily and let himself in the house.

'Right son, back to base, pronto. We'll be back at four tomorrow,' Inspector Allen announced, dropped his cigarette on the driveway and crushing it with his heel.

'But Sir,' Wells objected as they swung the gates open. 'He said he'd be out.'

'Exactly.' The inspected gave him a cheeky grin that split his face with pleasure. 'He'll be out, we're going in.'

**

The sheer volume of the drums almost knocked her out as she came cautiously through the double doors in the community centre. It had been advertised in the local newspaper and something about it had appealed to her. Always having been the first on the dance floor, and the last to leave it, Rebecca had been the life and soul of most family parties over the years. The thought of joining a local samba band to get back into a routine of weekly exercise, coupled with an overwhelming cloud of encouragement from her children, had rather forced her hand.

'Hi,' a nice lady with wavy auburn hair appeared by her side. 'I'm Angela, is this your first time?' Rebecca nodded with a smile and shook the woman's hand.

'Rebecca,' she said as the drums came to an abrupt stop. 'Is it always this loud?' The drummers were dressed in loose fitting white trousers with yellow tops. Some held drums on straps around their necks whilst others had larger ones fastened around their waists. A group of percussion players with smaller bongo drums, brass and wooden instruments and whistles lined the front row. A man of warm olive skin had his back to her, in contrasting coloured clothes, directing the merry band through the music.

'No, don't worry,' Angela laughed. 'We practice separately. They'll go off into the other room in a bit. Come on, I'll introduce you,' she offered, leading her towards a group of women in the far corner. 'Lexia,' Angela led her towards a woman about her age with a mane of dark hair held away from her face with a bright yellow hair band. 'This is Rebecca.'

'Ah, we speak on the telephone, I am so glad you come,' Lexia came towards her warmly. 'Welcome. Do not worry, we all friendly here,' she assured Rebecca with a light smile. 'Come, we start. You just copy me, you be fine,' Lexia smiled as the drummers drifted towards the back room, percussion instruments clanging against their legs like a dying chorus. 'Come come, ladies, we start,' Lexia called and Angela led her towards the centre of the hall.

'Come on,' she smiled. 'It's good fun,' she assured Rebecca as the other women took their places behind Lexia.

As the dance practise picked up pace Rebecca found herself enjoying it, swaying her hips to one side then the other, tipping her left hip up on the ball of her foot and pressing her heels down with a definite movement. They spun this way and that, drifting in lines and into a circle.

'Keep your eyes fixed ahead,' Lexia was saying as she demonstrated the spin. 'See, one, two,' she said, her head back to face the front straight away, her body twisted towards the back of the hall. 'Three, four,' she counted, completing the slow-motion heel-toe spin with her eyes fixed to the front. 'So you do not get dizzy, now, everyone, from the beginning.'

The band was rehearsing in the back room, their practised few bars of music temporarily overshadowing Lexia's CD player, but it didn't matter. The women were friendly, giggling and chattering between steps, a multitude in misshapen clothing for the weekly class. She was glad she realised with relief that she seemed to fit in effortlessly. Dreading a sight of leotard-clad super fit young women all in matching outfits she felt certain she would be the odd one out. 'It's not 1983 anymore,' Eliza had teased her when she had voiced her fears. She knew that but she hadn't been amongst an exercise class in a long time, probably since '83 trying to get her figure back after Samuel was born.

'So now, ladies, samba,' Lexia smiled widely as she hit the play button again. Rebecca copied the others and felt her body slip into the steps freely. A twist of the body, one foot crossing forwards over the other, the alternating arm to meet the twist, then the other way, stepping forwards into the middle of the circle until they were all bunched up together. A giggle or two erupted as the women clashed tightly in the centre of the hall. A spin out to samba back towards the invisible starting point of their circle.

The dancing felt natural, sexy, almost tribal movements that came easily and flowed smoothly. It didn't feel like exercise somehow, just partying.

Rebecca wiped her forehead softly with the back of her hand as the music came to a stop. She couldn't remember the last time she had been this breathless and realised that she was actually smiling, not out of sadness or fond memories, but happily.

'You do so well,' Lexia smiled at her as the ladies sipped gratefully at water bottles, waiting for the drummers to join them for a group practice before class disbanded until the following week. 'You enjoy?'

'Yes,' Rebecca laughed, 'it's so much fun. Thank you. Do you have space for me to join permanently?' she asked.

'Yes darling, write your name…' Lexia trailed towards her clipboard. 'Write your name here. You do so well, and I need a new lady. Three weeks ago one lady, she leave, so, welcome…' Lexia sipped at her water as Rebecca added her details to the list. 'We have performance in the town in the summer.'

'Performance?' Rebecca queried nervously, 'in the town?' handing the clipboard back to Lexia.

'Do not worry, it is just fun, you see. Be easy, you are natural at this, trust me.'

The drummers clanged their way into the room and assembled noisily at the rear of the hall. The man in the contrasting colours signalled to Lexia as the ladies took up their familiar spots in the hall again.

'It's just the same,' Angela whispered to her as they assembled in their circle. 'Just them playing instead of the CD,' she smiled. 'You're so good at this,' Angela laughed almost enviously. 'I've been doing this for ages and I still keep getting it wrong,' she giggled but the drums drowned out her cheeriness as they began to play.

'Wow, that was brilliant,' Rebecca smiled at Angela as the class came to a close. 'It'll definitely keep me fit. I'll see you next week,' she said, gathering her things together and waving as Angela took her leave.

'Bye, see you next week.'

Rebecca fastened her bag and was waving to the others and Lexia when she noticed someone approaching her. She made her way towards the doors but he was following her out into the sunshine.

'Hi,' he ventured. 'Paul,' he said offering his hand, his blue eyes smiling brightly. 'Paul Wood.' Rebecca shook his hand. He was tall, at least six foot, a covering of silver hair glinting in the daylight and his drum strap hanging loosely around his neck; the drum itself now securely locked away in the cupboard.

'Rebecca Houseman,' she smiled. 'Haven't I seen you before?' she asked, a sudden glimmer of recognition registering in his healthy athletic looking frame.

'Possibly,' he smiled, tying a string around his drumming sticks. 'I'm the manager at NatWest Bank, for my sins,' he laughed, a warm sound that made her feel at ease. He looked about five years older than her. 'I haven't seen you here before,' he commented, following her as she moved towards the car park.

'No, it was my first time today,' she breathed. 'Good fun but exhausting,' she smiled. 'What size drum do you play?' The gravel crunched beneath their feet as they walked towards the cars. Paul seemed to be following her.

'Medium,' he told her. 'My parents never let me have a drum kit when I was a boy,' he grinned peevishly, 'so I'm making up for lost time,' he laughed. 'I hope to see you again next week,' he smiled as he headed to his car, ironically parked next to hers.

'Yes, I'll be here,' she found herself lingering. 'Bye Paul,' she smiled, a shyness engulfing her as she unlocked her car. He was attractive certainly, but she was freshly widowed, she wasn't ready for attractive strangers.

'Bye, take care,' Paul smiled, watching her slide into the driver's seat before unlocking his own car.

Despite trying not to, she thought about the class, the fun, the friendly Angela and the lovely authentic teacher from Brazil, Lexia, all the way home and for the rest of the day. She thought about Paul Wood too. Clearly he had wanted nothing more than to introduce himself to her, and to learn her name. It was just a friendly greeting, a welcome to the band, she decided. Of course, that was it. Nothing more. Maybe he could help Neil out; after all he said he was the bank manager didn't he...

***

'She's my favourite teacher nanny,' George insisted, pointing at a woman across the far side of the football field. Rebecca looked at her grandson's English teacher, a woman of approximately her height with hazel eyes and a bob of hair that reminded her of milk chocolate.

'What's her name George? Rebecca asked, narrowing her viewpoint to see the woman in question. The football pitch was large, even for infant school players.

'Mrs Taylor,' George informed her. 'She used to be Miss Harris but then she got married,' George told her importantly. 'Will you have a different name when you and uncle Neil get married?' he turned to Katherine.

'Yes sweetheart,' Katherine smiled at her nephew, 'but to you I'll always be aunty Katherine.' George looked pleased at this news and ran away to join his friends who were huddling together for the start of the match.

The late April air was still warmer than expected and the sun was bright, the ground dry from a persistence reluctance to rain and the trees foliage full. Rebecca watched George and his friends dash around energetically. Children's energy levels never ceased to astound her. A banner stretched enthusiastically across the field, its stakes hammered with vigour into the ground. *Atwood Infants School* it read followed by *Come On Atwood.* Rebecca smiled. The days as a dinner lady when George's father was a little boy sprang to mind. Things hadn't changed all that much really.

'Mum,' Katherine's voice took on that charming quality she had held dear as a child, the voice of inquisitiveness. 'I've been thinking about the wedding.'

'Yes dear?' Rebecca asked, knowing what was coming and praying she would approve of the answer. Regardless of her opinion she would give her daughter the full backing she was clearly after.

A whistle caught her attention and the match was in play. George sprinted down the field in top form, his pass to a friend almost resulting in the first goal.

'What do you think about Samuel giving me away?' Katherine hid her blush that coloured her pretty face every time she mentioned her forthcoming wedding. Marriage to Neil, despite baby Craig's premature appearance, was still Katherine's future dream.

Rebecca turned to her youngest daughter in elation; it was exactly what she had thought herself, praying against hope that she wouldn't ask for Neil's father to do the honours. It didn't seem right that Neil's father had that slot as well.

'I think it's a wonderful idea darling,' Rebecca smiled at her daughter, gave her a quick hug. 'Will you tell Samuel?'

'Yes,' she breathed a sigh of relief. 'I'll ask him tomorrow,' her eyes sparkling with excitement. Samuel's son George was going to be handing out the corsages at the church, it would be lovely for him to see his dad walk his aunty up the aisle, his little steps following behind as the only page boy. Rebecca herself would be holding baby Craig in her arms, with Eliza's help no doubt as they took their seats near the front of the church.

A whistle separated the women's thoughts from them as a corner was awarded and the tension mounted. It was a critical game. If they won it would secure them a place in the coming play-offs. A draw wasn't quite good enough but they would have another chance the following week. If they lost it was all over and Rebecca knew how much this meant to George.

Sam and Tina were strategically placed on the other side. Every direction George happened to glance he would see a familiar face. It had been their custom since he started playing for the team aged just four and a half – ridiculously young really but he seemed to love it so. Rebecca thought about

Craig, he had loved the game. Every Saturday George and he had watched the league results at teatime with bated breath.

'What does he want to do this time, top goal scorer?' Rebecca asked Katherine.

'I think Tina said he wanted player of the year or some such title,' Katherine mused. Neil had little Craig at home. It was a rare thing for her to have a little time to herself without concentrating on her baby son. 'Mum, how are the dreams now?' she asked, her entire frame taking on that of a conspirator. 'Are they easing up?' She thought back to her hushed conversation with Neil in the waiting room and the intrusive man who seemed desperate to listen into their private conversation.

'No dear,' Rebecca sighed. 'They're not I'm afraid but I'm learning to live with them. I borrowed Neil's Internet the other day, when you were at the doctors, and I looked up a whole load of things about dreams and insomnia. There's too much really, I need to sit down and read it all properly.'

'Do you need to see someone about it?'

'I'm not sure darling; possibly, I'll make a decision next week. Let me read all this stuff first.' Rebecca looked at her youngest daughter with longing. Whatever was happening to her, the dreams that made her wake in a cold sweat, the grief at losing her husband so young, so unexpectedly, the fear of being alone in the world. It was all something she would deal with somehow, not anything she would voluntarily worry her children with. They were her joy, her delight, and her very own saviours on the gloomiest of days. It was her issue and she would deal with it, she decided; alone.

For a moment a cloud moved across the field and Rebecca followed the darkness as it shadowed the players, a rootless shape travelling towards the opposition's goal where it settled ephemerally and dissipated into nothing. Katherine was watching the action, the ball following the cloud, threatening a goal from the other side.

'Huh!' she cried. Rebecca turned to her daughter, her face frozen, her gaze fixed on the crowd standing behind the goal net. The cloud had vanished. A cheer erupted and the sun brightened.

'What is it love?' Rebecca asked, her daughter's face slowly softening to its usual pretty lines.

'It's him,' Katherine said, her gaze still focused on the crowd. The man from the doctor's waiting room with the curious eyes and the over-active ears.

'Who?' Rebecca asked; scanning the crowd without successfully spotting anybody she knew. A whistle blew for another corner kick.

'Nothing,' Katherine said quickly, turning to her mother, 'it's nothing,' don't worry,' a colour filling her cheeks with a rosy tint. 'My mistake.'

It was nearly half-time. Rebecca put on her bravest face as the whistle blew again and George approached, the light of life shining from him abundantly, coloured by adrenalin in his face, his eyes twinkling and his body glistening with the glow of exercise. If there was anything that could help her to get through, it was her family. They didn't even need to try, just them as they were, would be enough. Something had upset Katherine though. She wondered what, or who, it could have been.

Katherine glanced over at the man behind the goal net. He noticed her watching him, stared at her intently, and walked away. Glad that he had gone, and unsure why, she let herself be swept up in the half time euphoria of George's match but she felt cold, a sickly feeling creeping through her. That man, what was he doing there, he didn't have a child...

CHAPTER FOUR – SEPTEMBER 1959

The flash of the camera bulb blinds me temporarily as I leave the adoption agency, my hat slanted in an effort to conceal my identity. Another flash. I notice they are all around me. Swarms of them like vicious bees, clothed in browns and greys, no doubt hoping to blend into the any scene; lying in wait like predators, their pencils and notepads at the ready. The cameramen are weighed down heavily with large black machines on their shoulders, prepared to capture me on film without permission at a seconds notice. The backdrop of the adoption agency makes a picture worth a thousand words for them. Suddenly I realise I must get away. I do not think about how they will see it. I simply know I must get away.

My feet take on a surge of energy as I try to out-run the media. My caramel coloured skirt is not designed for running; it laps at my legs restrictively, its long hemline barring me from the freedom of distance and speed. Instead I am reduced to cunning if I am to stand any chance of losing them.

Instantly I realise I am running from one lion's den straight into another. Not that I particularly care but my father will not like this. It is bound to make a splash in the news, if not the national, then the industry news certainly. The odds on Michael and I will plummet overnight. Even this, selfishly, I am not swayed by. What I do care about is another argument. I am not sure I have the energy; my tactics will need to be laid out in my mind beforehand. I must conserve my energy for dance; that will save me. That will keep me going, keep me earning the money. I will need lots of money if my visit to the adoption agency is anything to go by.

The journalists are breeding I think, more seem to have appeared out of nowhere. I look up ahead and decide I will take a right into Curzon Street. I am only a fraction ahead of them, but if I do it cleverly they will mistake my meaning for going straight on towards Atwood town centre.

Breathless I round the corner a mere stride ahead of them. I spot a shortcut into the parallel street, an arched corridor of darkness between two houses. I dart into it as I hear their heavy clonking boots making the turn behind me.

Pressed back against the wall I hold my breath against the dank smell of stale water permeating the tunnel. My back feels damp against the brickwork; the chilliness seeping into my clothes makes me quiver. A trickle of murky water is oozing down the opposite wall in thick clumping splashes. Green moss edges the base of the bricks at my feet and travels along the ground like a directional aid.

I afford myself a glance out of the narrow opening, wishing for fresh air but not daring to move for fear of discovery. The horde of journalists thunder past the opening and spread out like a disease. I have outwitted them, this time, but next time I shall have to be more careful. I can hear them rummaging behind dustbins, the lids clattering and clanking on the ground in their haste to unearth me. The cries of frustration ring through the air and echo around my hiding place, circling me like a trap. I hold my breath and wait. They can't hang around long; no one would hang around here long, I think to myself. The area is not known for prettiness or prosperity.

For safety sake I force myself to wait in the darkness until I can be sure they have all gone. Even just one lone journalist would be more than I can bear right now. After what feels like forever I am ready to move. Gradually I peel myself away from the soggy wall and, with an involuntarily shudder, I tip toe through the tunnel out into the brightness of the other side. This can't be for nothing I decide, shaking my blouse free from its position stuck to my back, and realising the local charity shop will shortly have another outfit to launder and sell. I inhale deeply, keen to soak up the fresh air and free my nose from the vile stench of the tunnel. If I cannot out-run the media then I must find pleasanter places to hide. There isn't time to dwell. I have to be at the dance hall in twenty minutes and it is right across town. Hastily I make my way, my heels sounding on the pavement. Occasionally I glance over my shoulder but they are not following me. I am safe, for the moment. It is only a matter of time before they show up at my dance hall, or worse still, my house.

It is all Vivanti's fault of course, him and his silly posters. Michael and I are plastered across every rail station wall from here to Timbucktoo, life-size pictures of us in motion, strategically placed for the waiting crowds to gaze at as they line the platforms at Waterloo and Victoria. If it's not the posters then it's the newspapers, radio stations; the man is obsessed with publicity. Now, thanks to him, I cannot go anywhere without wearing a low hat or wig. I push him and his media craze from my mind.

I think about what the adoption agency has told me, the process one must go through in order to adopt a child, the many ways a child comes to be on their books. It is feasible, apparently, that my baby could have been taken there. The woman explained patiently how they undertake checks on paternity, where possible, but they didn't sound too robust to me. It would be easy to fake it, to pretend to be the parent. Naturally I didn't tell her my true purpose. If the press interview her she will assume I am looking to adopt a child, a young child or a baby. She will assume but she will be wrong. At the very least I must safeguard the fact of my baby's existence. If the press must print something then suspicions will have to satisfy them. They cannot have the facts. I must see to it that they don't gain possession of the facts. I must protect her, wherever she is.

I have nothing to go on but my intuition, nothing to base my search on but faith and determination. I check my wristwatch beneath the sleeve of my glove. Yes, I am dangerously close to being late. I hurry along the road, again another glance but still no one is following me.

When I arrive at the dance hall Michael is already there. There is no sign of Vivanti or the cleaning lady, Phyllis; who usually comes on weekday mornings to sweep, in what she thinks is time to the music.

'My God, what happened to you?' he asks. I remove my damp coat and hat and hang them up, peel off my gloves in silence. Without warning Michael takes me into his embrace, fingering my damp blouse in intrigue and concern. I let him hold me, feel his body close to mine and close my eyes. 'We don't have long,' Michael whispers into my hair. 'Viv will be here in a minute.' I nod, my hair growing static on his pressed black shirt. 'How are you?' His voice is mild, a casual question masking a whole series of unspoken ones. Slowly I look up at him.

'I missed you,' I tell him and he cups my face in his hand, brings his lips onto mine and answers in his own way. My mind races through time, back to a day when life was wonderful, to lying in Michael's arms, our bodies wrapped in each other's and twisted in pink satin sheets. Only the sunlight reflected our movement behind the locked door of the hotel suite, a shadow cast lightly over the room like a cloak of privacy.

Michael had not needed music; we had created our own rhythm, his vigorous naked body suspended over mine; dancing its way into my soul, and enveloping me in the tune of love. His hot passionate darts of movement, the sensuous feel of him melting my body into complete softness. Our lips insatiable, our bodies ravenous, our energy focused purely on each other.

'What happened?' he asks again. I blink back into the here and now with some reluctance. Softly I run my fingers over his chest and cast the memory to the back of my mind. 'You are ok, aren't you? I mean you're not hurt or anything?' Quickly I tell him about the media and he looks at me, a stunned expression staining his face. 'But they don't know, do they?'

'Apparently they do,' I say, unsure why he wouldn't realise that no matter what we hide, they always know. 'Oh come on, they knew what dances we were going to perform last year before we did. You didn't really believe my father when he said no one would ever know; did you?'

'Surely your father didn't tell anyone?' Michael studies me as he waits for an answer. I laugh at him, unable to stop myself.

'Of course not,' I sigh. 'He wouldn't dare tell anyone for fear of bringing it all back. I don't know how they know,' I say exasperated, 'they just do.'

'Look, don't worry about it,' he assures me, stroking my arm softly. I half smile at him, knowing he means well. He doesn't understand, I think. He'll never understand. How can a man possibly understand what it's like to carry a child, to give birth to that child, to love it with so much more intensity than you can ever believe exists, then to have it ripped away, your heart broken irreparably. A dull ache constantly resides in my chest. A part of me feels missing, empty, lost.

'They'll get bored and move onto someone else soon,' Michael is saying. He awards me a smile in an attempt to reconcile his own feelings on the subject. 'So, how are you?' he asks again, this time his eyes are searching mine for a true answer. I think about it. I feel terrible, my body aches from the sudden launch back into the daily routine, my head hurts from the nightly tears that threaten to drown me in my eventual sleep, and my jaw aches from the façade of smiling at Vivanti and my parents. The problem is I cannot lie to Michael. Instead I will sidestep the issue.

'I'll be fine,' I say. 'Listen,' I take his hands in mine and step back. 'I'm going to find her Michael,' I tell him, my own voice insistent and stronger than I feel. 'I mean it.' I want him to share in my excitement to reunite us with our child but instead Michael stares at me incredulously.

'I will find her,' I insist, pulling away from him and instantly wishing I hadn't spoken. The last thing I need is more objections. Naively I had thought he would be on my side, after all, she is his child as much as mine. I watch a shadow line his face and the fear in his eyes intensify.

'I meant, how do you feel, Joyce,' Michael says quietly. 'How are you?' he gestures in the vague direction of my abdomen with a face flushed with embarrassment. I swipe a hand aside as if my aching body doesn't matter. I'll get stronger I think to myself, I don't matter anymore, but she does.

'I'll be fine,' I say again. 'So, will you help me find her?' I ask, my heart sinking in realisation that he is too afraid to join me in the search for our missing baby daughter. These are the moments when I am most frustrated with him, why does he not fight for us?

'Is that why you were there, at the adoption agency? Searching?' He looks over my shoulder as Vivanti takes vast strides towards the entrance doors. Time is running out, again.

'Of course,' I say as if this should be evident. 'It's the obvious place to start. So, are you in or out?' I demand of him simply, losing patience rapidly. At this stage I decide not to tell him of my plans to visit hospitals, foster homes and the police too. He will be mortified. At best I know I can trust him to keep my secret, at worst he will do nothing.

'I don't think I want to talk about it,' he says, his eyes inspecting his shoes for minute specks of dust, 'not yet. I'm sorry,' he hunches his shoulders like a child. 'It's just too hard. Later,' he says as Vivanti swings through the doors like an actor taking the stage for the encore.

'Good morning my beauties,' he sings, opening all the doors around us with a clatter. The cleaning lady, Phyllis, appears behind him from the direction of the cupboard that stocks the mops, buckets and polish. Briefly I wonder how long she has been there.

'Ah, my dear lady,' Vivanti accosts the cleaning lady with energy and whirls her into his good books with an easy charm. She chuckles, enjoying the fleeting dream of the stage as he twirls her around the foyer. 'Can you give the floor a quick polish, I want to put them through their paces today,' he beams at Phyllis; a woman of indeterminate years with lines of wisdom around her eyes, a grey sheet tied around her hair and wearing, as usual, a stripey smock dress that does nothing to flatter her. She flushes crimson as Vivanti teases her shoulder with his fingers, threatening to twirl her again but instead he hurries her into the dance hall trailing her buffer machine behind them.

Michael and I stand there in the entrance foyer, facing each other, the space between us suddenly too large.

SPOTLIGHT EXPRESS – THE INDUSTRY'S CHOICE – 25 Sept 1959
CELEBRATED DANCER SEEKS HOME FOR CHILD

The well-known female half of the world's most cherished dance couple, Joyce Capelli, was spotted leaving a local adoption agency earlier this week. When questioned she fled the scene confirming the fact that she has something to hide. Could it be that the scandalous rumours earlier this year of a hushed up love affair were true? Could she be seeking a home for an unborn child? Pregnancy for the unmarried dance star would cast her into the shadows indefinitely. More intriguingly, who could the unconfirmed father be, if not her partner of the dance floor, the equally celebrated Michael Sutton?

The couple are scheduled to appear at the next round of judges' critique when the regional tournament commences, the world title championships and have a national tour commencing next year. We could see an opening for a new champion couple if Miss Capelli falls by the wayside into the realms of parenthood.

The newspaper hits the table with a thump, aided by my father's fist. All this is rather much for 7am I think. Ordinarily I would react but this time I am prepared. The teacups, however, are not. They leap into the air and bounce back down noisily with a clatter. Mother flinches, shaken with the sensation of an unwelcome surprise.

'What is the meaning of this?' my father shouts across the breakfast table, 'whatever do you think you're doing child?' He rises from his seat to take a stride about the room. 'The London world title is less than five years away, and the regional in three weeks. I thought you were working towards that?' he slams his fist against the wall in anger. I wonder if it hurts.

'I am searching for my daughter, father, nothing more, just as I told you I would,' I say calmly sipping my coffee and draining the last of the hot liquid gratefully. Wicked it may be, but given my belief in his part of her disappearance I am taking some small pleasure from seeing him squirm. It is true I hadn't intended my search to be revealed in quite so public a way, nor in its infancy, but since the camera flashed at me I have had time to reconcile with the idea that hiding it will be pointless from now on.

'Are you sure this is wise dear?' my mother asks me. I stare at her with bewilderment. Did she really think I was going to sit back and forget about her, my own child?

'Yes,' I tell her simply. 'I am sure it is.' I continue to butter my toast and nod when Rosa offers the coffee pot for a top up. 'Thank you,' I smile at Rosa. She vanishes; doubtless keen to escape the firing line.

'Dear God preserve us, you do realise what this will do to your career?' my father yells from the far side of the room. The early morning sun on the marble tiles is breath-taking. When I do not answer him he begins his striding back towards the table and hovers by his seat with uncertainty.

'Yes I do father, but I don't care. I want my baby back, whatever the cost,' I tell him, return the butter to the middle of the table and eat my toast. He stares at me dumbfounded and plonks himself back into his seat. 'You could save me time father,' I say without looking at him, 'just tell me where you sent her. I won't have to attract any unwanted media attention by searching then, will I?' I argue reasonably. He does not speak, simply stares at me with hot angry eyes. 'I'll go on looking so you may as well tell me now,' I threaten and sip my coffee. My mother doesn't speak, merely glances from him to me, wary.

'I don't know what you're talking about; all I know is that you've lost your senses child. I could forgive you once, you were upset, but twice!' his voice is rising like an eruption.

Here we go again I think to myself. 'How can you accuse me of such an act?' I do not say anything. What is there left to say except further recrimination? He treats me to a long cold stare then hurriedly finishes his coffee and gets up, his face crimson and his body agitated.

'I can't sit here like this,' he decides and marches out the room. My mother watches him leave the room, looks at me and closes her eyes. From the doorway I spy Rosa. I make my decision. My parents will not help me, but Rosa may. It is about time I spoke to her. She vanishes back into the kitchen as my mother begins to moan resignedly into her hands.

I continue to eat my toast.

The lights are bright, twinkling excessively as we await our entrance call in the wings. Around us the previous couples hover excitedly, a hint of anticipation at the forth-coming results mingled with nervous chatter. The noise bounces around my ears. I am trying not to listen to them.

Since the war ended Ballroom's popularity has grown, even more than before it seems. There were no competitions during the war and it feels as if the dancing world is trying to make up for lost time. The hunger is there for it certainly, the greed of the people behind me now just a flavour of what is yet to come.

The ICBD (International Council of Ballroom Dancing) was only established nine years ago and already it has changed the way these events are run. Up until this year it only awarded the Ballroom branch but now it recognises Latin American too. Vivanti says this will change things, make us even bigger stars. Maybe he will be proven right but for now I cannot think about that.

On the floor the couple before us are almost finishing their Foxtrot. I close my eyes; try to block it out, to hear only our music in my head instead of theirs. I must focus, concentrate, I must forget everything else for the next quarter of an hour. I must do this for Michael, and for the prize money that I can save from my father's clutches. I already have plans for this money, plans to track her down, which will demand payment.

I visibly flinch as the audience's applause sounds out. The previous couple are finished then, it is almost our turn. We will all dance together in heats of elimination next.

I can smell the sweat from those around me, the heat of the moment, the exertion and nervous energy poured into a regime that will last no more than a few precious minutes. From previous experience I know it can feel like an instant or a lifetime out there. There is no way to tell beforehand, only so much preparation that can be done. Practised steps, rehearsed routines, carefully created costumes, but in the end there is nothing anyone can do to help you with the nerves, the inner strength you need to step out onto the floor.

As the reigning champions we are scheduled to appear last. The previous couple; the promising mix of Desmond Basin & Elizabeth Winslade, surge past me in a cloud of euphoria and splash into the crowd of others waiting behind us; enmeshing themselves in the throng of waiting hopefuls. To add further pressure everybody, including those wishing otherwise behind us, fully expects us to win. I watch the band of ever-hopeful dancers snuggling together behind us, sequins, and sparkling outfits of all flamboyant colours, flushed made-up faces shining with glossy lipstick and overt eye shadow. Michael fingers my palms to draw my attention. I turn back to him to await the dreaded call out.

Three years ago I had stood here in the exact same spot, confidence streaming from me like a beacon, but now, I am simply not the same woman, and I feel it. I can barely stop shaking with fright. Michael takes my hand, gently applying a little more pressure to my palm for encouragement.

I look up at him briefly, his face cast in the shadow of the wings but I can still read the message in his eyes. It doesn't matter to him, or to me. With Michael I will always be enough. But to Vivanti and my father this means everything. Despite this Michael doesn't appear to have lost any of his confidence. Perhaps that will be enough; perhaps he will be enough to see us through this ordeal. I am wrong of course, the judges see everything in harsh reality, but I can pray. Life with my father will be unbearable if we do not retain our title.

We are about to dance the Argentine Tango and this is the regional championship; an annual event, for which Michael and I are entered automatically by my father.

This is a show dance. It doesn't count towards today's marks. The Argentine Tango sometimes falls under the Latin Swing title in Europe, but not in England. We have already performed our Foxtrot for the panel of judges. As the reigning champions it is considered polite to "give a little extra" Vivanti says, offering our services to the audience year after year, quite needlessly. I wish he had not offered us to entertain the crowd this year. Whilst we are dancing the judges will allow themselves a little extra time to check their scorecards. They will probably not be looking at us at all. Why then am I so nervous?

I must retain my core strength throughout the Argentine Tango, something Michael and Vivanti seem more confident about than I. The childbirth pains have all but passed but I am not yet as strong as I used to be and this dance is the hardest possible one we could have chosen.

'But this is your performance most spectacular my darlings,' Vivanti had protested when I suggested we swap for something easier. 'You are superb in it, you'll see, the winners you will be, I promise you!' he had spread his hands out as if seeing an invisible image, a premonition of our success, yet again. 'It will cement your title,' he insists, 'as well as your fabulous Foxtrot.' I am not so sure but it is too late for doubts, they are calling us out.

The entrance music is terrible. I try not to cringe. Michael offers me his hand, a wink and a smile, as he leads me to the centre of the floor. The applause of the audience is deafening, echoing around the dimly lit hall like a chant. I know that most of the audience will only have come to see us; our names are celebrated, unlike the other couples in this tournament. I have never come across another competitive event where amateurs and professionals can complete on an even playing field. If the rules were fairer we wouldn't be here at all in my opinion, one of the other couples would then have a better chance of taking their first glitzy step to stardom. If only they knew that it wasn't the glamorous world they thought it was. It is hard, painful, demanding, and yet it was what I wanted. What I thought I wanted. If I had known I would simply have settled for enjoying dance, without the pressure.

There is a strong spotlight that finds us instantly and I know it will follow us doggedly around the floor. A hush befalls the hall as the music starts and we take up open hold.

I can see Michael listening for the beat. Quickly I decide I will not worry about the beat, I will let him concentrate on that. After all, in this dance, I must follow his lead, even if he does fall off timing. It is all I can do to focus on him and his instruction, to hold my frame and my nerve.

I remind myself that the Argentine Tango is more about how we look, than what we do. Perhaps that will be enough to save me.

We start with a walk; I am going backwards as is custom for the woman, leaning into him so we are one apex. One, two, three, four, stepping on the beats of the music. I must keep my core strength; I remind myself, feel the tension riveted through my body, my legs stretching out far behind me with my weight over my toes, my heels never touching the floor as we caress the floor, the spotlight shining above, highlighting us, our passion mounting with every step.

Michael lets me feel the music for a moment, his hold of me growing stronger as we move. Gradually I feel his hand lowering, resting below my shoulder blades and I feel him gathering me into him like a precious jewel. I let him take my weight momentarily as I adjust into the position he wants of me. Only a couple as close as us could pull off this manoeuvre during the dance, to switch from an open hold into a more intimate stance whilst not detracting from the path around the floor.

This is Michael at his best, his true inner-self coming to the surface. It is sensuous, alluring, I am swept up completely by his command, his power over me. This is the dance during which I first realised I was in love with Michael; the heat, the drama, the intensity...he's so damn good at it.

Slow, slow, quick, quick, slow. One, two, three, four and into front Ochos; my feet painting out a figure of eight on the floor. I swivel around before him, a teasing movement, he leads me into them, commands my direction with ease. Then we're off again, a chase across the floor. It's a cat and mouse game, he catches me, I move away, taunt him, tease him, he rebounds a couple of steps and hastily chases me into a corner. I obey his instruction, he leans into me and I seductively wrap my leg around his, as he leans further towards me, my leg caresses his, rising tauntingly slowly up his until he moves back and I descend, a flick of my heel and backwards I go again, as he chases me, we dominate the floor to perfection.

The audience are enthralled but they are alien to me. All I feel, all I see, all my focus is purely on Michael, with him, every beat of the music, every step I take. It is not a dance you can learn by steps, it is something I feel, something I must give into, utterly and completely mirroring him, unconsciously moving in the direction he wants me to go. This is not something I can think about, I must surrender to him with all my soul.

I dare not look at him, my eyes fixated on the gap at the top of his shirt, mirroring his position, his body with mine, feeling his power as he seizes control of me effortlessly.

Charging me backwards my heels flick out, one, two, three, four, five, six and he captures me into a backwards lean. I wilt at his command and he pulls me back up, my body like a spinal wave as I revert to the position he demands of me, controlling my body in a bolt-like position. He careers me around another Contragiro and I take a wider step to keep in his mirror as we change direction around an invisible, irresistible, path across the dance floor.

We are already two thirds of the way through. I know this but I do not register the fact. I am under his spell, his control. He takes me across the breadth of the floor in one quick movement and we pause. I can feel my heart beating wildly; know that no matter what happens, he is my focus, my hero; the father of my child, my lover, and my leader.

I swivel into back Ochos this time, elegantly completing a Voleo, halting him; it is my moment to take the lead, briefly, before he charges me back towards the centre of the floor, a pause half way, a Cruce crossing my ankles and straightening up at his instruction, a Giro turning us as we progress further, eating up the floor with greed. He places his foot next to mine and I stop, statue still.

The audience are on the edge of their seat, the music momentarily faint. As Michael allows us to continue I step over his leg, seductively to the front and he throws me into a Gancho. Aggressively I hinge my leg around his thigh, one swift strong movement; sweeping back with gusto. He demands me to rock from side to side, before we take off again; we rock forwards and backwards, rebounding and acquiring the floor space towards our climax.

My ankles brush each other through Zero Point with each step I take, my toes slightly off to the sides as he steps outside of me and draws me into a Reverse Swivel. The final few moments are upon us.

I have no idea where we are, my focus is purely on Michael but I know we must be fairly central as he chases me the last few steps at rapid pace. With a violent twist he launches me into a back bend, he takes my right leg in his hand, my toes pointing to the sky and I let my body fall as we stop, my hair touching the floor and my gaze to the ground.

The audience erupt and I feel Michael release my leg and raise me elegantly to my feet. My breath is coming in gasps now as he bows, stands aside to indicate me to the crowds who are on their feet, their hands raw from aggressive clapping. I curtsey and await Michael's hand to lead me off the floor.

A strange elation fills me, oddly familiar but like nothing I've felt before. Never before have I battled so hard for such a performance. In previous attempts it has come easily, natural ability and dedicated training, sole focus and concentration, no worldly concerns to distract me. Today is different. Everything is different. I am pleased with myself. Irrespective of the result I know I have performed well, perhaps better than in previous years, spurred on by adrenalin, a real purpose for winning, a real goal to achieve. At last I remember the thrill of dancing, the real passion it has always evoked in me. Finally I feel more like myself again.

CHAPTER FIVE – MODERN DAY; APRIL

Rebecca packed the vacuum cleaner into the cupboard under the stairs and rammed the door shut. She would have to start the spring-cleaning soon. It would be hard to sort through Craig's things but she knew she couldn't put it off forever.

Jean bustled into the hallway the moment Rebecca opened the front door. Divorced and single, Jean saved all her chatter for when she met up with Rebecca.

'Oh my, Becca, what a day I've had,' she exclaimed, an armful of holiday brochures slipping away from her grasp, their glossy covers depicting families on the sandy shores of tranquil blue seas. 'The travel agents were packed, I had to wait for yonks just to get these,' she thrust the brochures at Rebecca as she let them slip onto the kitchen work surface. 'How are you my dear?' she paused for breath, kissing Rebecca on the cheek, her shapeless top brushing against her fleetingly.

'Ok,' Rebecca assured her friend. 'Tea?' she managed to chip in before Jean's flow recommenced.

'Oh yes dear lovely, gasping I am, simply gasping. Course I know all about grief from my mother,' Jean was saying, her platinum blonde hair bouncy and light with her movement towards the lounge where she found an armchair to collapse in with a loud sigh. 'And I don't just mean her death,' she babbled, blue eyes alive with excitement. Rebecca had heard the dreadful tale a thousand times before but she listened good-humouredly. Jean loved to talk, even the most morbid of subjects brought colour to her ample cheeks. 'That awful obsession of hers,' Jean continued, 'with the children I mean.'

The doorbell cut her flow and both women stared towards the hallway. Rebecca didn't know whom to expect but she certainly didn't expect the Inspector back again so soon.

'Mrs Houseman,' he removed his hat, tilted it at her and replaced it jauntily so it slid perilously to one side. 'Sorry to trouble you again,' he began as she widened the door. 'Thank you,' he grinned, wiping his feet and finding his own way into the lounge. 'Hello,' he grinned at Jean who was now flopped into an armchair, impatiently waiting to continue her story.

'Hi,' she drew herself up into a sitting position as Rebecca entered the lounge.

'This is my friend Jean Duchess,' she smiled. 'Jean this is Inspector Allen. Do you want a cup of tea Inspector?'

'Yes, that would be lovely Madam, a good strong colour, thank you,' he grinned at her, removed his coat and scarf and tossed them by his side as he sat on the settee, his hat now twirling on his fingertips.

Rebecca could hear Jean waffling onto the Inspector as she made the tea. It would not be easy, she feared, to answer whatever questions he had, with Jean there.

'I mean it's so hard isn't it. Can you imagine a woman not being able to have a baby?' Jean was saying as Rebecca brought the tray into the lounge. Oh dear, she thought, she would have to referee. 'I mean Inspector, my poor mother; she was driven to desperation she was, driven to it I tell you. Dear oh dear, and now Becca is getting these nightmares, my how I worry, I've told her you know; it's probably the grief. She'll be fine though will Becca; it's not as if she'd do anything so daft like my poor mother…'

'Sugar?' Rebecca cut in, her voice assertive.

'Two please,' Inspector Allen told her, accepting the cup and saucer with a grin. 'Perfect,' he mused admiring the strong colour of the stained liquid in his cup. He took large gulps whilst it was still hot and rested the half-drunk cup on his knee, the saucer on the arm of the settee. Rebecca poured out hers and Jean's.

'How can I help you Inspector?' she asked quickly before Jean could claim the flow again.

'We've got that mechanic down the station Madam,' the Inspector said, finishing off the last gulp of his tea with relish. 'Wells has him looking at mug shots as we speak,' he laughed, clattering his cup on the saucer and replacing it on the tray. 'He was bribed all right, and I think I know who by,' the Inspector told her as she took the other armchair, noticing for the first time that Jean was speechless.

'Who?' Rebecca asked, suddenly wishing she didn't want to know. If somebody wanted to harm her surely it was better all around if the police just took that person away. What was she supposed to do with that information anyway?

'Well Madam, I think I know who orchestrated it shall we say,' he removed a pencil from his pocket and chewed on the end. Jean grimaced. 'But there's somebody else behind it, someone who gave him the order... I'll get to the bottom of it Madam, don't you worry.'

'The ginger man...' Rebecca began.

'Oh no Madam,' the Inspector laughed, a deep throaty sound that resonated through the room vigorously. 'No, he made him up. That's why we've got him down the station, just to kill a bit of his time. No, no, there's a John Francis...' he paused to see if Rebecca registered the name. She didn't. 'He's a retired businessman, lives over in a fancy place in Keyes, he's behind a carefully organised car theft ring,' he mused, the pencil now gnawed sufficiently he stuffed it back into his pocket. 'Cars stolen to order. That sort of thing.'

'You're the one who was in the newspaper aren't you?' Jean piped up, her finger in the air and her eyes alight with intrigue.

'Newspaper? Probably, yes Madam,' he grinned. 'The mechanic at the garage where your car went...'

'Milton, the dying murderer, you're the one who caught him,' Jean screamed in delight. 'It was only a month or so ago wasn't it?' she squealed. 'There was a photo of you in court.'

'Yes, it was in the papers,' the Inspector grimaced. 'Still, never mind.' He turned back to Rebecca and Jean slumped into her chair, sipped at her tea sulkily.

'You were saying Inspector?' Rebecca prompted. 'The mechanic...'

'Oh yes, the mechanic, he's involved somehow, probably gets duplicate keys cut when he's got a car that Francis wants.

The customer takes his car away. Then, a few days later, with the duplicate key, it's stolen and delivered to Francis's house in Keyes where his client picks it up.'

'That's terrible Inspector,' Rebecca shook her head. 'What does that have to do with my car though? I mean nobody has stolen my car. Or do you think they will?'

'No, no, your car is safe. It's err,' the Inspector coughed, 'only specific models they're after,' he grinned.

'Oh I see,' Rebecca smiled. 'My old car isn't good enough for thieves hey?' she laughed. 'Well, I'm glad, but I've never heard of this Mr Francis though, why should he order my brakes be tampered with?' she asked him, her tea almost forgotten, a light cover skimming the surface like a seal.

'He did it at request of someone else. I'll be digging around him a bit later on Madam, don't worry, I'll find out who asked him to set it in motion. The mechanic got paid well for it, he only fed us that stupid ginger-haired twaddle when we asked, 'cos he doesn't want the theft caper to break up, see he gets a hefty chunk of the profits too.'

'Was it a one-off then, the brakes, or do they tamper with cars all the time?' she asked, replacing her cold tea on the tray untouched. 'Like a sideline?'

'I reckon it was a one-off Madam,' the Inspector narrowed his moustache with his fingertips thoughtfully, his gaze lost in a place neither Rebecca or Jean could see. 'That's why they made such a mess of the thing,' he grinned, 'thankfully.'

'Yes, quite,' Rebecca sighed. 'I still don't see why though.' The doorbell chimed again. 'Excuse me,' she said rising to answer the door and accepting a parcel from the postman. 'You were saying…' she smiled at the Inspector and put the parcel on the table next to the tea tray. It was an odd shaped box and she wondered briefly what it was. She hadn't ordered anything.

'I wanted you to be very careful Madam,' he cast a sly smile, eyed her curvaceous shape with a grin as she sat back down, 'you understand, don't you, that if the intent to harm you is still there, well, they didn't succeed the last time so…'

'They'll try again?' Jean finished for him. The Inspector nodded, his gaze fixed on Rebecca. She held her breath a moment and glanced quickly over at Jean.

'You get the point. Now, Madam, do you mind if I use your bathroom whilst I'm here?'

'No problem Inspector, the downstairs toilet is just at the back there, near the back door.' She half smiled as the Inspector left the room, reaching for the parcel. Jean was silent until she heard the Inspector close the bathroom door.

'You never said,' Jean admonished her friend. 'Why didn't you tell me?'

'I forgot, you know, what with...' Rebecca felt the tears prick at the backs of her eyes again and she blinked hard to keep them at bay.

'I know dear, I'm sorry. Do you want some help with that?' Jean asked, as her friend wrested with the parcel tape on the package.

'Maybe,' Rebecca accepted, 'I don't know what this is,' she said, 'but it's tied up well,' she stood to gain better leverage on the packet. Jean rose to help her and together the women stood by the mantelpiece ripping at the package. With a sudden burst the wrapping came away in their hands and a cardboard box fell to the floor with a thud and an unambiguous clicking sound.

The sound of the downstairs lavatory flush masked any further sound from the package as the Inspector stepped through the doorway to the lounge and the cardboard box on the floor burst into flames.

Rebecca screamed, sprang back and fell in the armchair. She couldn't see Jean through the flames, the heated wall between them menacing and lofty. Several tall sparks of golden red fire licked the air greedily as the women cried in fear. Rebecca felt her throat tighten and her entire body tremble hysterically.

'Get back!' the Inspector shouted, grabbing his coat and scarf and stretching them out over the flames. His hat fell from the fringes of his grasp, a victim to the heat that consumed the flimsy mucky fabrics in seconds. The burning smell of wool filled the air. Dark grey smoke flittered in bursts around them but the fire had died, a sudden death, its murky ghost haunting the room like a disease, spreading dark patches over her nice white ceiling and marking its ascent up the walls like a shadow.

Rebecca coughed, felt her tears falling and her shock vibrating through her as she sat, curled up in a knot of fright, in the armchair. It was Jean who came to her, tip toeing over the fire damaged carpet and dragged her to her feet, into an embrace.

Inspector Allen stood over the smoking hole on the carpet, his mobile phone in his hand. Painstakingly slowly he pushed the numbers to dial the station.

'Son, get over here, Mrs Houseman's,' he barked into the mobile. The women stood holding each other, waiting for instruction. 'Get a fire officer here too, forensics, the whole lot...no, sod the mechanic...just get here...quick son, quick,' he cut the phone off and pushed it back into his shirt pocket. Even his worn grey suit looked a nicer shade than the charcoal of her lounge. 'Are you both ok?' Inspector Allen asked; black marks on his face and hands from his close proximity to the flames. They nodded at him dutifully. 'I want you both to wait in the kitchen,' he said quietly, 'I'll have to take this up seriously now Mrs Houseman,' he tried a pallid smile but it had no effect. Rebecca was shaking. Someone had sent that package...what if she had been home alone?

'Come on Becca,' Jean was saying, leading her out of the fire-singed lounge, smoke still circling the ceiling like fog.

They sat at the kitchen table, the stunned shock only just settling in. Rebecca closed her eyes, wishing beyond all hope that Craig could be with her, to hold her close to him, to feel his warmth assuring her that the world had gone mad but would all be well the next day.

Within ten minutes the house was swarming with white-coated forensic scientists, a fire officer and two or three more uniformed police constables. She recognised the short plump one who was with the Inspector before taking charge of the proceedings inside the house, and wondered where the

Inspector had gone. Briefly she glanced down the hallway to the open front door and spotted him, out the front, chewing on the end of a cigarette with relief and greed, his face colourless and translucent.

'Well I was going to try and persuade you to come on holiday with me,' Jean was saying, her voice recovering quickly over the din of the extensive team at work in the lounge. 'But now I'm ordering you. We've got to get you away from here, and fast.'

'Ok Jean, whatever you say. Just give me a minute, I'm going to have a word with the Inspector,' she smiled at her friend. 'Can you put some coffee on?' She slipped away to find the Inspector and led him up the stairs.

'I think we can find you a new coat,' she was saying as Inspector Allen followed. 'I'm sure there's one in here that would fit you.'

'Really Mrs Houseman, it's fine,' Inspector Allen insisted but Rebecca was adamant.

'You save our lives and I can't even get you a new coat? Come now Inspector,' she managed a smile. 'My husband bought this many years ago,' she said, her voice almost lost in the depths of the wardrobe. She emerged, dragging a dark forest green Mackintosh out from the rail. 'It hasn't been worn in years,' she said presenting the coat on its hanger and dusting it down a little. 'Too small for him in the end,' her eyes brighter with the memory, 'too many café breakfasts I'm afraid,' she heard herself laughing lightly. Oh Craig, if only you were here, she thought.

'Café breakfasts hey, a man after my own heart,' Inspector Allen grinned. 'But really Mrs Houseman, you don't have to…'

'Try it,' Rebecca insisted, removing the hanger and handing the long green coat to the Chief Inspector. He cast a wide boyish grin and slipped the coat on. There were a few rips at the pockets and a dark blobbed stain on the sleeve but otherwise it was fairly smart. Half surprised he glanced in the mirror on the wardrobe door and smirked. Well, well, he never thought he'd find another coat he liked as much as his faithful charity shop purchase twenty years previously.

'Here,' Rebecca thrust a black scarf at him and pulled a forest green hat with a wide slanting brim out from the vast black magic that appeared to exist in her wardrobe.

'Thank you Mrs Houseman,' Inspector Allen treated her to one of his rare genuinely warm smiles that showed nothing except gratitude.

'The hat is a bit dated,' Rebecca half laughed. 'Craig used to wear it to go fishing, one of the kids bought it for him as a joke but it kept the sun off his face,' she told him, a tinge of sadness at seeing the hat on another man, but it was better than it sitting in the cupboard doing nothing. She had promised herself she would spring-clean. Redecorate too; she just hadn't planned on doing any of it quite so quickly.

'They won't know what's hit them down at the station,' Inspector Allen smirked. 'Well, well, what a day. I'll get this man, I promise you,' he said, his voice uncharacteristically stern.

'I know you will Inspector,' Rebecca said, suddenly absolutely sure that he would.

The blue slide loomed over her head, her sister hiding behind the steps. She was counting to ten. Mother was rocking the pram. Her baby brother's crying was slowly fading out as he gave up the fight against sleep. There was a park bench and a woman was sitting there. A grey gloved hand in hers. A smiling mouth telling her a story. Long dark hair, like hers, only shinier in the sun, gleaming, calling her over...The scent of freshly made ham sandwiches, flasks of tea and Victoria sponge cake with jam. A kind face with eyes as clear as night. Something familiar about the woman with her long dress-coat the colour of soft sand and a hat with a wide brim. Her sister running around the slide frantically, chasing her, trying to catch up...Climbing the steps quickly. A name...

It was three in the morning when Rebecca sat up in bed with a jolt. Clear as day she could still smell cream icing, see the lady, hear her say her name…no, it was gone. She closed her eyes and tried to clear her mind. No, it was no good; the name wouldn't come back to her.

Rebecca curled up under the covers and traced her mind through the research material she had printed off Neil's computer. What had the documents advised; establish fixed times for going to sleep and waking up, relax before bed, maintain a comfortable sleeping environment. She had done all those things; she had never had trouble sleeping before.

It was useless; she felt restless, twisted the sheets beneath her and got up. The night sky was starless as she drew back the curtains and opened the window a fraction. The cool air covered her skin in a fraction but she felt better, her body temperature returning to normality with ease.

Avoid napping it had said, well she hadn't napped. She had never been one for naps anyway. Avoid caffeine, nicotine or alcohol just before bed. She had never smoked, or drank heavily, only herbal teas in the evenings. What more could she do?

She traced her fingertips along the windowsill as the cool night air soothed her mind. Closing her eyes she let the air wash over her, feeling the sensation of cleansing. For her own sanity she had to find a cure, to free herself of the persistent dream, to find a way to stay asleep.

The new foundation had been expensive but it covered the dark circles that were gradually forming under her eyes perfectly. Moving deftly away from the window she sat on the edge of the bed and looked at the clock. The digits lit up the room dimly. 03:11am. That was another tip she had read; not to continually check the time during the night, but she found it irresistible.

Briefly she wondered if she might try the paradoxical intention suggestion she had read about in-depth. It wasn't that she had trouble going to sleep, the grief at losing Craig was eating into her sleep, that was true, but eventually her body would overrule and she knew at some point before 1am she would fall sleep. It was staying asleep that she suspected was going to be the long-term issue for her. The idea suggested to her by the NHS website was to try and avoid going to sleep, to fight it, to drag her body to the point of exhaustion that nothing could wake her until the morning dawn called. It was worth a try.

Suddenly chilly she closed the window and curled back under the covers. With at least three hours before it was decent to get up, she had no alternative but to stay in bed. Maintain regular sleeping hours, she reminded herself with dread. Here goes…she closed her eyes praying the dream wouldn't return.

'Oh my God,' Katherine screeched, taking in the damaged lounge. 'Can we touch it yet?' Rebecca nodded. Most of the photographs had been saved from the scorching torrent by the Inspector's swift action. For that alone she would always be grateful to him. A new coat and hat were a small price to pay for saving the family photographs, especially the most recent ones of Craig that shone out at her, untouched, from the otherwise depressive mantelpiece.

'I guess I had better start clearing up,' she sighed. 'Where's little Craig?'

'He and Neil are at home. I called Eliza and Samuel,' she gave her mother a half smile. 'They're coming over to help too, in about an hour.'

'Thanks love,' Rebecca sighed, surveying the room again with melancholy. So many years and so many memories of their life together all gone in a single moment. 'Ok,' she clapped her hands together resolutely. 'Fetch some bin bags,' she instructed her youngest daughter, 'cupboard under the sink, let's get started.' Katherine went to the kitchen obediently.

Rebecca pulled everything that could be saved, including the precious photographs and began building a tower in the hallway. 'Fill those with anything we need to throw,' she tried to smile brightly as Katherine returned, a roll of black bin liners in her hand and a blank expression on her face.

'What did the insurance company say mum?'

'Oh they sent an assessor round yesterday afternoon when the police were here, said I should send them quotations. It helped of course, that the police were here at the time. I've no doubt I'd still be waiting for them to answer the phone if that nice Inspector hadn't forced their hand.'

'Mum, what are you not telling me?' Katherine's blue eyes were dazzlingly clear, her lavender top reflecting her beauty even more than usual. 'Why is the Inspector still looking into a simple mistake by the garage?'

Rebecca held her breath. She wasn't sure she wanted to allow her children to worry about her. It was bad enough that Jean had been a witness to the proceedings and she knew she couldn't keep Jean from spilling the news all over town. Perhaps that was best though, to throw the culprit off his guard…It would be far worse if any of her family heard about it from someone else. Surely they would be hurt, upset that she hadn't chosen to tell them herself.

'Mum?'

'It'll all blow over love, I promise. They think someone is trying to harm me, but they're on the case…'

'Mum! How could you not tell me?' Katherine's wail only proved her suspicions; she was already hurt. Rebecca felt hot tears cutting her eyes. For Katherine's sake she could not let them fall.

'Don't worry sweetheart,' Rebecca tried to keep her voice calm, to control the growing fear that was tying her insides up in knots every day. 'The police are on the case. Anyway, until yesterday I didn't know there was anything to worry about. I forgot about it mostly…'

'Forgot?' Katherine cried; her hysteria mounting. Rebecca dragged herself over the charcoaled carpet and hugged her daughter tightly. 'You can't let anybody take you away from us,' she was sobbing, her tears melting into Rebecca's shiny hair. 'You can't, it's not fair. We've already lost dad…'

'Shss…' Rebecca soothed, stroking her daughter's back tenderly. 'I'm not going anywhere sweetheart, I promise. Everything's going to be ok.'

'You promise?' Katherine pulled back, looked at her mother directly.

'Absolutely,' Rebecca heard herself saying, her own voice stronger than she felt. 'Now, come on, we have to get cracking. I'm going to need your help to decide on the new colour and a new sofa,' she tried to laugh lightly. Katherine raised a smile and together the women began to tackle the fire-riddled room.

Jean had telephoned later that day with the news that she was returning, her mission to persuade Rebecca to book a holiday with her failed due to the excitement of the post. Rebecca was none too keen to go away but a part of her was glad of the excuse, to escape the madman who was trying to kill her. If anything it would be a relief, unless he followed her...she doubted Suffolk Constabulary's expenses extended to the Inspector accompanying her as a bodyguard.

Rebecca flicked through the brochures Jean had left behind. It did look inviting, there was no denying that. France, Spain, Turkey, Italy, Portugal, Egypt, the Canary Islands, they all looked so beautiful and perfectly peaceful.

She sipped at her coffee in the kitchen, the lounge unbearable to look at, stripped as it was to the bare walls and damaged furniture. Perhaps Jean was right, a holiday couldn't hurt and she could afford it. Warming to the idea she turned to the second brochure and tried to focus. She had never been on holiday without Craig before, well not since she was a little girl and her parents took her away...but even then it was usually in the UK. Money was tight. For the first time in a long while she wished her sister were there. A pity both her sister and little brother had chosen to move to Australia. It was lonely being the only one left. Of course she had a lifelong invitation but it wasn't the same as popping round for a cup of coffee on a Saturday morning and gossiping about the local news.

Their parents had died some years previously, a fatal car accident on the new motorway. Life just wasn't fair, she only hoped her children stood a better chance of a higher life expectancy than she was likely to achieve.

Rome looked nice, she thought, she would suggest that to Jean. It didn't seem to matter to Jean where they went, so long as they went somewhere. Briefly wondering if the children would think it wrong of her to go on holiday at this time she turned the corner of the page and picked up her phone. If she didn't call Jean she knew she wouldn't get around to it. Pushing her guilt aside she dialled the number quickly. Jean would book it and then it would be too late, she would have to abide by her commitment.

The Inspector would probably approve, she found herself smiling. Getting out of town was perhaps the smartest move she had made in weeks. Somehow she didn't think he would approve of the sunny climate of Rome though, perhaps Niagara Falls was more his style.

Rebecca felt a chill zip through her body as she managed to quell Jean's excitable insistence that she was going straight to the travel agents that minute. In a few weeks she and Jean would be soaking up the culture and the sunshine, sipping a crisp white wine on a romantically designed terrace balcony, and Paul Wood would be waiting to say hello at the Samba practise. Where had he come from, this guy she barely knew, an attractive stranger who kept randomly popping up in her thoughts, why did she keep thinking about him and why was she so keen for next week to come around? She shoved it from her mind with calculated force and started on a list of items to pack.

'You look like something out of the 1940s in that hat Sir,' Sergeant Wellington chuckled. Inspector Allen gave him a quick glance and plonked his slim frame into his chair wordlessly.

'It was a kind gift son,' he said, his mouth narrowing into a scowl, 'and I happen to like this hat,' he indicated the slanting forest green hat in question and removed it, admiring it keenly as he rested it on his desk. It covered the latest summons from the chief superintendent nicely, which was a bonus.

'Yes Sir,' Wells coughed clumsily. 'Quite, super wants a report on the car thefts Sir,' he said. The Inspector clicked his tongue against the roof of his mouth and drew a cigarette from his packet, lighting it without a word. He planted his feet on top of the monthly news bulletin with a thumping sound, the loose chippings from the car park outside now skipping free from the tread of his shoes and falling over the many files on his desk.

'Does he indeed, well give him one son,' Inspector Allen instructed. 'Tell him we're close to an arrest.'

'Are we Sir?' Wells queried, the hat comment completely forgotten. 'But Sir, we haven't even interviewed anybody,' he protested. 'What shall I say?'

'We don't need to interview anybody,' Inspector Allen told him, a perfect ring of smoke drifting from his mouth into the misty air of the office. The Inspector watched it with pride as it dissipated towards the office door and buckled. 'It's Francis son, we'll arrest him in good time, when it suits us. Just tell him we're gathering evidence to please the court.' He puffed out another smoke ring and grinned. 'That'll please him enormously son,' he laughed. 'Get onto forensics too. Tell them to meet us at Francis's place later today, about 4.30pm.'

'You can't do that Sir,' Wells objected. 'I mean you can't let them see…'

'Don't worry son,' the Inspector spun in his chair, his feet on the floor again. 'We'll get there 4.15pm, we'll be safely inside before the white brigade turn up. Wells was visibly relieved as Inspector Allen stubbed his cigarette out in the ashtray and closed the second draw of his desk with a slam. A white trail drifted guiltily from the seeping gap in the wood of the draw. 'Let's get out of here son,' he leapt to his feet, flipped his hat onto his head expertly, and bounced towards the door, grabbing his new forest green Mackintosh and black scarf from the stand as he passed.

'Right son,' Inspector Allen cast a good look up and down Broadbent Gardens. There was nobody in sight. 'Don't you hear the sound of a disturbance in there?'

'Oh no Sir, it's quiet...' Wells began, noticing the digital clock tick over at 4.15pm.

'It's eerily quiet isn't it son, let's go over there, take a quick look and make sure everything's ok. Bring that thing,' he poked a finger at the car radio. 'Come on,' the Inspector said, a grin craftily playing around his mouth. Sergeant Wellington followed the Inspector out the car and across the road. Slightly breathless, he reached his side as the Inspector was opening the iron gates, peering through the windows and tracing the walls around to the back door. 'Do you hear that son?' he beamed. 'Call the station, tell them we're entering this property on the grounds of public safety,' the Inspector smiled quickly, proceeded to wrap his hand around his new black scarf and smashed a small pane of glass in the back door.

'Sir,' Wells called.

'Radio in son, quick, do it now. It has to be this time,' he instructed, slipping his hands into a pair of white latex gloves.

'But Sir,' Wells was saying, punching his chubby fingers at the keys. 'It might be alarmed...'

'It isn't,' he grinned smartly, stretching out his long gloved fingers. 'I checked.' He threw a balled up pair of gloves at his Sergeant. 'Put these on,' he smiled. 'We must abide by the rules mustn't we,' he chuckled, waiting for Wells to receive a reply from the radio.

'All clear Sir,' Wells announced uncomfortably as the radio crackled into a thick silence. He unrolled the gloves and slid them on, the inside powder making his hands itch irritably.

'Marvellous son, come on, let's go and keep the peace,' he chirped, hooking his hand through the broken pane and unlocking the door. 'Chase up the forensics team son,' the Inspector was calling as he crunched over the tiny fragments of glass on the doormat and headed straight through the kitchen into a vast open plan hallway, where a beam of daylight was flooding through the opaque glass of the front doors. 'I want them here to give Francis a bit of a scare.'

'Yes Sir,' Wells said, sidestepping the glass and following the Inspector into the richly carpeted hallway as he mumbled into his radio again. 'What are we looking for then, Sir?' Wells asked, clipping his radio safely back onto his belt.

The Inspector had found his way into a vast living room complete with a grand piano, expensive surround-sound home cinema system and three large corner sofa groups. A dark mahogany cabinet sat primly in the corner, probably stuffed with vintage liquor and crystal glasses.

Wells followed the Inspectors roaming eye as he scanned the room, the objects sliding easily into his photographically accurate memory.

'I've no idea son,' Inspector Allen paused, smiled wildly at his Sergeant and released his chewed pencil from its entrapment in his pocket for further torment. 'But we'll know when we find it. Let's check out the study. He must have one...' his voice vanishing, pencil stuck between his teeth as he sauntered off out into the hallway and towards one of the closed doors. 'In here, son,' his voice called, a soft firmness that Sergeant Wellington knew only too well. It meant a breakthrough.

'What Sir?' he trotted towards him, pushed the study door a tad wider and found the Inspector peering through some open files on a large wooden desk, the richness of the furniture's aroma thick in the air. 'Oh, what's that?'

'This, son,' the Inspector grinned happily, 'is our next move.' He presented the Sergeant with a business card advertising the delights of an exclusive club for the world's elite. 'Note down the details son, we'll pop along there later.'

'Allen,' a thin voice sang through the air. Wells trotted away to greet the forensics team. The Inspector glanced quickly around the room to see if he could find anything else of interest. A photograph of Francis, his arm around another man's shoulders, a shorter man with dark hair, quite a bit younger, dark eyes and a crooked smile. Both men wore tuxedos', shiny black shoes, the backdrop a plush hotel lobby.

A cupboard stood proudly by the window. Inspector Allen twiddled with the handles. They drifted open casually. Francis should really lock things away properly, he grinned to himself. Another shelf full of files, photographs with labels and dates on them were stacked neatly on the shelves. He selected one folder and laid it bare on the desk, revealing photographs of cars with the registration plates clearly visible, and duplicate log books. Another sheet caught his eye; a detailed list of names, records of monies received.

Inspector Allen sank his pencil back into the depths of new forest green coat pockets and blew out an imaginary smoke ring. Bingo.

'What the hell is going on? Get out of my house.'

That'll be John Francis then, Inspector Allen thought casually, sliding the files back into the cupboard and standing freely in the hallway where he could plainly see the forensics team trying to keep the owner of the property at bay.

'You!' He spotted the Inspector who inclined his hat at him casually. 'What do you think you're doing? Aren't you supposed to have some sort of search warrant?'

'Good afternoon Mr Francis; we meet again.'

'Where's your warrant? I'll have you for this,' he was shouting, his face a nasty shade of red and his eyes bright with anger.

'You really must try to calm down Sir, we're the police, remember?' Inspector Allen treated him to a sly smile. 'Nothing to worry about. You see the thing is Sir,' he began strolling about the safety of the hallway. Francis was trapped on the other side of the forensics team who were detailing everything in the vague vicinity of the broken glass. 'There was a suspected disturbance Sir, we thought we heard noises from inside the house,' he spoke calmly; tweaking his moustache, 'and do you know what we found?'

John Francis stared at him coldly. The light streaming in from the hallway reflected off Inspector Allen's grey hair, and flickered over his head.

'One of those little glass panes was broken Sir,' Inspector Allen whistled, rocking slightly on his heels. 'You know you really should invest in an alarm system, house like this,' he grinned, waved his hands around him to indicate the luxury.

'Lucky we were in the area Sir,' he concluded with a smirk. 'Are you almost ready lads?' he addressed the team in white coats.

After a chorus of nods they began to pack away their equipment.

'Don't you worry Sir,' the Inspector smiled at John Francis coyly, removed his white gloves slowly and stuffed them in his pocket. 'We don't think the culprit got much further than the kitchen. I expect he heard us coming and legged it.' The team, duly briefed by Wells on arrival about what to do should Francis appear, were packed up and out in a matter of seconds. 'We'll take these samples here,' the Inspector strolled happily towards the angry Francis, who stood by his back door, his face puffed out with hot air, 'and we'll trace the intruder for you.' Inspector Allen passed close to John Francis as Sergeant Wellington waited on the perimeter of the doorway, waiting for the sprint towards the car. Allen wouldn't hang around once he actually commenced his stride…'Unless he wore gloves Sir,' Inspector Allen spoke so quietly, almost in the man's ear. Francis flinched. 'Goodbye Sir, I'd get that fixed if I were you,' he pointed to the broken glass, grinned quickly and strode out towards the car.

CHAPTER SIX – EARLY OCTOBER 1959

There is a soft knock at my bedroom door. I lean up on one elbow from my position on the bed, surprised. I am not expecting company. It is Sunday and, as usual, Michael and I have been to the Hammersmith Palais to practise. I always enjoy these sessions, without Vivanti's eagle eyes, other dancers around us. We have so many friends there too, real people who live in the real world, with real lives to tell us about.

The soft knock taps again. The evening is growing late and I have retired from my parents company as early as I could excuse myself. I wonder now who it could be.

'Come in,' I say, hoping it will not be my father demanding my return to the lounge. Rosa's head peers around the door tentatively. 'Oh hello Rosa, come in,' I smile at her, relief too great to mask.

'Miss Capelli,' she begins, closing the door and twiddling her thumbs around her apron strings cautiously. 'I hope you mind not that I speak with you now,' her eyes downcast and her voice quiet.

'Of course not Rosa,' I smile at her encouragingly. 'Have a seat,' I pat the end of the bed but she does not sit. Instead she abandons the apron strings and pulls up a chair. 'Now,' I try to catch her eye, 'what's wrong?'

'It is not I Miss, I, err, I…'

'Don't worry Rosa, you can tell me,' I insist, now sitting fully upright and curious. The dying sun is shadowing the room in a half-light as we sit, relative strangers who have known each other my entire life, anticipating a conversation that will evidently border on the fringes of propriety.

'I hope you not mind Miss, but I am worried about you. It is now three months since your baby, she was taken.' I feel my blood run cold at the mention of it. I hide my eyes in an effort to shield the inevitable sadness from Rosa. It is not her fault. I nod silently. 'I worry about you Miss. You do not recover quick enough.'

'I'm tired Rosa, that's all, it has been difficult, with the regional championship...' I try to reassure her, touched by her concern.

'Oh yes Miss,' Rosa interrupts; her hands now on top of mine in earnest. 'I understand. You work very hard. You do very well to win, I think. I know it must be very hard for you.'

'Yes,' I answer shortly, my breath suddenly shallow. 'Yes, it was. But now there is a little time for rest. I have some time now,' to find her, I think.

'Is there anything I can do for you Miss, anything more?' Rosa looks at me, her big eyes wide and hopeful. I begin to wonder.

'You knew didn't you Rosa, from the start I mean, you knew I was going to have a baby?' Rosa nods at me in answer. 'I thought so.'

'I feel sorry you are sent away from here Miss. I could take care of you. I tell Madam but Sir, he say you must go.'

'I know Rosa, I know,' I pat her hand. 'It's all over now. I promise you I am fine. There is something...'

'What Miss?' Rosa leans forward, her big eyes wide with longing. It is at this moment that I realise I am possibly the reason Rosa stays in our employment. It is true she is well paid; she has comfortable, even luxurious quarters of her own, treated like one of the family. She could do much worse. Yet when I watch her serve my parents there is no feeling. When she pours my coffee it is always with a smile. 'I will help you Miss. I remember when you were a little girl, very sweet you are.' She smiles at me quickly, flutters her eyelids in case she has gone too far.

'Rosa, I want to find my daughter,' I tell her suddenly. 'I have been searching for her but I have not found her yet.' I look at Rosa's face. She does not register shock. 'You are not surprised,' I observe.

'Of course I am not surprised,' Rosa takes my hand in hers. 'I think I too would look. Yes, I will help you.' She is nodding insistently, pleased to be of service. I am grateful but I must also be careful. I must not put her livelihood in jeopardy.

'You understand don't you that my father does not approve, if he finds out that you help me…' I begin, but Rosa is shaking her head violently.

'I do not care about this,' she says. She looks adamant, her eyes steely and keen. 'It will be secret, yes?'

'Oh yes, definitely a secret Rosa. If we are discovered I will say you had nothing to do with it,' I promise her but again she shakes her head, dismissing the very thought.

'I am not afraid,' she says, her voice strong, her face up and her chin defiant. 'I am not sorry to help you, I am not in regret.'

'Thank you.' I lunge forward to hug Rosa. In a second we slip into the comfortable status of two women who have struck up a pact, no longer employer and maid. Rosa is now my ally.

The search continues without success and I grow restless, despondent. It is Rosa who supports me, who rallies my spirit and who stands by me. My parents, aware I have not given up, do not ask about my progress nor bother to insist I quit. They are resigned to the fact that I will not be told. They do not realise Rosa has been assisting me and, despite her assurances of allegiance, I will not allow them to learn of this fact. It is not for her to take the fall, should any trouble arise.

Vivanti knows nothing. Michael knows but refuses to speak about her. I know this is his method of handling her loss, but I am frustrated by his lack of input. I want him to be on my side. When something happens he will be, and I know that when I need him, he will be there for me. I just wish he would join me in seeking her out. I sigh at his reluctance; only too aware I cannot convince him. My efforts are better placed in searching for her.

During my quest Michael and I adorn ourselves with medal after medal. We win every competition and national title there is to be won. Vivanti is driving us hard for the world title and exhaustion alone sends me to sleep at night.

During the evenings I pour over the census and the records I have obtained from the registry offices around the country. I search for any female child who could be the right age, I dig into the background data, the history, I try to find out where she came from, anything, any scrap of detail that may be falsified. If there is a trail I follow it. Any remote chance she could be my little girl…any remote opportunity; I take it, just as someone took mine before me.

AUGUST 1964

I cannot believe how beautiful she is. Her father's sparkling dark eyes look out at me from a distance as I marvel at her hair, long and black as coal, like mine. She lets out playful yelps as she darts about the climbing frame with her sister. I wonder if she knows. Is there some inexplicable feeling deep down inside her, a spark of recognition when she looks at me?

Unconsciously I shrink back into the park bench, my eyes never leaving her. I know it is her birthday and I know she is five years old. Her sister, fair haired and blue eyed, does not seem to mind that I am here, watching them playing. I am not entirely sure she has even noticed me, but my little girl has. Odd really, I don't even have a name for her. I never got that far…Tears prick at the backs of my eyes and I wipe them away quickly. The last thing I want now is for some kindly old lady to befriend me, offer me handkerchiefs in return for a life history.

The summer heat is stifling and consequently the park is busy, children feeding mouldy slices of bread to the ducks, running around the play area and fighting for their turn on the blue slide.

Parents sit in collective groups on blankets spread out over the grass, and wooden picnic tables, having first cleaned away the undesirable remnants of the ducks.

I sit alone, on a bench by the path, away from the maddening crowd. I wonder when I will find the strength to approach her. I know I will, some day. It has been two years since I found her, finally, completely by chance when strolling in the park, my hopes having taken yet another beating.

I knew it was her, my baby, instinctively, I just knew. What I don't know is what happened, how she came to be living with this particular family. The parents look nice but then, I remind myself, they could be the very ones who stole her from me…Somehow I don't see it. They look like ordinary people, saving their pennies for the summer treats of ice cream and candyfloss when the Fair comes to town. They have another child too, one I have never seen, hidden by the frills of the pram that the mother is gently rocking to and fro. How can that be fair? They have two adorable children, why must they have mine as well?

I watch as she and her adoptive sister run around the play area happily. Her adoptive mother calls out to them and they run to her soundlessly. The woman presents her with a present, wrapped up in bright paper with a ribbon. I see her open it, her little eyes alight with glee and happiness and I wish I had been the one to give her that. She unwraps a floppy red hat and plops it on her head cheerfully, running away to play with her sister. She stands in front of the large blue slide that seems to be their favourite and waits for her sister to find her. I watch her sister creep up behind her. I watch their girlish giggles, as it's her sister's turn to hide. My heart feels heavy and I wonder if things might have been different had I found her much earlier, when she were younger, much less settled into this family and their lives.

Every conceivable path to follow in finding her has been trodden and in the end, she was just there, right in front of me one day. When I think of the number of hospital nurses, policemen, adoption agency workers, social workers and foster parents I have irritated over the years, I wonder that I am allowed to wander freely in the park at all.

I feel slightly faint, dehydrated, adrenalin zipping through me at having finally found her; mingled with a heavy dose of fear. What if she doesn't know who I am? Can I just bounce into her life now, announce that the woman she thinks is her mother in fact isn't? How can I take my rightful place now? Wouldn't it destroy her?

I wipe away another tear harshly as I watch her and her adoptive sister chasing each other towards the swings. The air is sticky and suddenly I feel rather sick. Rising from the bench I notice her watching me. I smile at her as brightly as I can and hope to God that I will not frighten her. She waves at me and I find myself waving back, a ridiculous excitable wave. My little girl, she knows, she must know…I wave frantically. Her sister catches up with her and suddenly they are in a playful tumble, my presence forgotten. I watch her and her sister sprinting happily around for a moment. I touch my face, realise I have been crying, feel the loneliness break my heart, and walk away.

'Ah, come my darling, come, there is much to do today,' Vivanti tells me, as always, as I enter the dance hall. I dump my bag unceremoniously on a chair, my face greying with distaste. I watch Michael stretching out by the far corner.

'There is always much to do Viv,' I complain as he retreats towards his music sanctuary with a derisive nod of annoyance.

'For you yes, my beauty,' he calls over his shoulder. 'What is wrong with you? Five years we work towards this moment, the London title,' he sighs. 'I get you shape back, we work hard, yes, hard, we work very hard every day. I give my life, for you,' he splutters, points suddenly at Michael, 'and you.' Sure, I think, you were the one who moved my legs for me. I just stood here waiting for you to move me like a puppet, of course, how silly of me to forget.

Michael gives me a look of exasperation and I relent, but only for his sake. I know he wants this title, and a little part of me wants it too, always has. Only, five years ago, I had something worth a million and one titles and if I had to sabotage our chances in this to get my baby back then I would. Furthermore I'd do it without hesitating, regardless of Michael,

Vivanti, or my parents. Michael is pleading at me silently. I know he is right, if I annoy Vivanti now we'll both pay for it for the next seven hours.

'I'm sorry Vivanti, I'm having a bad day, nothing more,' I attempt a smile at him as I slip into my shoes. He practically leaps into my arms, his pink V-necked sweater clinging to his frame like a wrapper.

'I know my beauty,' he takes my hand and spins me towards Michael. 'I know, the pressure, I understand. Now, to work my beauties,' he flicks his long fingers into an invisible clef of music. Michael and I take the hint and our starting positions. Vivanti, in his skin-tight black ballet leggings, takes a seat; mercifully hiding the parts of him I am far more familiar with than I'd like.

'I've found her,' I whisper into Michael's ear as he leads me into a back basic to start and a ladies turn. He looks at me quizzically and I nod emphatically, completing my turn with the final Cha Cha Cha chasse.

'Where?' he whispers back as Vivanti fiddles with the record player and the music picks up pace in an instant, throwing Michael's count out.

'In the park, come, tomorrow,' I whisper as he leads me into hand-to-hand steps underneath ourselves, 'she's beautiful,' I breathe. 'She has your eyes,' I promise him.

'That's wonderful my darlings,' Vivanti calls over the music, his long fingers lacing together a funnel through which he calls to us, 'a little concentration if you please, focus now. Just four weeks I have,' he sighs, dismantling his funnel, 'just four weeks to get you ready,' he says to himself.

I avoid giggling at Vivanti. Michael resumes his face of concentration, leads me into a forward and back basic followed by a New York and spot turn.

'Please,' I persist, 'please say you'll come.'

'No,' Michael says shortly as he sends me with a back step into Rope Spinning, forcing me around his back with his hand over his head and a spot turn to finish.

'What?' I almost scream. 'Why?'

'Concentrate!' Vivanti shouts and cuts the music. The needle scratches across the record recklessly. 'What point if you do not concentrate,' he claps his hands together with the beat of his words. 'You must focus,' he pulls us together into his little huddle. I am dragged by his remarkable strength for such a skinny little man, forcibly into the hold. 'Listen,' he takes our hands and taps them. 'You must listen to the music,' he closes his eyes. 'Now, feel the music, close your eyes, listen, let it eat up your thoughts,' Vivanti is humming, tapping his hands over ours.

Neither Michael nor I close our eyes. Instead we stare at each other over the oblivious Vivanti. It is bad enough that I have lost my baby but I never wanted to lose Michael too. I feel guilty at our diminishing relationship. Despite my better judgement I have never managed to free myself from the emotional hold Michael has over me. It would be inaccurate to say we had a relationship now, but we have come together in times of emotional insanity, stress, guilt over our lost child, love even, just that in its purest form. It is true; I do love Michael even though he frustrates me beyond reason.

I feel bad that I haven't been there for him, I have become utterly absorbed by finding our daughter. I have neglected him and our relationship, which could so easily have been saved and turned into something magical. If only he would talk to me I think, if only he would talk about her. It would help. Instead he has buried his feelings deep inside and even I cannot break the shell.

In moments of irresistible temptation we have fallen back into each other's arms, always hiding our love from the world. He has supported me, held me whilst I have cried desperately on his shoulder. He has been good to me. I stare at him now and I wonder when I became such a terrible person, when I stopped appreciating him. Now I want him to take the step I know he can never bring himself to take, and instead of understanding him, I am getting angry with him. When did I become this person? This isn't me I think silently, this isn't who I am.

'I just don't think I can face it,' Michael mouths silently at me. I stare him out and look away, blink away tears. 'Sorry,' he mouths again.

'Now, you get you,' Vivanti decides. 'I can feel you get it now, the passion, oh la la, the passion, there is the heat now. Let's dance,' he spins away towards the music station and we take our starting hold. There is heat all right Vivanti, I think, but not the sort you meant.

'I'm sorry too,' I whisper as the music starts. Michael looks into my eyes and I see the same look of love that I saw that first day of my return.

'That's it,' Vivanti cries triumphantly. 'Keep going,' he shrieks. 'That's it, you have it.' He is leaping up and down at the side like an excitable fan. 'You are sure to win the world title, the best you two are,' he enthuses as Michael takes me from a back basic into the Fan followed by a Hockey Stick, an pen basic and a Full Natural Top. We complete the dance.

'Now, I think that must be the opener for the tour my beauties, yes, yes, I think,' Vivanti is clapping as he fiddles with the record again, wiping a smear off with his legging-clad thigh.

'Tour?' I question. 'What tour?'

'Your father has arranged a tour, for after the title competition,' Michael says. 'I only found out myself earlier today. He is adamant that we'll win and he wants us to showcase the country. It'll boost income,' he sighs, only too aware of my hatred for my father's greed.

'I bet it will but I don't want to go on tour,' I protest. I do not want to leave the town. What if I miss her, what if she moves, I won't be able to trace her, I'll be starting all over. I can feel the panic rising in my throat. 'Why must we go now, I mean we don't have to, I've only just…' I can feel the tears burning the backs of my eyes. I cannot stop them from falling. Vivanti is watching me curiously.

Michael takes my hand and drags me away towards the corner of the hall. He pulls me into his chest. Vivanti is about to approach us but Michael raises a hand and he halts in his tracks, back treads silently towards the music collection and busies himself needlessly.

I attempt to resist Michael but he is too strong, my tight-knit fists pushing on his chest until I relinquish all effort and cry into his shirt.

'Put something light on Viv,' Michael instructs. Vivanti is, for once, lost for words, but complies with Michael's command deftly and spends the time fiddling with his records, clearly in discomfort. Eventually he finds some soft music and plays it. I stand in Michael's hold, transfixed by grief, utterly at a loss as to how to overcome the tour.

'Why,' I whimper. 'I don't want to,' I cry. He holds me in his embrace tightly until I stop whimpering. Gently Michael strokes my hair and I feel calmer. He cups my face in his hand and wipes away my tears.

'Don't worry, we'll sort something out,' he whispers. I lean into him once more. Vivanti doesn't speak.

SPOTLIGHT EXPRESS – THE INDUSTRY'S CHOICE – 9 August 1964
SUTTON AND CAPELLI FOR THE LONDON WORLD TEN TITLE?

The heat is on as London boasts the World Ten Dance Title event. This prestigious world title is every dancer's dream. Understandably every UK professional dancer is out to win it this year as our capital hosts the event. The heat dances are being scheduled around the top London hotels. Each couple must complete all ten dances plus a showcase dance of their choosing if they reach the final round. The winner will attain top marks from the judges' panel on every dance, if they are to make it to the final round.

The odds are stacked sky high for the celebrated couple Sutton and Capelli. If the rumours about Capelli were true we wouldn't be seeing them as they rehearse night and day for the big day. Scandalous rumours would have you believe that Capelli had a child, but no evidence to support the fact has been forthcoming and what mother could out-class the rivals of Riches and Iceni as smoothly as Sutton and Capelli managed last month at the medals contest. Yes, if you're a betting man, put your money on Sutton and Capelli for this one.

Riches and Icenci are tipped for second place, their only rivals being the wild card newcomers to the industry, Beradi and White. In addition, the quietly confident Walter and Rayner practice for stardom. For the full list of entrants contact the box office for a programme, on sale now.

The highly competitive world of dance may look like spandex and stardust but believe me; the heat is definitely on, with the title tied to a hefty cash prize, that's bound to make the competition interesting.

Watch this space; in two weeks we could be crowning the new king and queen of dance the world over, and we all know who is marked for the post.

Tickets are available at the box office. Bank cheques accepted.

Michael and I are alone, sitting in my room looking over sequences from previous tournaments. We will have to perform all ten dances to perfection; Foxtrot, Rumba, Waltz, Cha cha cha, Ballroom Tango, Paso Doble, Quickstep, Samba, Jive and Viennese Waltz, plus our showcase Argentine Tango in order to win the world title.

We have less than two weeks until the big event. The very thought of it makes me edgy. If I am ever going to win this thing then Michael is the partner to take me there. We have such unison on the dance floor that I am swept away by him. If only we could achieve that same level of harmony over our missing daughter.

'I think this one was the best we ever managed for the Paso Doble,' Michael says now, handing me a photograph and sequence sheet from one of our early tournaments. I glance at it quickly, flick on a bedside lamp as the sun sets outside, dimming our view.

'Yes ok,' I concur easily. 'What about the Jive, I like this one,' I venture and Michael nods happily flicking through the remainder of the sheets. We are supposed to present Vivanti with our choice tomorrow so he can coach us into a state of exhaustion and nervous tension for the next two weeks. 'Michael?'

'Yes?' he answers, still lost in the many sheets spread out over my starry bed-sheets.

'I'm scared,' I confess. He abandons the sheets and rests down beside me. 'I don't want to fail you,' I whisper. 'My head just isn't in this.'

'You won't sweetheart,' he says, looking into my eyes. 'You could never fail me; remember that. I know it's scary but it's what we've always been working for, we may as well give it our best shot now that it's coming up.' I nod at Michael silently. 'Would it help if we could postpone the tour?' he asks me.

'Yes, that would help,' I agree sadly, 'but how long can we put it off? My father will never allow me to cancel it,' I sigh. 'I wish you'd come with me to see her,' I look deep into his eyes to see if he will relent. Instead he draws me into his hold and I let him take me, cover me with his body warmth.

'I'll talk to your father,' he says simply. 'Get him to postpone the tour with no definite date.' I know deep down that this will not make a jot of difference, but for the moment it feels nice.

'And…' I brave a repeat of my question.

'I'll think about it,' he agrees. 'I'm just…'

'I know,' I smile at him. 'I know.' He kisses me lightly and I smile my appreciation at him. I am still not convinced he will come with me to see her but thinking about it is a long way from a straight no.

'I think that right now though,' he whispers in my ear seductively, his warm breath tantalising me as he shuffles his body over mine for a snug fit. 'We should work on our rise and fall,' he teases, his lips dangerously close to mine.

'Well Viv is always saying we need to remember musicality,' I giggle. Michael caresses my lips lightly, his delight airy, his feeling overshadowing us both with ease.

I let him unclasp my clothing, feel his urgency driving him, feel his warm fingers working their magic until I know that the real Michael, the version I admire so much, is about to surface.

I find myself kissing him back with a passion I had forgotten I felt. My mind has been so preoccupied, my body following its lead without question, my life ordered by control. I have forgotten how I feel about Michael, but it takes him just a second to refresh my memory, and for those feelings to burst forth. Suddenly everything fades into the background, and all I need is right in front of me.

Chapter Seven – Modern Day; May

Sergeant Wellington logged the urgent request for an official search warrant with due diligence, relieved that John Francis hadn't caught them in the house before the faked forensics visit had commenced. Sometimes the Inspector took one too many risks, but Wells knew he wasn't afraid to take the rap himself. He had never yet let his Sergeant take the blame for any of his infamous hunches that had gone spectacularly wrong. Fairly shrewd though, he smiled to himself as he filled out the last few entries on the request form. Hardly ever caught out, suspected of breaking every rule in the book yes, but never proven. It was good fortune for them that Allen had decided to take up his career on the right side of the law, Sergeant Wellington laughed to himself quietly; if he were a villain they would have had a hard time catching him out.

Marking urgent on the request form and emphasising it heavily, Sergeant Wellington wondered what the Inspector had found to merit this second official visit. Whatever it was he had better hope that Francis wouldn't remove it before they got there.

Rebecca swirled around the hall happily. It was a pure release and she loved it. She had recommended the Samba School to Jean with enthusiasm but being of the lesser energetic tendency, Jean had declined the invitation to join her this week.

'Ladies, very good, now, like this see,' Lexia was demonstrating a step. 'It is like water, like a wave,' she was saying from the tips of her toes until she was about to lose balance, then crashing forwards with a controlled movement, her arms imitating the waving motion of the sea. 'We dance the steps for the goddess of the sea,' she smiled brightly, 'then like this,' she continued the demonstration with two smaller waves involving her feet in tiny steps forward with the arm waving motion, her finger tips gentle and seductive. 'Now, you try,' Lexia stood back as the group attempted the new step.

Rebecca felt incredibly sensuous. It was almost as if she could feel the history of the dance reaching to her through the ages, the feminine struggles of the day overcome by the strength of the movement, the power of the gods by whom so many of the steps seemed to be inspired.

'Now, like a waterfall,' Lexia was saying, as they followed her lead through a step-ball-change dainty path across the floor and into a crouched position where they were letting their fingertips cascade down from above their heads, as if catching the falling water in their hands. 'Yes, very good, very good.'

'Last year we did the one with lightning and thunder,' Angela was whispering as the group followed Lexia through the next section of movement.

'Lightning?' Rebecca whispered back with intrigue.

'Yeah,' Angela gasped as they attempted another leaping wave. 'Arms like swords, a kind of spinning round with fingers pointing to our heads,' she breathed out the words as they came to rest whilst Lexia started the CD for the last run-through. 'A kind of feet shuffling thing,' Angela tried to remember and laughed, 'don't count on me to remember though,' she giggled.

'It goes back a long way doesn't it, all this?' Rebecca observed.

'Oh years, Lexia will tell you if you ever want the history. They're all mostly about women though, goddesses or one thing or another. It's supposed to represent fertility and that sort of thing. Quite sexy really,' Angela smiled, 'that's if you don't copy me,' she laughed heartily. Rebecca found herself giggling like a little girl and suddenly she wanted to join the summer performance. It would be fun, and Craig would have encouraged her she thought, a tinge of sadness swiftly swept away as the CD started.

'Right, from the beginning,' Lexia was instructing, taking her lead in front.

'Here goes,' Angela smiled, 'let's see if I can get it right this time.'

After the last run-through the drummers joined them, as before, for the final practice. The performance was scheduled for July so they had plenty of time to practise. Rebecca found herself searching the sea of faces lined up with instruments, a flicker of guilt crossing her eyes as she spotted Paul in the second line back. Wasn't it far too soon for her to be remotely interested in talking to Paul? After a lifetime of happiness with Craig and more years than she cared to count, how could it be that she felt drawn to his company? It was ludicrous; they had barely exchanged two words. Decidedly she swung her gaze back to her new friends, began organising her things to leave.

'Hi,' his voice instantly recognisable behind her back. She spun up and around, a shocked expression colouring her eyes.

'Hello again,' she said softly, finding his eyes magnetically locked into hers. 'How did it go today?' she shook herself free of his gaze, busied herself needlessly with her floppy bag that had become her weekly dance bag, stuffed in the half drunk bottle of water with her new soft pliable ballet shoes that kept her feet clean. Some of the women danced in bare feet. Lexia had promised to order her some dance trainers for the performance in town, their split soles making them flexible and yet suitable for outdoors, but the ballet shoes were fine for rehearsals.

'Ok,' Paul shrugged his shoulders dismissively, 'some of the newcomers are just learning the ropes so we're repeating quite a bit at the moment,' he smiled. 'How was your week?'

Well, let's see, Rebecca thought, someone is trying to kill me, I can't sleep and when I do I wake in fits of cold sweats, a persistent dream that I can't understand, a fire destroyed lounge and an insurance claim to file, redecoration to do, desperately trying to make it through each day without breaking down in tears and missing Craig...

'Fine,' she said shortly, 'yours?' she attempted a smile as she realised she could no longer reasonably play for time with her floppy bag. Paul said something she didn't catch as she slid her bag on her shoulder and waved to her new friends, accepting that Paul was probably going to accompany her to her car regardless. 'Actually,' she paused in the sunshine, 'there was something I was hoping to ask you...'

'Yes?' Paul's voice was eager, his smile bright. She noticed a sparkle in his blue eyes and felt a blush colouring her cheeks. Ridiculous, she chided herself.

'Oh it's nothing really...' embarrassment gripping her as they headed to the cars, parked exactly the same as before.

'Anything. Tell me,' Paul insisted.

'Ok,' Rebecca paused by the cars, shielding her eyes from the sunlight that appeared to have singled her out with force. 'My son-in-law, he has just started up a new business and...' she wrestled her mind for words but she felt them choking her, the blush deepening. 'I was wondering if you'd...'

'Of course, look take my card,' Paul smiled, 'have him call me. I'll do anything I can to help him. Hang on,' he dashed to his car, rifled through the glove compartment desperately. 'Here,' he produced a business card. 'Take two,' he smiled, 'if you ever want a lift or anything...'

'Thank you,' she felt his fingers against hers as she took the card, a tingle, gone in a moment. 'I'll tell him,' she tried to smile, 'thanks.' Suddenly she was afraid, she had to leave. It was all too soon and she wondered what Craig would think if he could see her now...'I've got to go,' she said quickly. 'I'll see you next week,' she tried to smile brightly.

'Looking forward to it,' Paul's smile reached his eyes with warmth as he waved lightly and waited for her to get into her car.

'Bye,' she waved out the window and drove away quickly, her heart hammering in her chest with a growing fondness for a man she hardly knew, and guilt, for the man she could no longer have, but would love for all eternity. Whatever was she supposed to do?

The sign was grand, the lettering stretching across the white brick wall with a conceited air of elitism. Belvadere Club was a private establishment, according to its gold plaque by the doorbell. The front door was locked but DCI Allen rattled the handle vigorously none-the-less. Sergeant Wellington pushed the bell and the Inspector grinned at him sheepishly.

'Worth a try son, worth a try,' he shrugged his shoulders. 'Got your notepad Sergeant?'

'Yes Sir, but why, Sir? You don't usually want me to take notes.'

'I do today son, take them, lots of them, doesn't matter if they don't make any sense. Just take them,' he lifted a finger in the air as if that would explain his unfathomable reasoning as a terse voice spat out at them from the intercom.

'Atwood CID,' Sergeant Wellington called into the microphone. There was a rustle and a note of panic at the other end. 'Open up,' Wells demanded. A click indicated the door may be open and Inspector Allen wrenched on the handle instantly, pulling the heavy wooden doors free from their superior locking system. He flashed a toothy smile at his Sergeant and strode into the darkness of the Belvadere Club.

'Come on son,' he barked, 'let's see what we can find in here…' his voice fading into the thickness of the air inside the club.

Dingy and narrow corridors led into vast open spaces with long bars and tall stools, pool tables dimly lit with low-hanging lamps, the sound of cues smacking the balls across the faded green felt tops. A stain of alcohol and tobacco hung in the air like a fog. No sign of anybody smoking though, the Inspector thought grimly, taking out his pencil and robustly chewing on the end, his teeth settling into the familiar marks.

He would have liked to enter the club as a stranger, not as a representative of the law. There was something odd about the silence, an expectation almost…as if a swift transformation had occurred in the blink of Wells announcing their arrival and before the door had been opened. It was just a gut instinct and he knew he had got many wrong in the past, but as the Inspector took in a sweeping glance around him, he knew he was right. There was more to this club than met the uninvited eye. He just had to find a way to scratch the surface…

A row of suited gentlemen lined the bar, hanging limply off stools and sipping at their shots of whisky. They hovered around the pool tables and eyed the Inspector and his Sergeant with open suspicion. Inspector Allen let his fingers trail along the wall; the paintwork, a deep maroon colour and thickly applied to leave a bumpy finish had a heavy wooden frieze splitting the walls in half. There was a slight crease, he felt it; stopped. The silence seemed to deepen. The man behind the bar flinched, paused in polishing the freshly washed tumblers, his eyes following the Inspector's gaze at the wall.

Inspector Allen grinned at his audience.

'DCI Allen,' he produced his warrant card like a whip, the smudgy marks unnoticeable in the dim light of the club.

Crash. Splintered glass fanned out at the barman's feet, a flinch from the men at the bar and a grin from the Inspector. The barman stooped to collect the broken tumbler.

'This is Sergeant Wellington,' Inspector Allen thumbed at his Sergeant quickly who held up his warrant card and proceeded to remove his notebook and pencil from his pocket. The Inspector strode purposefully towards the men by the bar, their solid silence faltering.

'Oops daisy,' Inspector Allen smiled at the barman who emerged from the floor with a dustpan and brush in his hand. He said nothing, tipped the broken glass noisily into the bin and proceeded to polish the remaining glasses. 'Nice place you have here,' he commented, his usual opener, and stared suddenly at a man with a covering of dark hair shining across his head in the bleak light. 'You,' he accused, 'what's your name?'

'Fisher,' the man grunted defensively. Inspector Allen cast him a sly smile and spun round to ensure Wells was taking notes dutifully. The Inspector watched Fisher carefully, he knew him, he was sure he had seen him before…and his name definitely wasn't Fisher.

The men watched Wells writing down Fisher's name, their eyes keen and their minds frantic. The Inspector grinned at them all happily as the door opened and a man stood frozen in the doorway. He let out an audible sigh and closed the door behind him. From experience John Francis already knew there was no escape from the Inspector.

'Ah, Mr Francis,' Inspector Allen's smile split his face as he strode toward the man as if he were an old friend. 'Join us, won't you?' he indicated an empty bar stool. John Francis stared at the Inspector with clear hatred and took his seat.

'Large scotch,' he hissed at the barman. The others watched him. Inspector Allen nodded at Sergeant Wellington who fiddled with his notebook to find a clean page. 'What'd you want Inspector?' Francis complained; his white hair almost transparent in the darkness of the room, 'can't a man have any peace?'

'Not when he's nicking cars he can't, no,' the Inspector shot him a glare and a thin smile. 'I'm here to question you Mr Francis, on suspicion of receiving stolen goods and orchestrating car thefts. My Sergeant here will do the honours, won't you son?' he smirked boyishly. The other men began to turn back to their drinks and hushed conversations ensued, leaving John Francis to face his fate alone. 'Take him somewhere quiet son,' Inspector Allen beamed, his gaze not leaving Francis's face. 'There must be a room we can use somewhere, probably hidden behind that wall over there.' The Inspector didn't fail to notice the barman's flinch.

'Can't I finish my drink first, hey?' John Francis shouted, his voice booming under the low ceiling and his face flushed with frustration and anguish.

'Oh yes Sir,' the Inspector almost sang. 'You better had Sir, make sure you enjoy it won't you Sir; it'll be the last one for a while. Come on son, accompany him to a nice comfy place where we can have a little chat,' he voice evenly stern. Sergeant Wellington led John Francis away from the bar and out to the maze of available doors off the dingy corridor.

In his wake the other men had resumed conversations, their laughter now beginning to crack the silence. A sense of enlightenment and relief swept over the bar. Inspector Allen noticed some music for the first time, now turned up slightly by the barman.

'You, what's your name son?' the Inspector jabbed a finger at one of the men along the bar. The conversation dulled, fear beginning to spread again.

'Nicholas,' the man spoke densely, his voice heavy with sarcasm, laden with guilt. His probing eyes had no effect on Inspector Allen. He was the man in the photo at Francis's house.

'Um yes, what'd you know about Francis then?' Inspector Allen asked, his voice the only sound over the low music. The men were listening intently whilst trying to appear uninterested. Inspector Allen's toothy smile spread slowly, it was often the affect he had on people and it amused him greatly.

'He's alright,' the man with dark eyes insisted. 'Whatever you think he's done, you're wrong,' misguided loyalty underpinning his voice.

'Alright, hey, um, well we'll soon see about that.' He grinned peevishly. 'And you, Nicholas,' the name rolling slowly off his tongue, 'what do you do then?'

'Nothing, nothing at all,' the man insisted, returning to his drink and abandoning the Inspector.

'Can I get you anything Inspector?' the barman looked up, breaking the silence with a curt voice. Inspector Allen smiled.

'Couple of straight answers perhaps son,' he said, his pencil now chewed to perfection and back in his pocket. 'About the sort of establishment you run here, but I'll pop back for that later,' he promised with a wide smile and sauntered off towards the door, pausing briefly by the wall that had intrigued him earlier. 'Old place this, isn't it?' he remarked. The barman only nodded, his polishing motion severely concentrated on the glass tumbler. 'Um, interesting,' he hummed, tweaking his moustache; then he spun on his heels and marched away to interrogate John Francis.

The room Sergeant Wellington had found looked like an office, an untidy one at that, papers strewn around the desk and files stuffed with papers that couldn't possibly fit.

'Do you mind?' Francis was shouting as Wells peered at the documents curiously. 'This is a private office, my office as it happens…'

'Yes I thought it might be,' Inspector Allen cut in, his tall frame narrowly missing the top of the doorframe. 'I must tell you Mr Francis that we have a search party at your house as we speak. Don't worry Sir,' he smirked. 'We have a warrant.' The Inspector nodded at Wells who continued to unnerve John Francis by studiously scribbling at his notepad. 'Did they give you an update son?' he half whispered to Wells.

'Yes Sir, they rang just as I was escorting Mr Francis in here Sir, they found a business card and some documents stating that Mr Francis is the owner of this club Sir,' Wells informed him, looking baffled.

'I thought as much,' Inspector Allen said quietly. 'Won't you take a seat Sir?' he directed his instruction at Francis, striding towards him and backing the white-haired man into a chair, his face dangerously scarlet.

'So what?' John Francis screamed and his arm flapping. 'It's not a crime to own a club.'

'What else did they find son?' Inspector Allen swivelled on his heels towards Sergeant Wellington quickly.

'Log books Sir, lots of them, records of car sales…'

'So I've bought a few cars…that's not illegal either,' Francis yelled, attempting to get up but Inspector Allen stood in front of him, barring his exit from the room. His towering height loomed over the captive with a wicked grin and narrowing eyes.

'I think I'm going to have to ask you to accompany me to the station Mr Francis,' the Inspector said levelly. 'Our superior will want to talk to you about all this.'

George dashed past at lightning speed, dribbling the ball expertly between two small framed boys from the opposite side, flicked his foot unexpectedly and the ball shot through the air towards his team mate, who shot it into the back of the net with an easy kick; the keeper flopping lamely to the ground.

Rebecca smiled at Tina's motherly squeals of delight as George and his teammates were buried beneath the mass of players in a moment of glory. Seconds later the game was back on, the whistle had blown and Rebecca watched her grandson sprinting down the side of the pitch, his legs a blur and his face flushed with the warmth of exercise. He was a lovely child, she thought, smiling at Tina who was leaping up and down in encouragement. She and Craig had been so pleased when Samuel had presented Tina to them, even then she had known, somehow, that Tina would make a lovely wife and a truly superb mother. Craig would have been so proud, she thought, a tinge of sadness threatening to overwhelm her. He would have been leaping about, like Tina, offering advice from the side lines.

'Whoa!' Tina's gush of anguish at the failed attempt at another goal shook Rebecca from her daydream.

'Hi mum,' her daughter lightly tapped her shoulder, approaching her from behind. Rebecca hugged Katherine quickly.

'Hi love, I didn't know you were coming today.'

'Neil's working,' she smiled lightly, fiddling with the sunshade on the pram, in which baby Craig was sleeping peacefully. Rebecca glanced over her baby grandson and wondered if he too would have his cousin's football skills.

'It's lovely to see you dear,' Rebecca's voice was lost in the cheer that erupted that very moment. Tina overpowered Rebecca with an embrace, her little feet bouncing up and down in the excitement.

'Hi Tina,' Katherine said, giggling as she watched her sister-in-law release her mother.

'Isn't it great,' Tina hugged Katherine quickly, her sun-blonde hair mingling softly with Katherine's shining darker shade. 'They're winning,' she squealed and reverted her beautiful lavender eyes back to her son's team, engrossed in the action. The team were now moments away from the winning result they needed.

'I'd never have guessed,' Katherine whispered to her mother with a hidden smile, then raised her voice slightly over the din. 'Do you think I'll be doing that in a few years?' Rebecca cast her daughter a smile and a nod. It was inevitable. George's team were putting in a good enough performance to win the season's trophy. George was bound to teach his baby cousin a thing or two about football one day.

As the final whistle blew Rebecca watched George and his teammates slapping each other playfully, leaping about in spurts of adrenalin and exuberance. She greeted George with a big hug as he approached his mother; his legs caked in mud and his shirt almost black, a large smear down the side of his face but the brightest smile lit up his eyes.

'Well done, you were magnificent,' Rebecca laughed as George grinned, a flash of his grandfather in his eyes momentarily. Rebecca held her breath. It was gone in a moment.

'Thanks Nana,' George was smiling, his face flushed, 'I'd better go,' he called as he went to re-join his friends.

'I'll see you later,' Tina gave her a big hug as George ran off. 'Thanks so much for coming,' she smiled brightly, 'Sam's working today,' she explained, 'it's nice for him to have us here.'

'Any time love,' Rebecca assured her, 'besides you know I like to watch him.' Tina waved at them and went after George towards the cars. Rebecca and Katherine began strolling towards the edge of the playing field.

'Did you walk down love? Rebecca asked.'

'Yes, I had the pram and it's a nice day,' Katherine smiled but she was looking around the pitch, twisting as they walked slowly towards the path.

'Looking for someone?' Rebecca followed her daughter's gaze.

'Oh no, no,' Katherine said, 'nobody. Come on, let's go.'

'Oh yes,' Rebecca smiled at the thought of Paul. 'I've met someone who I think may be able to help Neil out with the business. He's the local bank manager, very nice man.'

'Very nice man,' Katherine repeated; a sly smile on her lips. 'Very nice.'

'Don't be daft,' Rebecca heard herself sound sterner than she intended. They had reached the edge of the playing field and were down on the path, the traffic quietly humming by their side.

'You're only human mum,' Katherine said gently. 'Dad went so young,' her voice calm and her gaze forward, over the pram where baby Craig was still peacefully oblivious. 'None of us would think less of you if you ever,' she paused, the words somehow inadequate. Rebecca patted her daughter's hand clasped around the pram handle with a silent nod. She and Craig had never been wealthy in the bank balance stakes but she considered herself one of the wealthiest people in the world when it came to having everything that truly mattered, her family, her children, grandchildren; surrounded by love and support every day, even through the darkest of hours.

'Nobody could ever replace your father dear, and I'm not ready anyway,' she finally spoke, 'but thank you.'

'So he's a bank manager then?' Katherine prompted. 'Where'd you meet him?'

'At the Samba school I told you about. He's in the band, plays a drum. Apparently it's an act of rebellion because he wasn't allowed a drum kit when he was a child,' Rebecca heard herself giggling, failing to notice the recognition of admiration in her daughter's eyes. 'Anyway, he told me he was a bank manager and I thought he may be able to advise Neil. I've got his card here,' she rummaged through her handbag, 'somewhere,' she muttered, her voice lost in the depths of her bag, 'here,' triumphant, producing the card and handing it to Katherine.

'Thanks mum, I'll give it to Neil,' Katherine smiled warmly. 'It's all right,' she said softly, 'you are allowed to make new friends you know.'

There was even more colour in Jean's ample cheeks than usual, her voluptuous form happily spread over one of Rebecca's kitchen chairs, the brochures open on the table.

'I'm so pleased we're actually going,' Jean enthused, her blonde hair bouncing around her face as she shoved strands of it behind her ear, continuing her flow. 'It'll be just what you need Becca love, you see. I expect you're glad aren't you Inspector?' Jean cast a quick look over at the Detective Chief Inspector who sat opposite her at the table, his strong coloured tea cup, drained, in front of him on the table and his mouth partly open ready to answer. 'I mean, get her away from here, from all this madness,' Jean continued. The Inspector closed his mouth and watched Rebecca who sat between them, her face going from one to the other as if on an elastic band.

'Mrs Duchess,' the Inspector managed to chip in.

'Yes that's right Inspector, though I'm really a Miss again now. I reverted to my maiden name again Inspector, after I got rid of that evil swine of an ex-husband of mine. My mother was from here you know, though she raised me in Cumbria.'

'I'm sure the Inspector doesn't have the time…' Rebecca attempted but Jean didn't hear her.

'Terrible time she had of it my poor mother, such an awful obsession it was. An illness really,' she insisted, leaning forwards over the table. Rebecca couldn't help but smile as the Inspector noticed Jean's cleavage spilling out over the table as she thrust herself as far forward as she could.

Inspector Allen was not shy when it came to admiring any woman who happened to cross his path, but Rebecca could see him grimace and tilt his empty cup for want of distraction. It wasn't Jean's fault that she had no dress sense at all. Today she was wearing a floppy shapeless outfit, no doubt influenced in style and colour from the recent holiday booking, and the unusual summer climate in spring, which did nothing to enhance her curvaceous body, nor protect her ample bosom from defaulting to its most unflattering, if comfortable, position.

'More tea, Inspector?' Rebecca asked over Jean's story.

'Um yes Mrs Houseman, thank you,' the Inspector grinned, his respect for the intelligent woman by his side growing rapidly.

'It's such a shame but there you are. She had me in the end so that put a stop to all her silliness.' Jean paused momentarily and the Inspector opened his mouth to speak. 'Still, I know all about desperation you see Inspector,' Jean continued. Rebecca smiled at the Inspector as he accepted defeat into silence and ran the brim of his hat between his fingers.

'These dreams of Becca's I mean,' Jean was saying. 'It's all about desperation. They're 'bout children too aren't they dear?' Jean didn't wait for confirmation. 'Playing in the park and all that aren't they?'

'Dreams...' Inspector Allen piped up as Rebecca placed his tea in front of him. 'Thank you Madam,' he said quietly as Jean waffled on regardless.

'Yes, dreams about meeting a woman, a stranger wasn't it dear? Well that poor woman probably isn't real, but you know these things filter into our heads, Becca dear, you've probably met someone who suffered like my poor mother, maybe it's me talking about her that has you dreaming...'

'Mrs Houseman,' Inspector Allen's voice was assertive, cut Jean's flow instantly. She cowered into her chair and accepted the tea Rebecca handed to her. 'Just a couple of questions,' he lowered his voice, tweaked at his moustache calmly. 'I was wondering, if you could tell me about yourself, just a little bit. It just may help me catch this lunatic.'

'Oh she's had a lovely life Inspector,' Jean insisted. The Inspector cast Jean a glance that reminded Rebecca of her old headmaster. She suppressed a giggle as Jean slumped into the chair and sipped at her tea quietly.

'Nothing out of the ordinary Inspector,' Rebecca began. 'Usual thing, Craig and I married when we were both quite young and we had our children...'

'I was thinking more about when you were a child Mrs Houseman.' Inspector Allen drained his teacup, sighed happily and selected his pencil from his coat pocket.

'Oh ok, where to begin…' Rebecca sipped her own tea. 'Ok. My parents died sadly, an accident. My sister and brother both moved abroad some years ago but when we were little it was all quite normal.'

'And you lived…' Inspector Allen waved his pencil then stuck it back between his teeth.

'Here, in Atwood,' Rebecca told him. 'Not that far from this house actually,' she smiled.

'And your earliest memory Mrs Houseman, what would that be?'

'My earliest memory?' Rebecca half smiled. 'What an odd question. I don't know, I'll have to think…possibly playing with my sister, my brother arriving.'

'You said arriving,' the Inspector pounced, shot up from his chair. Rebecca and Jean flinched at his rapid movement. He began to pace the kitchen, his mind racing. 'Not being born, arriving.'

'Of course he was born but I can't remember him being born, I was too young,' Rebecca corrected him. 'I was probably taken away anyway, at the time. It wasn't like today,' she smiled. Inspector Allen grinned at her and sat back down suddenly.

'How long have you had these dreams Madam?' he asked, his voice trailing into a barely audible whisper. Rebecca wondered if he didn't want Jean to hear him.

'Not long, you can't really think my dreams have anything to do with…'

'I don't think anything at the moment Mrs Houseman,' Inspector Allen assured her with a toothy smile. 'How long?'

'Just about…' Rebecca wiped a stray tear away. How much longer could she expect these instant bursts of emotion to attack her? 'Just before my husband died.'

'Just before. That's interesting.' The Inspector slid his moustache between his long nicotine-stained fingertips and blew out an imaginary smoke ring.

'Is it?' Jean lurched forward over the table again. 'Why?'

'I'd better be going,' he said, shooting up from the chair, his height seeming a lifetime away from Rebecca's seated position at the table. 'Thank you Mrs Houseman,' he afforded her one of his rare genuine smiles and glanced towards Jean. 'Miss Duchess,' he inclined his hat, plonked it jauntily on his head and strode purposefully towards the front door. Rebecca hurried after him to reach the front door.

'Thank you Inspector,' she said, opening the door and spying a waiting car blocking her driveway. The driver was the man who had accompanied him before.

'Oh by the way Mrs Houseman,' Inspector Allen said, spinning on his heels to face her from his stance on the doorstep, the sunlight blinding them both. 'We've had to let old greedy-guts go.'

'Who?' her voice inquisitive, shielding her eyes from the light with the back of her hand.

'The garage mechanic Madam,' Inspector Allen flashed a thin smile, 'but don't worry, I'll get him, and his fellow crooks.' Rebecca smiled at him. He was such an odd man but strangely amusing. 'Oh, and by the way Mrs Houseman,' he continued, 'I'm taking up the case of your husband's murder too. I won't be resting until I've caught the culprit.' He nodded at Rebecca resolutely and marched towards the waiting car. Rebecca watched him slide into the passenger seat with ease.

'Quick son, back to the station.' Wells started the ignition. 'Check out the two from the club, Nicholas and Fisher,' Inspector Allen instructed as he waved at Mrs Houseman on the doorstep. They turned the corner towards the station.

'Why Sir?' Sergeant Wellington enquired, indicating towards the town centre.

'Fisher, we've met him before son, called himself something else though, can't think what...' his voice dying in the speeding sound of the tyres on the road as they sped towards the traffic lights, zipping through a fraction before the red shone. Inspector Allen pulled a cigarette from behind his ear and lit it quickly, puffed greedily. 'Did time a few years back. Check him out. I know I've seen him before and it was something deeply unpleasant. We'll get him proper this time,' he announced with a wide smile.

'What about Nicholas Sir?' Wells asked, opening the windows and pointing the car towards the police station car park entrance. There was barely time for the Inspector to finish his cigarette, he would have to be quick if he didn't want to be caught smoking in the police car.

'He looks fishy,' the Inspector said sharply, blew out a large smoke ring and smiled. 'Besides, he knows Francis and I don't like him son, his eyes, they keep avoiding me.'

Sergeant Wellington manoeuvred the car into a space as slowly as possible as the Inspector took a final puff on his cigarette and crushed it between his fingertips with satisfaction. Inspector Allen swung his long legs out the car and strode towards the entrance to his lair.

'A lot of people avoid you Sir,' Wells chuckled to himself, locking the car.

'I know son, but this one won't get away with it,' the Inspector shouted over his shoulder, already several long strides distancing them. Sergeant Wellington reminded himself that Allen's hearing was impeccable, either that or his intuition was astounding. Either way Wells was sunk, every time.

CHAPTER EIGHT – SEPTEMBER 1964

I can hear them downstairs, the heat of their words staggering towards me as I descend the staircase slowly, creeping down one step at a time. I do not want them to see me. I have no desire to join the conversation.

'But Sir, Joyce is exhausted, and so am I,' Michael protests. I press my body up close against the wall and hold my breath. I cannot take any further steps down because the wall falls away and the handrail is insufficient to hide me. My flimsy heels will sound loudly on the marble steps and I hold my frame, afraid to move.

'Tough,' my father roars, I can imagine him flapping his arms around, a drink in hand, pacing the room like a tiger in captivity. I can picture Michael now, standing straight, his posture always one of his strongest assets, his weight carefully measured between his two feet and his full height extended in a match for my father. His dark eyes will be bright at the moment, that sparkle that comes alive when he sets his mind on something.

The sunlight from the glass front door shines up at me on the stairs. I squint in the blaze of the morning's light. It is chilly but unusually bright for the time of year. The lounge will be bursting with sunshine this time of the day, the blinds drawn to deflect the glare. Mother has gone out shopping and Rosa is in the kitchen preparing the Sunday roast. Father hates Sunday roast but it is the one thing my mother has always succeeded in getting him to have. In England all respectable families have Sunday roast, according to her, and he has never been able to prove to the contrary. I wonder now if she maintains the tradition simply as a little victory.

'It's too much Sir; I assure you that I am not ready. We'll have to postpone, at least until the New Year,' Michael's voice carries well.

'The New Year.' My father's booming voice is unnecessarily loud. 'Certainly not.' I hear him guzzling his drink rapidly. 'I may be able to give you a couple of weeks,' he relents, 'but the New Year?' he shouts again.

'I'll not be going anywhere until January,' Michael stands his ground. I feel a buzz of admiration warming me from the inside. I have never heard him so brave. 'There is no point Sir, in your sending Joyce anywhere without me. I'm sorry but we're just too exhausted at the moment. The public will have to wait,' Michael concludes. I hear his footsteps coming towards me. I hurry back up a couple of stairs as quietly as I can.

'Michael. Do not walk away from me,' my father's voice is hoarse now, raw with emotion and strain. 'Let's talk about it, come back here.' I hear Michael falter, turn around, that familiar sound of heels spinning on the marble tiles.

'Mr Capelli?' he questions my father, voice hard. I smile; finally, the version of him that seldom surfaces appears to be making more of an entrance these days.

'Ok, ok,' my father concedes. 'But early in the New Year, no longer than that.' There is silence. I can only imagine the two men facing each other, a mutual respect expanding, filling the air like a cloud. 'Tell Joyce will you?' my father asks but I hear him walking away quickly, no longer interested in waiting for an answer.

'I will Sir,' I hear Michael say to my father's back. Quickly he turns and heads for the door. From my hiding place on the stairs I watch him leave the house, my heart fluttering. I wonder how I can ever thank him for buying me time. Now all I need to do is figure out how to get my baby back before midnight strikes on New Year's eve.

I am in full control of my own finances now, of course, but unbeknown to me my father has always been a step ahead. He has tied a lot up in investments, probably wise investments, but still, I am unable to take it out of these schemes for another two years and right now all I need is working capital, a sizeable sum and some more time, with which to concoct my plan.

I have found her, I know where she lives. I know who her adoptive parents are. I do not believe, although I have no proof, that they are the ones who took her. What I do not know is how she came to be adopted, what happened to her between leaving my side at the hospital and ending up housed with her adoptive family. More importantly, I have no idea how to approach them or what I will say if I ever muster up the courage to do so.

I hear the car draw up outside. Mother is home. I mount the stairs, retreat to my room.

I wind my scarf a little closer around my neck as I set out towards the park. Mother was not aroused since it has become my habit to take a walk on a Sunday afternoon. I know they take her there most Sunday's. Soon the weather will be against me, I cannot afford to miss a Sunday until then. The Hammersmith has been put on the back foot.

It is too much to hope that Michael will accompany me but at least he appears now to better understand that I am not quitting on our baby. I will never stop wanting to see her, never stop longing for my mind to provide me with a way of bringing her back into my life.

They are already here I notice, spying on her adoptive parents at a picnic bench up ahead, wrapped in coats and gloves. Her sister is alone on the swings. Where is she? I look frantically ahead, my heart racing, my eyes narrowing to view, no longer caring if her adoptive parents notice me. The breeze laps at my sides and I gather my coat in closer, my view still strained ahead. Where is she? Where is my baby?

'Hello,' a small voice sings by my side. I look down. I see a floppy red hat and a stream of dark hair, two small eyes – Michael's eyes – looking up at me inquisitively. I realise I am holding my breath, my gloved hand on my chest in ambivalence.

'Hello,' I say; squatting down on the path, my coat and dress creasing at my knees. My voice sounds hollow, faint, my head feels light. She is so beautiful.

'You're here every week,' she observes. I can't stop myself smiling at her. Her voice is so sweet, soft and charming like music.

'Yes,' I whisper. 'How are you?'

'Oh I'm fine thank you,' she tells me, peering out from underneath the large folds of her hat. 'My mum always calls me sweetie,' she extends her hand gallantly. I take her tiny fingers in mine, the soft fabric of her red glove brushes against my grey ones fleetingly. I look into her eyes and I see her smiling back at me. I see my own reflection, my own confidence as it used to be once upon a time.

'What a pretty nick-name,' I smile brightly at her. 'I'm…' I find my voice dry up. I want to tell her but I am afraid of frightening her. 'Joyce,' I say finally. 'Is that your sister?' I ask her. I am half afraid she will run away, but unsure what to say to her. The long rehearsed speeches in my head, the longing for this moment, and the lines of practised words fail me completely. Instead I am stunned into a wordless state of love and grief all wrapped up around us by the chilly September breeze.

'Yes,' she says simply. 'That's Charlotte. I call her Lotty. She's ever so naughty sometimes,' she giggles. I think this is the most precious thing I have ever heard. I manage a small giggle in return. 'You can't tell her I said that,' she confides, bringing her gloved finger to her lips.

'It's our little secret then,' I say, my smile wider than ever. 'I promise.'

'You're ever so nice,' she beams. From across the park I hear Charlotte call her name. I don't want this to be over yet. My mind races for something else to say but I am a blank, utterly absorbed in looking at her sweet little face, her creamy complexion, not as dark as mine, but brighter than Michael's. A tinge of sadness threatens to choke me as I picture the little family we might have been.

'I have to go now,' she says matter-of-factly, 'maybe I'll see you again next Sunday. Goodbye,' she smiles and turns to run. After a few steps she stops, turns brightly and waves at me again. I raise my hand quickly but she is gone, her sister still calling her away.

Vivanti is selecting the music to match our choice of dances for the world title championship. I feel a little distracted today, I have not slept well, tossing and turning all night replaying my brief conversation over and over in my head. Memorising every fraction of her face, her little hands, her voice so soft and musical...

I look at Michael and all I can see are her eyes. I look in the mirror and all I see is her hair, her face shape and her little nose. With a hint of irritation I hear Vivanti calling me. I shake myself from my little dream world.

'My darling, what are you thinking about eh?' he says, dragging me towards the floor where he and Michael are ready to begin. 'You must think only of your footwork, feel the music,' he is saying. I know, I think, you have given me the same lecture for years. 'Now come, my beauties, to work, eh? We start with a little Salsa, just to get you warmed up.' Vivanti flits away to start the music. Today he is in his white ballet leggings again with another one of his flounced rainbow coloured tops that puff outwards like a balloon when the breeze takes it by surprise.

I see Michael wait for the beat as the music begins to fill the hall. We march on our toes, one, two, three, pause, five, six, seven, pause; our weight ever so slightly forwards into each others hands. I wonder what she is doing today, Monday, surely she must be at school by now...

Michael leads me into a Cuban Basic, one, two, three, pause, five, six, seven, and pause, a Mambo. I hear Vivanti sigh loudly but I ignore him. I wonder if she likes the same subjects as I did. We take the marching steps again.

'Michael you push her hand further down, she does not know what you want her to do, push further down,' Vivanti calls from the sides. Michael passes me a look and I smile. We continue into the Cucaracha side steps, another Mambo and a turn.

'No, no, you forget eh?' Vivanti stops the music. 'My darling,' he pulls me aside. Remember, you turn in a straight line; you do not go to the side. We are dancing the Salsa not the Rumba' he flicks his hands up the air in some gesture that is supposed to make everything clear. 'Come on my darling, you know all this, just focus my beauty, focus.'

'But Viv, I didn't go to the side,' I protest. I see the irritation crease his face. Michael gives him a look of pleading.

'You did a little my darling,' Vivanti insists. I sigh and Michael pats Vivanti on the shoulder.

'Let's continue,' Michael suggests but Vivanti will not relent.

'Now remember,' Vivanti says. I am not really listening to him but I humour him for Michael's sake. 'You turn straight in front of Michael. You are on a plank of wood yes?' Vivanti says, pushing me aside and taking his stance in front of Michael. He turns around, his arms lining his sides, 'you see, I am directly in front of Michael, I do not go like this, eh,' he takes a step slightly to his right. 'No, no,' he insists, stepping back, his arms lining them again. 'I stay here, eh? Come now my darling, you are tired. I know you know this. Focus, that is all. Now, let's try again. We are just warming up for a little. There is much to do, much to do,' he continues, shaking his head and walking away to his music sanctuary.

The music starts again and I try to concentrate. I want to tell Michael all about it but I see in his face he is focusing on the music. He does not look at me. A sweep of annoyance fills me as I stamp out the steps angrily.

'Ah yes, that is much better,' Vivanti is calling. 'Superb my beauties, superb,' he sings from the sidelines. After several minutes of praise he stops the music and we move onto the practise pieces. With less than ten days until the world title competition I am beginning to get nervous and I know that Michael feels it too. Mistakes are creeping into his moves, ones so basic he would never normally make.

'Are you nervous?' he asks me as Vivanti fiddles with records.

'Yes,' I smile briefly. 'You?' Michael nods. I see Vivanti is almost ready with the next song. 'I spoke to her,' I say quietly. Michael does not speak. He looks at me half in bewilderment and half disbelief.

'What? When, how...?' he stammers, turning me around as we Quickstep across the hall into a Quarter Turn and a Progressive Chasse. I wonder how to phrase it succinctly. 'Well?' he hurries me.

'Shss...focus,' Vivanti calls from the side lines. Michael leads me into a Lockstep and a Spin Turn, eyeing me keenly, waiting for my reply.

I smile at him and say nothing.

My feet hurt, my back aches, and my body is rigid and stiff. I sink gratefully into the hot water and rest my head back on the towel hanging over the edge of the bath. I close my eyes. It has been a long day. Vivanti pushed us further than either of us thought we could physically manage.

What will be the point of the championship title if we are both too tired to attend, I wonder, knowing that we would never be that lucky. Our entire future depends on it. If we win we are set for life. If we lose we will have to go on like this year after year, until we appease our parents and Vivanti.

'Just think sweetheart,' Michael had said today, away from Vivanti's earshot, 'if we win this thing we can ease back. No more seven hour days, six days a week.' My preoccupation with my daughter had overtaken my mind and suddenly I knew he was right. There will be nowhere else for my father to push us. Vivanti only follows my father's orders, after all. Without my father's silent background pressure we will be free. The idea is appealing. I could spend more time with her; find out where else she goes.

Usually I would play music but right now all I want is peace and quiet. I slide my body deeper into the bubbles and try to quieten my mind. I must learn to relax if I am to have any chance of winning the title. It will be no use to Michael or me to be pent-up with frustration and anger. It is hard though; there is so much to think about. I can't stop running my argument with Michael through my mind.

'What are you doing Joyce?' he had demanded the moment we were alone today. Vivanti and Phyllis were long gone. We were supposed to be practising our opening piece. 'Why now? With the title coming up you can't afford to...'

'Can't afford to what Michael?' I had yelled angrily. 'See my daughter, your daughter. For Christ's sake, I only said hello, am I not entitled to, after all I've been through...' My tears had burnt my eyes, fallen heavily and without warning. 'You can't stop me,' I had stabbed my finger at him and he took it, pulled me into him, fought my resistance until my tears subsided into a more even flow, then I spun away from him. 'I will see her again,' I sniffed, 'and I will talk to her. Why can't you come with me, just once, why won't you look at her?' I screamed, my anger boiling over into an emotional tidal wave.

'I told you I can't, didn't I?' He wrestled with his sports jacket, shoved his arms into the sleeves. It hung on him awkwardly as he shuffled it into place. 'Why are you always pushing me Joyce? I told you, I just can't,' his voice rose uncharacteristically. I stared at him in disbelief. In all our years of dancing together, the training, the competitions, frustrations, nerves, spotlights; all our love for each other, physically and verbally expressed, our grief at our lost child, fears, hopes, dreams; I had never known him to raise his voice to me, not even when I had screamed at him.

'I...I don't think I can,' softer this time, so quiet I almost missed it. 'It's too hard,' he whispered, bringing his hands to his face.

I stood watching Michael, my own body rigid with grief and guilt, my face stained with tears and my hair static with the day's movement. I had never seen him express such sadness and my heart felt heavy for him, guilty for pushing him too far. I took a tentative step towards him, led him towards the chairs. He slumped into the chair silently, bringing me down onto his lap and comfortably into the crook of his shoulder. For moments we sat in the chair, he tying knots in the cords of his jacket, I wondering where we go from here.

'I'm sorry,' I sniffed, my tears lessening, softly dampening his shoulder. He kissed the top of my head and tossed the jacket cords aside, shuffled me into a position where he could look at me.

'One day it might be different,' he told me.

As I blink my eyes now, the bubbles cooling around me, I wonder what he meant by those words; one day. If only that one day would come sooner. Perhaps my little family picture is feasible, if we win the title. Suddenly all that matters is winning the title. Everything could change if Father has no more cards up his sleeve. I close my eyes and picture her face. One day.

The envelope is cream, the handwriting richly scrawled across the sheet, the ink thick and blotchy. I look at it with intense curiosity, unwilling to open it in front of my parents but finding the temptation unbearable.

'Good morning dear,' my mother smiles, her blonde hair a little frizzy from the shower. She takes her seat at the table as usual. 'Good morning love,' she smiles at my Father. He nods at her and ruffles the newspaper as Rosa pours out the coffee with precision. Father grunts a type of thanks to Rosa. She pours for mother and me, leaves the pot and vanishes into the kitchen.

'Morning mum,' I smile at mother. She looks fresh today, cheerful and bright. The last few years have been a strain on her and lately I have begun to avoid arguments with Father, mainly for her sake, and partly because I see now that they resolve nothing. Father is not a man to be trifled with, least not by me. Michael managed to succeed with pushing the tour date back. I sincerely doubt I would have had the same luck if I had broached the subject personally.

I wonder what will happen if we do win the world title. Certainly Father will be even keener for us to take the tour, his assumption that we will win it already set in stone in his mind, but surely the title will afford me greater clout; greater powers of persuasion for me to lead my own course, for a change.

'You look nice today mum,' I volunteer. She rewards me with a smile. Whilst I will always be disappointed with her lack of strength against my Father, I begin to understand why she doesn't try harder.

At the age of twenty-two I might still seem very young to most but since my pregnancy five years ago I have grown so much. Sometimes I think mother sees that and against all odds we have grown closer together. Despite this, I do not confide in her. I do not want to hear her trying to dissuade me; it would only serve to weaken the bonds between us that are still rather fragile.

'Thank you dear,' she says, buttering her toast. 'How are rehearsals going?'

'Fine thanks,' I tell her shortly. 'We're almost set I think,' I announce.

'You'll win for certain,' my father says from behind his newspaper, ruffling it crossly as he flicks over a page too many.

'It'll still be tough,' I attempt to warn him.

'Nonsense,' he claims, putting the paper down. 'You'll walk it,' he insists. When I do not reply he picks up his paper and scans the stock market results.

'Of course you will dear,' my mother smiles and he grunts a sound of agreement as he studies the share prices.

I sip my coffee, my gaze attracted by the envelope. It is begging me to open it. I take another swift gulp of coffee, almost burn my throat, scrape my chair back across the tiles and rise to my feet.

'I'm sorry, I'm quite busy this morning,' I announce. 'We have that party performance tonight,' I remind my parents and quickly walk away before any protest can arise.

Upstairs I tear at the envelope. The letter inside is neatly folded, the handwriting perfected with a flourish. The paper has a scent to it, a pleasant mild scent of perfume. Greedily I unfold the single sheet and begin to read.

I write to you with deep regret and guilt. I think you have now found your little girl and I want to tell you that I think you are right to believe that she is the one so cruelly taken from you at birth.

I know what happened to her. If you want me to tell you then go to the Duchess Hotel in Atwood on 26th September. Look at the events board for a room number. I will meet you there at 10.30pm. This information will cost you £500. Do not reply. Destroy this letter once read.

The party is a great success as far as I can see. Couples of varying degrees of ability take to the floor with relish, keen to jive to the band. It is a birthday party and we are scheduled to appear, to dance for them, as a special surprise for the birthday girl.

I feel tired and worn out, my feet ache from today's long rehearsal and ideally we could do without this but the booking was made months before, and it would be highly unprofessional to back out at the last minute.

The crowds begin to hover as the dance floor clears and we appear. I should be nervous but I'm not. We are simply performing our showcase Argentine Tango followed by a quick Waltz around the floor and we're on our way. I have on my most faithful trusted little black number and my trusty black heels. Compared to the title performances next week this is a walk in the park.

As the music starts Michael smiles at me, a shy smile designed purely for me. One day, I think, one day. As we wow the crowds I am wondering whether I should tell him about the strange note I received this morning at breakfast. I am not inclined to tell anyone, not even Michael. Surely he would try to dissuade me from going. Perhaps I could talk it through with Rosa.

A loud applause brings me back into the present as I take my final spin and Michael throws me into the backbend dip in dramatic climax.

As I change into a long pretty pink evening gown Michael takes the microphone and toasts the birthday girl. After our

Waltz around the room there is just time for me to change into casual clothes, before we say our goodbyes, pieces of birthday cake thrust into our hands as we leave. Vivanti trails behind us carrying bags of costumes and shoes.

'Did you pick up the envelope?' Michael turns to Vivanti.

'Oh yes, I have the fee, 16 guineas,' beams Vivanti, 'and extra, they were very impressed.' Vivanti looks smug as he climbs into the passenger seat. I wonder if he has practised the look from my Father. 'So my beauties,' Vivanti sings brightly from the front seat as we load the car with our bags that he has so thoughtlessly left at our feet. 'We have just eight days to go. I want you as the lark tomorrow my darlings.' We hop into the back seat, grim faces at his remark.

'I guess that means early then,' Michael mutters.

Vivanti always hires a driver when we perform anywhere, usually the same chap, nice man, flat cap and a cigar in his mouth that he never lights.

'Evenin',' he smiles in the rear view mirror. 'Homeward bound is it?'

'Yes please,' Michael says politely. 'Thanks.'

'Oh Miss,' the driver says, 'there's another note waiting for you.'

'Oh?' I enquire. How on earth would he know?

'Popped by your place earlier, your mother, she wanted a ride to the theatre she did. Said another letter had come for you, left it on the table for you, said I should tell ya like,' he chews on his unlit cigar.

'Oh right,' I say, unsure what to make of this. 'Thank you,' I manage and avoid Michael's glance.

'Another letter?' Michael's voice is curious.

'It's nothing,' I tell him. 'Nothing.'

The moment I am safely in my bedroom, the others long past the end of the driveway, I tear open the envelope, the same as before; thick cream quality paper with thick ink scrawled impatiently across the page.

Go to room number five. It is on the second floor. There will be no name other than yours on the board.

I fold the letter and lock it in my jewellery case with the first, close my eyes and pray I am doing the right thing.

CHAPTER NINE – MODERN DAY; MAY

Rebecca felt her insides burning her, a scorching sensation. She breathed deeply, felt her face reddening, her throat constricting her.

'Becca? Are you all right?' Jean screamed, slamming her cup onto the saucer instantly and rising.

Rebecca tried to speak, to scream, anything, but her words were stuck, lodged inside her like a sponge. She began grappling for air, her hands at her throat and the fear engulfing her, the sounds around her muffled suddenly, like the popping sensation on an aeroplane.

Through her wide eyes she spotted Jean lunging towards her like a puma, pulling her onto the floor. She felt as if she had shrunk from the world, a tiny speck calling out soundlessly from the centre of her body, desperately trying to be heard. From somewhere in the depths of her consciousness she knew Jean was putting her into the recovery position.

Her eyelashes flickering, determined to retain consciousness, she watched Jean shouting into the phone, the sounds distant and faint. Tossing the phone frantically to one side she felt Jean take her head in her hands, stroke her face. Her eyes felt so heavy, flickering open and closed. Jean was saying something, she couldn't hear it, she tried to make it out, to read her lips but it was too hard.

A sound pierced her soul, a Siren, insistent and booming. Jean was still talking to her but she felt so tired, so hot, her pulse racing, her heart hammering in her chest. It was all she could hear. It was so hard to keep her eyes open…

A scent of bleach filled the hospital ward. Rebecca wished it weren't all happening so fast. The room felt like it were spinning. She felt disorientated, drunk and unstable.

'Mum,' Katherine patted her hand tenderly. 'Are you feeling better?' Rebecca tried to focus but her eyes felt so heavy, tired. 'Mum?'

'Yes dear,' she mumbled, squeezing her daughter's hand lightly. 'I'll be fine,' she whispered. The antidote the doctor had given her was strong, taking effect quickly and forcing her body to sleep, to rest, to fight the reaction. She would have to stay the night but something told her it would probably be the best night's sleep she had had since the dreams started and particularly since Craig's death.

'The doctor said it was an allergic reaction of some sort.' Katherine looked at her mother, her face a little puffy and her eyes wide and tired. The Police had already been and taken the evil envelope away, suspected poison. Rebecca nodded and closed her eyes.

'How could they be so careless?' Katherine raged through clenched teeth at Neil who stood holding baby Craig. 'Some stupid satisfaction survey,' she thumped her right fist into the palm of her left hand, her eyes on fire. 'I'll sue them,' she announced, her voice rising slightly.

'Shh, come on love, let her sleep,' Neil whispered, his free hand on Katherine's back and leading her towards the waiting area beyond the ward doors.

'That damned insurance company.' Katherine was crying now, her tears hot and thick, running rapidly down her face.

'It'll be all right,' Neil cradled her into his free arm, baby Craig nestled comfortably in the other. 'The police will get to the bottom of it. You know that odd Inspector told me it wasn't actually from the insurance company.'

'What?' Katherine burst free of Neil's captive hold. 'You mean it was meant to…' Neil reclaimed her, led them to a sea of waiting chairs and handed baby Craig to her.

'I'll get some coffees,' he said. Katherine watched her fiancé's back as he ventured on the mission for coffee.

The waiting room was empty, sparsely furnished with a selection of blue chairs, a table lined with out-of-date magazines and a play area stuffed with Lego bricks and children's colouring books. The lights were dimly lit for the evening, shadows of the passing traffic from the corridor flickering across the seats like a slide show. A creepy silence prevailed as Katherine kissed baby Craig lightly and closed her eyes, the horrors of the event pasted on her mind. Even closing her eyes didn't save her from thinking about the wickedness that might have occurred.

The insurance company had paid out quickly and it was true, the decoration was now complete. If a real satisfaction survey existed her mother would probably have ticked excellent in every box. Was Neil saying that someone else had sent the survey with the pre-paid envelope to her mother on purpose, the lethal substance already gummed into the sticky seal, just waiting of her mother to lick it moist... The reaction was strong and instant and, according to the doctor, could have killed her if she hadn't such a strong constitution or been rushed to the hospital in the nick of time. The police would, of course, suspect it to be another attempt on her mother's life. They had acted quickly, removed the envelope in an instant and it was now, apparently, undergoing rigorous tests with their forensics team.

Who would want to harm her mother this badly? It just didn't make any sense. She didn't have any enemies, had never upset anyone in her life, certainly not to this extent... Katherine thought about the man at the football game, the same man who had peered at them at the doctors' surgery. She shook her head. She knew she was being irrational. He was a stranger. No, it had to be someone they knew... Even Jean had agreed it was likely to be somebody they knew. What a horrible thought.

The brakes failing, the fire-riddled parcel, now this...it was something that happened to other people. It could have come straight from a twisted movie plot about world domination or something equally barmy. It just wasn't what she expected for her kind-hearted mother. Wiping a tear away she wished her father could be with her. He would have known what to do.

Neil handed her a cup of coffee and she sipped at the steaming tasteless liquid gratefully, as he sat, his arm draped around her shoulder. Rebecca would be staying the night in the hospital so there was nothing to wait for but Neil knew Katherine would go nowhere until the doctor had spoken to her.

'I never thought I'd say this,' Katherine sighed, grateful that the room was devoid of other relatives, 'but thank heavens for Jean.' She managed a half smile. Neil squeezed her shoulder and smiled back with a slight chuckle, his own coffee now almost drained.

'Good job she was there,' he agreed quietly, a shadow passing over his face. Neil stroked little Craig's face with a light finger as he slept in Katherine's arms.

Around them the hospital was in full flow, its hectic schedule carrying on as they sat on the fringes of sanity in the empty waiting room. Nurses and patients scurried past. People were being pushed in wheelchairs; doctors in white coats, visitors looked lost and haggard, trawling past the waiting room entrance, their expressions strained with confusion as they paused momentarily by the door. It was a wonder baby Craig could sleep through the mayhem.

'I'll never think badly of her again,' Katherine sighed. Jean was a babbling noisy woman, whom they found irritating most of the time, but Rebecca seemed to find her amusing.

'Do you want me to find the doctor?' Neil offered. 'We should be getting the little chap home really.' Katherine nodded, lost in thought. If Jean hadn't called the ambulance... It didn't bare thinking about.

'Be back in a minute,' Neil whispered, finding a nearby nurse to consult. Katherine looked into her baby son's face, his bright eyes waking and blinking at the harsh hospital lights. She nestled him closer to her and stroked his face gently. Life could be so cruel at times.

Sergeant Wellington handed the warrant to the Inspector and took his seat, hidden suddenly by the mountain of files on his desk. A thin haze of smoke trailed from the Inspector's desk draw, its scent lifting the air and drifting lazily towards Wells' desk. The Inspector slammed the draw closed and sighed happily.

'Oh blimey Sir, not more car thefts, what are we gonna tell the super?' Wells exclaimed. DCI Allen watched his Sergeant shuffle the mountains either side of his desk and his round pink face peer through the gap at him eagerly. 'He's already chomping at the bit at us for that arrest you promised him.'

'Don't worry son,' Inspector Allen assured him, his voice rough, followed by a light smirk. 'We've got him now,' he waved the warrant in his hand. 'Send the boys in son, let's see what else we can pin on him shall we?' he swung his legs from his desk with a light thud on the floor. 'Spot of attempted murder perhaps, how does that sound?'

'But Sir,' Wells objected. 'We haven't got any proof against Francis for that.'

'We will have son, we will have.' Inspector Allen rose; pulled on his forest green mackintosh and slid his hat casually onto his iron-grey hair. Sergeant Wellington put the call through instructing the search team to meet at the club immediately. 'You forget the logbooks son; that's proof enough if we get him to cough to it too,' Inspector Allen said quietly, his fingers thinning his moustache thoughtfully. 'Anyway, what'd you dig up on Fisher?' he demanded, his voice booming in the hazy room, his stance tall by the door waiting for Wells to join him.

'Fisher Sir,' Wells said, pushing his squashy form out from his chair with some effort and following Allen to the doorway. 'Formally known as Bateman, did a five-year stretch back in the early nineties, explosives, intent to kill, Sir.' Sergeant Wellington clicked the car keys in his pocket with a smile as the Inspector grinned.

'Good work son, good work.' Inspector Allen launched forwards and out the office, his cigarette in his fingertips awaiting the open air. 'What about Nicholas?' He spun around quickly, halting Wells unexpectedly.

'Nothing on a Nicholas Sir,' Wells said. The Inspector was off again, Wells hurrying to keep pace behind his progress along the corridor, his speed half-fuelled by his need to light his cigarette.

'There will be soon then son, soon. Just a feeling I've got,' he chirped. 'Quick son, in the car, I want to go back to that grotty club.' He waved the warrant around, simultaneously bounced through the entrance double doors and lit his cigarette. Wells pushed the doors out his face and followed the Inspector to the car. Another search was about to reveal something. The Inspector's hunches were often wrong but his loyalty to them was concrete.

Outside the sky was greying, threatening rain, the clouds heavy and shifting slowly. Wells unlocked the car and clambered behind the steering wheel.

'When we get back son,' Inspector Allen said, puffing a thin trail of white smoke out the window into the cloudy sky, 'I want you to trace Mrs Houseman's family tree son. Not the official one, look deeper. Go back to her date of birth, find out where she was born, find people who were there at the time, interview them.'

'But why Sir?' Wells asked, exiting the car park as a stream of squad cars roared ahead of them; the search team. The car engine hummed quietly as Wells sped up to join the end of the possession.

'Because there's a reason some lunatic is trying to kill her and I think it has to do with her identity. Just dig son, if I'm right you'll find something,' he grinned, puffed out another smoke ring and tossed the cigarette out the window. 'It'll be big news too,' he predicted.

'I'll call round Sir, ask her about it...'

'No,' Inspector Allen barked. 'You'll tell her nothing son, nothing. Clear?'

'Yes Sir,' Sergeant Wellington agreed. 'Right Sir. Nothing.' Wells flipped the sun visor down, the dark clouds already making way for the streaming sunlight. Spring was definitely warmer and much dryer than usual. The news was full of stories about the consequences of the drought. Some people were never happy.

'Good. Now, quick son, we've got evidence to find, if we're really lucky we may even find something to help us fit up Bateman, or Fisher, or whatever the little swine is calling himself now, with the murder of Craig Houseman.'

'You think that the husband's murderer is the same person behind the attacks on the wife now Sir?' Wells enquired.

'Absolutely son, absolutely. It's all tied up somehow. We just need to find out how,' Inspector Allen grinned.

'What about Francis Sir?' Wells asked, racing up behind the last squad car in the line as a Vauxhall moved out his way. Wells was sometimes glad he hadn't gone down the wrong side of the tracks; he wouldn't want to be Francis right now, or Fisher. The trail of uniform ahead of them would put the most hardened criminal off.

'Francis is in on it too son, I reckon. He's just the type to kill at a distance, not to get his own hands dirty. That envelope gum is right up Francis's street. But they're sticking together son, I just wish I knew why...' his voice fading as Wells turned the corner at speed towards the Belvadere Club.

'You mean their motive for wanting Mrs Houseman dead Sir?'

'Exactly son, what does a nice woman like that do to deserve their little games, hey?'

'I'm not sure Sir,' Wells confessed. 'We're here anyway Sir,' he announced, pulling up by the kerb. The road was now swarming with police cars and several of the neighbours had ventured to the ends of their driveways to investigate. It was a nice street with expensive properties, ladies who had only leisure on their day's agendas'. An entire fleet of police cars were probably the highlight of the year for the social coffee morning gatherings.

'Good son, let's go and create chaos,' Inspector Allen grinned. 'My favourite past time,' he whispered, his lips thinning into a determined line.

Rebecca sat in her newly decorated lounge, a cup of tea on a tray on the coffee table and a magazine sprawled open on the settee by her side. She was glad to be home, away from the hospital, but the lounge didn't yet feel like home. It was lovely; a pastel shade of coral paint adorned the walls, a beautiful canvas print of red poppies on the far wall, the family photos back safely along the mantelpiece and a new, extremely comfortable, scarlet three-piece suite. The insurance pay-out had been excessive and she still had a small sum left in the bank, spending money for her holiday with Jean.

She sipped at her tea and glanced around, missing the familiar shape of Craig embedded in the armchair, the scent of him in the room long gone, dusted away by the smoke and drama of the parcel. Wiping a tear from her eye she flicked idly through the magazine; bored instantly by its tawdry content, and sighed. She had contemplated not going to the Samba School today but the desire for company overwhelmed her.

The doctor had suggested she rest and the dancing was hardly a rest. Her body felt weary and she knew she looked a fright, her face still slightly flushed from the medication and her concentration levels pushed to survive a magazine article, let alone a highly-choreographed dance routine; but something deep inside her wanted to go. Was it just to see Paul? No, she shook her head, felt dizzy and closed her eyes. She enjoyed the dancing more than she ever thought she would. It was a mixture, the need to feel like a woman again, which the dancing would definitely give her, and the need to feel alive, as opposed to the zombie she felt like at present. It would be nice to see Paul too, she admitted to herself with a shy smile. His cheerfulness would make her feel better.

Instinctively she got up deciding she would run a hot bath. She had a few hours before Samba, perhaps a bath and fresh change of clothes that didn't smell of the hospital's disinfectant would make her feel better. Then, she would be ready to go.

Rebecca sat behind the desk, her freshly painted fingernails flicking through the sheets of printed information. Neil was interviewing for a receptionist, each candidate taking a seat in the limited space before her.

'I'll value your opinion,' Neil had told her, 'see how they cope, sitting out there waiting for me.' To be honest she had been glad of the distraction, pleased he had asked her back to hold the fort, instruct the candidates where to wait. Hardly able to openly read a novel she had brought along the data about sleep, insomnia and dreams. It was all valuable, informative and useful yet none of it made any real difference. If the situation didn't improve soon she had promised Katherine she would seek professional help. But what sort of help should she seek? There were so many options...

'Hello,' she smiled as a young woman approached her. 'Can I help you?'

'I'm here for the interview,' the young girl said, long dark hair and eyes wide with anticipation. 'My name's Sharon Bottle.'

'Take a seat, Mr Carter won't be a minute,' Rebecca told the girl, watched her smooth out her skirt and sit down carefully. She ticked the girl's name off the list discretely and returned to her printed sheets, hoping she wouldn't need to consult them much longer. The obvious place to start was the doctor, but she didn't want to start anywhere. Craig would have told her to go to the doctor, eventually. She knew that, and had he been around to tell her she would probably have gone. But now...now she didn't want, no, that wasn't true. The real issue was that she didn't believe anyone could help her move past losing Craig. A large part of her wasn't ready to move past it. One day she would sleep again. The single most helpful thing she had read in the density of the available information was that if her body needed sleep, it would take it, despite her trying not to let it.

'Thank you Mrs Grate, I'll be in touch,' Neil was saying, shaking the hand of an older woman as they approached the side of the desk. Neil came to Rebecca's side. 'Who's next?' he whispered as Mrs Grate left the office, a shaft of cool air in her wake. Rebecca nodded at the girl sitting quietly, trying to blend into the scenery, 'oh, right. What'd you think?' his voice even softer.

'Seems nice,' Rebecca said. 'Nervous, I think.' Neil smiled and stepped cautiously towards the waiting area.

'Miss Bottle?' he extended his hand. The pair vanished into the office behind and Rebecca sighed at the material, folded it back into her handbag and waited for the next candidate to arrive. She was sick of worrying about it.

Paul hadn't been at the Samba School last night and today she felt despondent. She felt guilty for missing him, for even noticing his absence at all. Lexia had taken them through the final chosen steps for the performance in the town and she had scribbled down the steps as quickly as she could. It gave her a purpose at least.

With a start she realised the telephone was ringing.

'Carter Financial Advice,' she spoke crisply into the line.

'Oh Becca dear,' Jean bubbled down the line, 'I thought you were there today. Your Katherine answered your house phone, she said you were there helping out that nice young man of hers. Just wanted to see how you were doing today?'

'I'm fine thanks Jean,' Rebecca laughed. 'That nice young man of hers is going to be her husband in about three months you know,' she said.

'Oh I know dear, lovely isn't it? I love a good wedding. So, you're ok today?'

'Honestly, I'm fine, my face is still a little flushed but I'm ok.'

'Oh Becca dear, you have just been poisoned. That evil insurance company, I hope you're going to sue them…I'm so glad you're on the mend dear. I can't imagine…well I just can't imagine. What did they think they were doing? You gave me quite a scare you know; I shall never forget it…'

Rebecca listened to Jean rattle on. She knew she would hear the story several times over the coming years. That rather peculiar Inspector had told her the survey wasn't from the insurance company, they had denied ever sending any such document out to her. It was yet another attempt on her life, but she saw no reason to enlighten Jean on that score. It was bad enough that her family were pressing her to take it seriously, but what was she supposed to do? The strange police Inspector she couldn't help but like would sort it all out. He had that air of determination about him. Dogged, she smiled to herself; that was the word for him.

'Oh when they stuck the Siren on, aren't they loud…' Jean was enthusing. Rebecca accented agreement in the relevant places.

Silently she pondered what to buy for Jean, chocolates and flowers seemed so trivial. What did you get for someone when they quite literally saved your life by phoning the ambulance just in time?

Katherine and little Craig were waiting for her at her house, she would ask Katherine what to buy for Jean. It amused her that Jean managed to irritate most people with her endless verbal stream of, mostly pointless, gossip; including her poor Katherine, but Rebecca liked her. As much as her family were supportive, for which she was truly grateful, her children couldn't possibly understand some aspects of her grief. They were too young and fortunately they hadn't experienced the pain of losing someone they loved as much as she had loved her husband. Admittedly they were grieving over the loss of their father, but that was a very different type of ache.

Jean was funny, witty, easy listening, seldom requested much of an answer, and right now she could learn a lot from Jean about learning to live on her own again. It wasn't as easy as people made it look.

'I know, I'm looking forward to it too,' she said, suddenly aware that Jean had moved onto their holiday. 'I'll start making out a list of things to pack soon.'

'Excellent. I'll pop over later this week dear and we can have a proper chat about it. We don't both need to take a hairdryer do we? Oh and how about a plug? Have you got one of those things, you know, with the two pins instead of three?' Jean's frantic breath was heaving down the line, trying to keep up with the pace of her chatter. Rebecca smiled.

'Yes I think so, somewhere,' she laughed.

'Oh we'll sort it Becca dear, I'll pop over later, better go now though, I'm supposed to be helping sell cakes at the charity bash down the church hall. I'll catch ya later Becca dear,' and Jean was gone. Rebecca smiled as she replaced the receiver. Despite what people said, Jean did make her forget herself.

'So, do you think any of them are any good?' Katherine wanted to know when Neil and Rebecca came into the new living room. Baby Craig gurgled at her and she happily took her grandson from Katherine's arm as the couple began to discuss the candidates frankly.

A comforting scent of cooked chicken sailed through the house and Rebecca took Craig to investigate the kitchen. Katherine had been busy in their absence. Rebecca smiled to herself. Of all her children it was her youngest who always took the trouble, and never expected any recognition.

'I reckon experience counts for a lot more, what do you think mum?' Katherine was asking as she followed her fiancé into the kitchen, where Rebecca was cuddling baby Craig affectionately, and feeling more cheerful than she had in days. Her baby grandson was a magical cure all by himself. 'Experience or qualifications; which should rank higher?'

'You want both, obviously,' Rebecca said, her gaze warmly fixed on Craig's snug little face. 'Experience will always help in a new position but it's no good if you need qualifications you just haven't got,' looking up, 'who are you talking about?'

'Mrs Grate has ten years' experience as receptionist at a doctor's surgery,' Neil explained, 'nice woman, knows how to handle people, but she doesn't have any computer skills and ideally I want the receptionist to be able to type a few letters. Sharon Bottle,' Neil sighed, 'on the other hand, has all the computer skills you could shake a stick at. But she's fresh out of college and she's shy. I'm not sure she would cope well out front, exposed like that.'

'What's more important?' Rebecca enquired, filling the kettle for tea absent-mindedly as Katherine took Craig from her to feed him. 'Is the typing the most pivotal part of the job?'

'I'm not sure it's more or less, I should probably have advertised for a receptionist come secretary...' Neil sighed, 'oh, perhaps I should advertise again.'

'Perhaps,' Rebecca agreed. 'You'll find someone; don't worry. Why not give them each a trial run?' Neil nodded thoughtfully as Rebecca poured hot water into the teapot and moved it to the kitchen table. 'See how they get on, the young girl may surprise you and the older woman may pick it up quite quickly. People are so keen for work these days Neil, I'm sure they'll try their best if they've got any sense.' The three of them sat down.

'Katherine darling, you didn't need to do all this,' Rebecca touched her daughter's hand affectionately. 'I'd have managed.' She began to separate the mugs and poured in a splash of milk.

'I know mum, you always do,' Katherine smiled, re-positioning Craig slightly, to his minor protest, 'he was asleep,' she smiled at him, 'and besides, you were helping us out today, can't expect you to prepare a feast for our entire family brood on top can we.'

'Oh yes, thanks for recommending that guy at the bank to me,' Neil chipped in, 'he was really nice. We're meeting next week; he's going to help me put together a business plan.'

'We've got a business plan,' Katherine objected.

'One written the way the bank want to see it,' Neil smiled at Katherine, 'not quite the same thing.'

The day slipped past in a blur as Eliza and Chris arrived with her granddaughters Charlotte and Christine. The girls were beautiful, there was no denying it. All four were in the garden watching Samuel, George and Neil playing football, their discarded jumpers as goal posts. Rebecca dished up the roast chicken, predictably with Katherine's help whilst Tina sat chuckling at them out the window, holding baby Craig happily. Dinner was raucous and happily rowdy but by the end of it Rebecca felt exhausted, her energy completely spent at keeping it all going without Craig by her side. His absence was all the more obvious and she found herself swallowing tears through the meal, punctuated by laughter as George and the girls teased each other in the merciless method only children knew how to adopt.

When everyone had finally gone, the washing up done, the lounge restored to order and the house quiet, she sank into the new settee with a large glass of wine and let her tears flow freely. Craig smiled at her from the mantelpiece. He would have loved having the kids there, it had been the most important and treasured part of their lives; the ultimate good things to come out of their marriage, that and their love for each other.

Still, when all was said and done, she admitted to herself, they were still exhausting on mass. Raising her glass and smiling back at her husband who peered out the silver frame, 'to you, my darling.'

The smell of perfume. A soft floral scent, pretty. Long dark hair, patches of blue, gloves…a woman in a long coat. A park bench…a name…the news broadcast…Craig, his face, trying to tell her something. His eyes wide, life slipping away…

Rebecca sat up in bed, her head dizzy from the sudden movement. She reached out blindly for the glass of water on her bedside table and took several long gulps. Three thirty in the morning. There was no way she could get up now. She closed her eyes resolutely and sank back down into the warmth of the duvet. No, she didn't want to dream, not any more. Her soft tears spilt onto the pillowcase as she tried to block it out.

What had he tried to tell her? Something about the news broadcast. If only she could figure it out, then maybe the dreams would stop haunting her. Maybe Katherine was right. Perhaps she did need help, just to move past it, to make the dreams go away.

'What's this son?' Inspector Allen flipped over a jiffy envelope, its sender a mystery.

'Oh that Sir,' Sergeant Wellington said, reading from a memo on his desk. 'You intercepted Mrs Houseman's post Sir. This came earlier today when we were at the club. It's a CD apparently,' Wells read further down the memo, his voice running low on oxygen, supping noisily as he reached the base of the memo. 'Hypnotherapy CD Sir, designed to help you sleep. This one has been tampered with,' he sat heavily in his chair; the arm rests bowing sideways.

'Is it indeed,' the Inspector mumbled, his chair squealing in protest as he slumped into it and ripped the jiffy envelope open savagely.

'It's been altered Sir,' Wells explained, his eyes now lifted from the remains of the memo and watching the Inspector's progress. 'To make her take an overdose of sleeping pills.'

Inspector Allen paused; looked cautiously at the CD and then at Sergeant Wellington. He flipped it over, studied it carefully then slung it towards Wells.

'Play it son, let's have a listen.'

'Here Sir,' Wells said, proffering a leaf of paper. The Inspector grabbed it and read down the text. 'It's a transcript of the CD Sir.' The inspected nodded as he read on. 'Good idea of yours Sir, to intercept her post like that; this could have been nasty.'

'Yes well, our culprit seems to have a taste for sending things by post doesn't he,' Inspector Allen mused. He read the transcript twice, let it drop to his desk and thought for a moment. Wells waited silently. 'How'd we get on then?' he asked suddenly, his voice booming again.

'You mean today Sir?'

'Yes son, fill me in.' Inspector Allen put his feet up on his desk, crossed his ankles, slipped his cigarette from behind his ear and lit it, waiting, his expectant smile widening as he puffed out another trail of white smoke. A few thin files filtered to the floor as he shuffled his feet into a comfortable position.

'Well Sir, the logbooks found at Francis's house and club are enough to convict I'd say, the records of sales we already had match some contacts we found in his address book at the club. That'll get us Francis for the car thefts.'

'True son, where is he now?'

'In custody Sir, we have to wait until he's had his meal,' Wells informed him. Inspector Allen rolled his eyes. 'Ok, get the grease monkey back in here son, we'll nail him too, now that we've got Francis.'

'Right Sir. There was also that stuff about Bateman in Francis's club office Sir, probably enough to blackmail Bateman into doing anything Francis wanted.'

'Agreed son, agreed. If Francis knew about Bateman's past…' his voice faded as he tweaked his moustache and blew out a large ring of grey smoke, admiring it with affection. 'If Bateman didn't want his new identity of Fisher ruined he'd have caved under Francis's command,' the Inspector concluded. 'Good work son.'

'So Fisher, or Bateman,' Wells coughed, chewed distastefully on a mouthful of smoke, 'was behind the explosive parcel sent to Mrs Houseman?'

'Yes son,' Inspector Allen blew out a strong line of smoke, stubbed his cigarette out in the brimming ashtray and slammed the second draw closed on his desk with force. 'It was Francis though; he's the driving force,' he declared.

'Forensics report here, Sir,' Wells read from a creamy sheet on his desk, his eyes studying the lines of text carefully, 'says Bateman rigged the thing cleverly. It was only activated by some gismo in the wrapping, Sir. Any amount of tossing around the post office van and it would be absolutely fine, until she started to get under the wrapping.' He glanced up at his superior who appeared to be lost in thought.

'He's a clever swine all right,' Inspector Allen mused, twisting the end of his moustache thoughtfully, 'But why son, why?' thumping his fists heavily on the desk as he swung his feet to the ground.

'Maybe Francis will tell us Sir,' Wells suggested.

'Never son, he'll never tell us. The only way we'll crack him into a confession is if we know more than he does.' The Inspector paced the office like a tiger, his feet striding around quickly, pausing, striding back towards the corner and brushing past the dying plant carelessly. 'We'll start him on the car thefts son, we can nail him for those, get the mechanic in here. We'll hang the two of them off each other until we've cracked that.' Inspector Allen stuck his pencil between his teeth, paced some more as Sergeant Wellington dialled uniform to pick up the garage mechanic.

'That'll faze them at least,' Wells agreed. 'There was also the hidden casino Sir, you remember, behind that wall in the bar. You noticed it before Sir, the crack in the wall....' Sergeant Wellington's voice lowers into insignificance as he stared at the Inspector. DCI Allen looked delirious. He pointed a long finger to the ceiling with a beam.

'Yes son, of course. That's it! Listen, I want you to dig into Mrs Houseman's birth line, concentrate on that, and don't forget about Nicholas. He's involved somehow, I know he is.' Inspector Allen pointed his chewed pencil at his Sergeant enthusiastically as he opened the office door. The light from the corridor flooded in, framing him in the doorway, his head almost touching the top. 'I'm off to frighten Francis,' he announced with a grin from ear to ear, turned and fled down the corridor towards the interrogation rooms. 'Get me a constable to sit in,' he bellowed over his shoulder.

CHAPTER TEN – SEPTEMBER 1964

It is slightly cold, the sky a shade of grey and the clouds almost non-existent as I sit on the bench by the path. Rosa gave me a wry smile when I left the house. Despite all her help I have not told her where I go to see my baby. It is for her own protection really, her defence against questioning should any arise in my absence. When I think about it the notion is daft, my parents do not know that I have found her, only that I searched. Perhaps they think I have given up…unlikely I surmise. They know me better than that.

I am worried about the world championships, worried about how I will keep my head on the task at hand, despite knowing full well that when that damned spotlight finds us my body will obey Michael's' leads without question. It is an odd thing really, my ability to switch off at that precise second. It is not like that in rehearsal, much to Vivanti's annoyance, though he knows nothing of our dilemma.

If we should win I am even more hopeful that the tour can be cancelled, despite the opposite being favoured. If we win the options are unlimited, endless, our dreams, anything we want… One day, Michael had said, one day. I know he has grown tired of the pressure too, and I know he would like us to have a normal life together, the three of us. If we win the normal life could be ours, how to fit our daughter into the jigsaw is slightly trickier, but there must be a way. There must.

From around the bend of the path I see her. She does not wear the hat today. Instead she has on a woollen knitted thing that resembles a tea cosy, matching multi coloured gloves and scarf. She skips with her sister along the path towards the play area. The woman, short with a flame of red hair and wearing a long cream coat, is pushing the pram with the unseen child tucked cosily inside and the man, tall and lean, strides by her side. He wears a suit beneath his long dark overcoat, and I decide he must be an office dweller, something in banking perhaps, in the city, or parliament.

I had not noticed it before, not having paid much attention to anyone in her sphere other than her, but they look wealthier now, more so than before. Promotion for him at work, maybe, or a sudden windfall, inheritance…? Whatever it is, it may explain a lot.

I watch her and her sister mount the steps to the large blue slide. Her sister is behind her, eager to reach the top. She races ahead up the steps, stumbles slightly and loses her footing on the flimsy bars. My heart skips a beat and my body freezes at once. I am on the point of rising from my seat, but she recovers instantly. A childish yelp and she is on her way, safely, down the large blue slide, her near accident long forgotten.

How easily children overcome obstacles I think. I wonder if my instant fear would have melted, over time, had I been able to raise her normally. Bumps and scrapes, the usual sort, I would have dismissed them as everyday occurrences. Mothers the world over cannot possibly be on such thin ice as I am right now, not permanently, the planet would be over-run with nervous wrecks. The woman with the flamed hair doesn't flinch as much as me, she watches clearly, but she doesn't flinch quite so visibly. There must be a level of natural caution that comes with experience.

When she gets up at the bottom, her sister almost crashing into her, she sees me. I smile and wave. She waves back and runs to the steps again for another go.

I watch them play for a few minutes. Unexpectedly she starts to venture my way, her sister following. The woman with the red hair eyes me sceptically as the girls approach. I note that she does not remove her glance from my little girl or hers. A stab of anger hurts me, how on earth could she think I would do anything harmful…then gratitude springs into play; if she is this watchful my baby will always be safe. Oh I wish things were simpler. They reach me.

'Hello,' she says, that same sweet voice making me feel a hundred times better.

'Hello,' I answer her. 'Hello,' I address her sister, fair hair, equally long, with blue eyes and a rounder face. She looks pretty I decide, together they will make a stunning duo of heartbreakers in later years.

'This is Charlotte,' my little girl says, 'she is my sister.' She points suddenly to the woman with red hair who is blatantly ignoring her husband's conversation in favour of watching us. He does not appear to notice her neglect. I am amused by this, the suited gent who sees only his own little world; and I hope he is a different being at home.

'That's mum and dad over there,' Charlotte joins in the pointing. For the first time I notice that Charlotte does not have her mother's red hair either and the man seems to have brown hair. I wonder if Charlotte too may be adopted.

'Let's wave,' the girls say and wave in unison. I politely acknowledge the woman and she seems to unclench slightly, a small wave in return. 'Can you tell us a story?' Charlotte requests.

'Yes, if you like,' I agree, unsure how to begin. They sit cross-legged on the grass before my feet. I look at them both, their expectant faces, the little eyes waiting for me to begin, and their noses slightly rosy in the cold. How I wish it were all much simpler. The woman with red hair has turned back to her husband, the casual glance over her shoulder now and then.

'Ok,' I start. No words enter my head, only the truth. They are waiting. I unwind my scarf, feeling slightly flushed. 'Once upon a time,' I say, stammer a little but they only smile at me. 'Once upon a time there was a little baby girl. Her mother loved her with all her heart, more than anything else in the world,' I look at my daughter; feel my throat closing up and my words choking me. I take a deep breath quickly and glance over at Charlotte to regain composure. 'But a nasty man arrived in the middle of the night,' I put on a different voice, a deeper one and they giggle delightedly. I smile brightly and wish I could take her home with me. 'He whisked the little baby away,' I say, 'the poor mother was heartbroken and she started to look for her baby but she couldn't find her.'

'Ah, that's a sad story,' Charlotte sighs, 'what happened to the little baby?'

'The little baby was safe,' I improvise quickly. 'The policemen catch up with the nasty man and they put him in jail,' I decide. The girls clap happily. 'But the police do not know who the mother is and so they give the baby girl to a nice lady and man who will look after her. They are very nice and the little girl grows up to be very beautiful,' again I feel my eyes burning with threatening tears. I blink furiously to stop them falling. 'She is very happy and she has a sister who is very lovely.'

'Do they have a brother too?' my daughter asks me. I glance quickly over at the pram. The woman with red hair acknowledges me this time without a hint of concern.

'If you like yes,' I turn back to the girls, 'a young brother; he is very small and cries a lot at night,' I hazard a guess. They seem delighted at this, their little smiles wide with giggling.

'What about the nasty man?' Charlotte asks.

'He is in jail,' my daughter informs her, a nod of satisfaction as if that seals the deal forever.

'Yes, that's right; he is in jail forever because he has been very bad. The policeman had to lock him up. But the little girls and their baby brother were loved very much by their mum and dad and together they were a very happy little family.'

'The End,' Charlotte almost sings.

God, I hope not.

'Thank you that was a nice story,' Charlotte says. My daughter is smiling at me. A tiny part of me wants her to believe, but I know in this case ignorance is bliss.

'Will you tell us another story when we see you again?' she asks me.

'Of course I will sweetheart, any time you like,' I feel the tears choking me now and blindly manage to hold the worst of them at bay.

'Thank you, we had better go now,' she says happily. 'Goodbye,' she waves as she and Charlotte sprint back towards the slide. I wave a polite acknowledgment to the flame-haired woman who casts me a smile and a nod as she returns to her husband's, no doubt, boring tale.

Safe now that no one is watching me the tears begin to stain my face with a speed that would rival the rapids. I get up, turn to leave, walk very slowly away from the park. The chill has now reached me again and I wind my scarf tighter around me, pull my long caramel coat in closer and tilt my hat. When I reach the gate I turn back briefly but the children have vanished. Frantically I look around, spy the family heading off in the opposite direction.

'Bye sweetheart,' I whisper, 'for now.'

'You silly child,' my father yells. The ornaments on the mantelpiece wrestle with stability as he launches his bulky frame from the ledge towards me. I notice the heat in his brown eyes, the gleam of the sun from his greying hair and the shine on the balding patch in the centre of his head.

I turn towards my mother as he comes towards me like a charging bull. She is cringed in the seat at the far side of the room. In an instant I know she will not help me.

'It's my business,' I tell him, spinning on him at the last fraction. He falters on his footing and steps back from me quickly. 'I'll do as I please,' I tell him, my eyes defiant. I hold my stance, my body tall, and my posture perfect. 'You shouldn't read my letters anyway,' I accuse him; snatch them back from his fists. A corner tears in his hand and he discards it on the floor with vehement. In a heartbeat I spy Rosa peer through the doorway and vanish, quietly closing the doorway into the sanctuary of the kitchen.

'If you weren't so damned secretive child I wouldn't have had to take them off you, would I?' he retaliates. Having refused him the information at breakfast and foolishly having had them in my pocket, he had noticed, insisted I tell him what they were. When I hadn't, we had ended up in here, arguing, again.

'I am not a child,' I insist, my voice level and firm. 'I am twenty-two father, old enough to make my own decisions and

I'm going to this hotel,' I thrust the letters, crumpled in my fist, at him and turn to leave.

'You can't go. They're only after your money. For God's sake Joyce, think about it, please,' my father reasons, his hands lay out before him as if offering some invisible plate of wisdom.

I have, of course, thought about this already. I face him once more, if only to hear him out for my mother's sake. She sits silently in the chair watching the battle with her usual uneasiness. She sips at a tall glass of Pimms drowned in cucumber-favoured lemonade. It's the trendiest drink over in Soho and I wonder how she knows about it, seems so unlikely...she doesn't normally drink, especially at this time of day. I wonder if we are driving her to it...? Momentarily I am distracted but my father snorts loudly at my silence, convinced beyond logic that he has made his point.

I look at my poor mother sipping her drink, and feel sorry for her already. Over the years she has seen my father and I spar for ownership of a decision, an outcome, a whim, some things worth fighting for, others not so. She must have seen an even keel of results over time. This time I will go though. It doesn't matter what he says. I have made up my mind. I have to know and instinct tells me I will find out. This isn't a hoax.

'I have thought of that,' I tell him. I keep my voice level to add weight to my words. 'But something tells me this is genuine. I must go. I've seen her myself,' I say, taking a step closer to him. He looks at me, his eyes cautious and sad. 'I've seen her father, I know it's her.'

'But you can't know Joyce, not really. You haven't seen her since she was a baby. This child,' he splutters, paces the room. 'She could be anybody.'

'He's right dear,' my mother stands up, joins us in the centre of the room. I feel hemmed in, suddenly I feel as if I can't breathe.

'Do you really think I can't recognise my own daughter?' I ask my mother. 'Are you seriously telling me you wouldn't recognise me if you didn't see me for twenty years?' I turn on my mother, rightly guessing she cannot answer that.

'But Joyce,' my father interrupts, seeing my mother's weakness folding his case with ease. 'Think about it, if it's a hoax it could ruin everything.'

'Why?' I insist, 'what on earth is wrong with finding out?'

'Oh Joyce, if it's what I think it is, some greedy swine after your money, he'll take the cash, give you nothing. It's probably a journalist.'

'That's all you care about it isn't it?' I accuse my father, an anger boiling inside. 'Money.' I watch my mother retreat to her chair and sit down, her head in her hands. She cries softly.

'You will have the title in two days,' he reminds me, his voice calm now, patronising. I cringe at him. I don't need a reminder. 'Think about it Joyce,' he asks again, 'this could ruin you. Michael and you will win the title, then you'll be the world's greatest.' He spreads his hands around him.

I see now, dumbfounded as to why I haven't seen this before. It isn't my dream; it was never my dream. It was his. A failed dancer himself he had given me natural ability and trained it to fulfil his own destiny for him.

'What do you think will happen to you if the next day the papers are full of this rubbish, scandalous rubbish, everything you've worked for,' he sighs. 'If not for me then think about Michael,' he says. I listen to him quietly, knowing he is talking sense but all the while thinking to myself, I am going. I will go. I will find out what happened to my baby. 'It's bad enough that they caught you a few years ago,' he continues. 'Just think about it Joyce, please.'

'I'll think about it,' I say, my eyes hard and unyielding. I watch him take a deep breath. He knows I'll go through with it. He turns his back, leans against the mantelpiece again and I walk away.

I sit on my bed after dinner and re-read the notes from the unknown writer. They promise to fill in the gaps, the part I made up about the nasty man and the policeman. Who could really know what happened, and how?

Could the writer be the guilty party? The first line starts with regret and guilt. Casting this over my mind I cannot think of an alternative solution. Do I want to meet the person who stole my life? How do I know what I will do when confronted by this person? I think about it carefully for a long time, re-read the notes until the nice cream pages are crumpled with anguish. I will defend myself, I think. I must take some sort of defence with me. Just in case.

I hear the telephone ring downstairs. It stops after three rings, when I guess Rosa has picked it up. A commotion is heard and I open my door to hear. My father is shouting, something about the bank.

'That damned man,' I hear him roar, his voice bouncing around the open staircase clearly. Poor father. I wonder about his health some times, he must be his own worst enemy. I dare say all that shouting does him no good at all. My mother's soft soothing tones do not reach me but I picture her there, by his side, trying in vain to calm him down.

'What are you talking about woman, what do you know of it?' he answers her, his voice now strained and wilting. He used to be able to sustain his roaring state much longer. When I look at him now, I notice his greying hair, the lines about his eyes more prominent than before. 'He ought to know better,' he is saying, now distinctly quieter. 'I've a good mind to take my gun to him.'

'Oh no Roberto, no, please!' my mother's soft voice suddenly afraid and reaching a new octave.

I close the door, uninterested in his financial dealings. As the door clicks softly into place I smile. Of course, father has a gun.

The darkness draws in like a blanket and the house is very quiet. All the lights are out. I have been waiting for this moment. I put my slippers on and tiptoe soundlessly out of my room, down the staircase and into father's study. The door creaks slightly and I hold my breath. There is nothing. No sound from the upstairs. I swing the door quickly to dull the creak and enter the study.

It is richly furnished, a large oak desk filling the best part of the room. Lines of bookshelves adorn the walls but they do not contain books. There are a few manuals advising investments but mostly there are box files. I have not been in here in years. Ordinarily I would not enter but tonight I have a mission to fulfil.

There is a musty smell in the room. I look around for its cause; find nothing, just my father's presence stained into the air, his aftershave lingering. I wonder what he has in the files. Curiously, I take one from the shelf, prop the others up with my hand in fear they will crash to the floor in a noisy mess. I glance around, listen intently, but there is nothing, not a sound. Taking a paperweight from his desk I lean it against the remaining files on the shelf and take my chosen one to the desk.

I leaf through the sheets, all rows of numbers, nothing interesting. Underneath the sheets I find a photograph. I slide the blind back a little so the moonlight floods the room.

The photo is of us, taken many years ago. My father and mother are standing close together, my father's arm around her shoulders. They smile out from the centre of the photo, she cuddling a baby close to her chest – me I suppose. I stare at it, unable to account for its presence. I wonder why he hides it here. I put it back hastily and return the box file to the shelf. As I turn around I notice, for the first time, that the one wall without lines of files is covered with photographs, mostly Michael and I at various stages of our glittering dance career. In the centre of them all is a picture of my mother. She is young, the moonlight now shading half her face, giving her a translucent beauty. She looks just like me but with the fair hair. Her eyes, blue like mine, are a slightly smaller shape. I can see myself looking out through her eyes. I blink, look again, notice her young face, her lips bright and curved into a smile, her eyes sparkling.

I stand back, glance at the wall, my certificates of various dance achievements framed and all over the wall, the photographs of Michael and me. We entered so many competitions in the early days. It was the only way to make a name for ourselves, the judges watching us for a split second; we had no choice but to dance before them, time after time, after time.

I notice one photograph in particular; it is of me last year. Michael must have been standing by my side but he is cut out of the frame. I am smiling, accepting the glittering glass plate at a championship final. I can barely remember which one; we have won so many. A feeling washes over me, guilt. Perhaps under his wrath he is proud of me. How could I not see this before?

Suddenly I feel awful. I shouldn't be in here. I rifle through the desk draw as quickly as I can to find his gun. It shines out at me, the metal picking up the moonlight in a sparkling blaze. Slowly I remove it from the back of the draw, hold it in my hand. It feels heavy, cold and frightening. I click the barrel open but it is empty. Perhaps that is enough, I think, just to scare. More afraid of myself than anything I might do with it, I slip it into the pocket of my dressing gown; redraw the blinds and close the desk draws.

I take one last look at the photographs on the wall. Oh daddy, I sigh, did you really take my baby?

CHAPTER ELEVEN – MODERN DAY; MAY

Rebecca tried not to listen but it was so mysterious, inviting, intriguing. Whatever did they want Jean for? Unable to stop herself listening at the closed lounge door she decided to take the ironing upstairs, to distance herself as far as possible from temptation.

Jean was being interviewed in her lounge by the tall Inspector with the chewed pencil wedged between his teeth. It was beyond her comprehension what the interview might consist of. Jean didn't know anything, surely…Perhaps it was simply her account of the explosive parcel. Yes, that must be it, she decided, a statement.

The Inspector was working furiously on the case and she knew he would get the culprit in the end but she was beginning to wish he would hurry up. The numerous attempts were, she was loath to admit, beginning to frighten her.

From the depths of her wardrobe she heard movement below. They were finished. Descending the stairs in a fashion she hoped didn't look as hurried as it felt, Rebecca plastered on a smile.

'Inspector,' she said, opening the front door as he flipped his hat onto his head and nodded goodbye to her, his pencil now safely in his coat pocket and a cigarette in his fingers, ready for the split second the door was opened. His Sergeant trotted after him and the two sped away in their sleek blue car.

For the first time Jean looked lost for words. 'Shall we have some coffee?' she suggested. Jean nodded glumly. 'Don't worry,' Rebecca smiled, wondering what the Inspector had said to stun Jean's verbal flow so effectively. 'It'll be all right.'

If she were lucky Jean would tell her all about it over coffee.

***

Inspector Allen grinned to himself silently as Sergeant Wellington drove them towards the red-bricked unassuming house that belonged to the last link in their chain. Finally, a motive was beginning to take shape in his mind; a motive that could easily explain Craig Houseman's murder, the attempts on Rebecca Houseman's life and the car thefts.

'Is this the place Sir?' Wells enquired, slowing the car to a crawl outside the house. An ordinary but immaculately kept Rover sat on the driveway, its paintwork gleaming in the mid-day sun.

'I think so son, yes, I think so,' Inspector Allen swung his legs out the car and strode towards the metallic grey Rover. 'Yes, this is the place,' he decided. 'Come on son, let's go,' he pointed his long finger towards the front door and made his way, his open forest green mackintosh flapping by his sides with its own energy.

Sergeant Wellington hurried to lock the car and joined him as he was pressing the doorbell. It chimed tunelessly for a moment. A bulky shape blurred into vision behind the frosted opaque glass and opened the door.

'Good day Sir,' Inspector Allen smiled, removing his hat and holding it over his chest, its wide brim covered the breadth of his wiry height with ease. 'Mr Henry Sutton?'

'Yes, how can I help you?' the man asked, his blue eyes cautious and his dark blond hair neatly shaping his kind face. Sergeant Wellington produced his warrant card. 'Oh, you'd better come in,' he widened the door, pressing his healthy well-built frame against the wall.

'Thank you Sir,' Inspector Allen grinned quickly, flashed his smudgy badge at the man and sauntered down the hallway, the creamy carpet stretching ahead and lighting a path towards a neat lounge. Frosted smoked glass and ebony furniture, a gleaming black leather settee and a magazine rack with the tidiest papers he had ever seen. He surveyed the room in a sweeping glance and grinned chirpily. 'Just a couple of questions I think you can help us with Sir,' Inspector Allen said, his voice thinly mocking.

'Take a seat,' Henry gestured towards the black leather. Inspector Allen eyed the seating sceptically, eventually committing, with some reluctance, to the armchair by the window.

'Are you familiar with the Belvadere Club Sir?' he asked suddenly, his fingers narrowing his moustache as he spoke. Sergeant Wellington perched on the edge of the settee, the squelch of leather creaking under him.

'No Inspector, I'm not, but my brother is a member, I think.' Henry sat comfortably in the other armchair, crossing one leg over the other, his pressed dress trousers neat and smooth.

'Oh really, is he indeed. And what is your brother's name Sir?'

'Nicholas,' Henry answered, straightening his navy tie that complimented his pale blue shirt to perfection. Inspector Allen whistled softly and nodded at Sergeant Wellington to take notes. The rustle of Wells' notebook sounded loudly in the otherwise peaceful room. 'He isn't here I'm afraid,' Henry continued. 'He lives on the other side of town. Was it him you wanted Inspector?'

'Most probably Sir, most probably,' Inspector Allen smiled quickly. 'How long has he been a member at the club, do you know?

'Oh a long time,' Henry thought, 'at least ten years I'd say. He's rather fond of socialising Inspector, a little too fond if you take my meaning,' his voice lowering and his eyes burning in embarrassment at the carpet. 'We're quite different individuals, Inspector,' he decided, looking up again with some jolt of confidence. 'You wouldn't think we were brothers at all.'

'Um…Quite.' Inspector Allen looked around the room, 'this is a nice place you have here Sir, what is it you do for a living?'

'Me? Oh, I'm a projects manager for a local property company, Inspector. In fact you're lucky to have caught me at home, just stopped by to pack a few things. I've got a business meeting in Kent tomorrow so I'll be heading off shortly.'

Inspector Allen watched Henry flatten his trousers with his palms, impeccable taste, neat and calm. A businessman probably with a background in on-site construction, coupled with a head for figures. That would account for his healthy active frame, his sharp mind and his quick thinking. The house was of average size but it was furnished with expensive tasteful pieces, his success embedded in his surroundings, a subtle message for those who chose to read the signs. A clock ticked loudly in the background. DCI Allen suspected that Henry liked it not only for its obvious quality and accuracy, but for its stability too.

'What can you tell me about your brother Sir?' he asked suddenly.

'I knew it,' Henry heaved a deep-hearted sigh. 'What's he done this time?'

'This time? Well, nothing I can prove Sir,' Inspector Allen smiled hastily, 'yet.' He glanced around the room, not an ashtray in sight. The smoked glass table was polished beyond a shine. Henry probably wouldn't approve of stray ash. He pulled out his pencil and settled his teeth into the comfortable marks, watching Henry close his eyes and shake his head in despair.

'You'd better tell me the worst of it Inspector,' Henry braved another look at the DCI. 'I'll get a diluted version from Nic, if that.'

Sergeant Wellington looked up from his frantic scribbling, his spiky brown eyebrows lining his eyes, wide with surprise. Inspector Allen nodded at him and afforded Henry a moment to compose himself. He bit down hard on his pencil and cleared his throat. This wasn't going to be easy; the man was visibly distressed at his brother's latest antics.

'There was an illegal casino at the club Sir,' he launched into his story, 'until earlier this week.' Resolutely he stuffed his pencil back into his coat pocket. 'We shut it down,' he grinned. 'It's my belief that your brother, Sir, he was partial to the hidden casino and I suspect he has built up gambling debts.'

'Regrettably Inspector, I'm not surprised,' his composure now regained, if a little shaky.

'Did you know about the casino Sir?' the Inspector asked; his voice low and sympathetic.

'No, I didn't, if I did I'd have tried to stop him going there Inspector, honestly, I would. Did you know he's been married twice?' Henry heaved another sigh, flickered his eyes closed fleetingly. 'Married wealthy women too, heiresses in their own rights, divorced with a pretty packet each time but still that wasn't enough for him. I expect he's on the lookout for another poor young girl with a rich father to bail him out. I've tried Inspector, I've tried to reason with him many a time but I'm afraid I'm wasting my breath on him now.'

'Well he'll have to find somewhere else now Sir,' Inspector Allen said, 'at least for the moment we've closed that particular avenue of pleasure for him.'

'So, it's illegal gambling then, is it? This time?' Henry surmised with disdain, his face colouring a pale shade of rose pink, the worry lines beginning to crease his brow.

'You say this time Sir, been in trouble before has he?' Inspector Allen enquired, knowing only too well he would simply ask Wells to dig a bit deeper the moment they left the black and white palace.

'Yes, I'm afraid so. Same sort of thing, but never with the law. I knew it would come to this one day. I'm only glad my father didn't live to see it.'

'Does he have a car, your brother?' Inspector Allen asked, nodding at Wells to ensure he was still noting the conversation diligently.

'He's had several over the years, always sold them to raise capital though. I don't think he has one at the moment. But then, I haven't seen him since the funeral.'

'Your father's funeral, would that be Sir?' Sergeant Wellington peered over his notebook. Henry nodded and Wells began scribbling again.

'I'm sorry to have troubled you Sir,' Inspector Allen struggled to raise his tall frame from the low level chair. 'Don't worry Sir; we'll sort it all out.' He flipped his hat onto his head and grinned. 'Would he ever get involved in car thefts Sir, do you think?' Henry looked at Inspector Allen, his eyes a tinge of sad inevitability.

'If it meant financing his gambling then I'm deeply afraid he may be persuaded,' Henry said quietly. 'But he would never be the ringleader. He just doesn't have the grey matter Inspector. Awful thing to say about your own brother isn't it?'

'Yes Sir, it is.' Inspector Allen followed Henry to the front door. 'Thank you Sir,' he said, lifting his hat slightly. Sergeant Wellington ran after him towards the car.

Henry sighed again, closed the door and lifted his mobile phone from the hall table. Patiently he leafed through his extensive list of contacts and activated a call.

'Paul? Hi, it's…yeah, I know. Bit of bad news that's all, I'm all right. Listen, I've got to go away tonight but are you free tomorrow evening?…Sure, what time?…ok, I'll meet you there…thanks mate. See you tomorrow night.'

Henry pulled on his jacket and slid the phone into his pocket. It was time to go to Kent but the thought of talking his concerns over with Paul the next evening was quelling his fears slightly.

Paul Wood was a nice guy, level headed, a good friend. When it came to his brother there wasn't anybody who could actually help or dissolve any of his disappointment but, at the very least, he could always trust Paul to listen and not to blabber it about town.

Rebecca was changing into her ballet shoes, listening as Lexia briefed them on the schedule for the performance in the town. Somewhere from the blurry outskirts of her vision she sensed him approaching.

'So, we start, yes,' Lexia was calling as they assembled into their pre-arranged places. The chatter rumbled through the air like a cloud. He was coming closer and she knew he was aiming for her.

'He likes you,' Angela half whispered, thumbing over her shoulder towards Paul Wood.

'Nonsense,' Rebecca insisted, her cheeks colouring faintly in betrayal of her own words. 'He's a friend, that's all.' The drums were already practising in the other room and she wondered why Paul wasn't with them, the rhythm beating around the hall with its contagious charm.

'Hi.' His smile was so bright Rebecca felt herself weaken. 'How are you?'

'I'm fine, you weren't here last week,' she accused. He half smiled at her. Angela slunk away but Rebecca could just see her. Lexia was fiddling with the music CD. Two seconds and they would start.

'Sorry, I had a late business meeting and it ran on a bit, by the time I managed to free myself it was too late to come.' The sound of the drums, dulled by the thick walls, hummed towards them in the crescendo of the piece. Paul looked over his shoulder.

'Oh,' she smiled at him despite herself and deflected the knowing smiles that were filling Angela's giggling eyes. 'Hadn't you better, err…?'

'Yes I should join them,' he said quietly. 'Just one question; I was wondering, would you like to go for a drink sometime?'

'Um…' she stammered. The answer was yes, but she felt odd about it, as if Craig were still holding her back. Angela was nodding enthusiastically behind Paul's back, her head looking as if it were stuck to her by thin stretched elastic.

'Maybe next week,' Paul persisted, his voice light. 'You can think about it,' he shrugged his shoulders and began to step away, his reluctance to leave her clear but his path towards the drums threatening to claim him.

'Sure, why not,' she blurted out, afraid suddenly of losing the opportunity to talk to him. She heard her own words echo back at her and clasped her hands together to stop herself covering her mouth. Her palms felt clammy suddenly and her heart felt as if it had flipped over involuntarily. Her wedding ring burnt into her fingers and she tried not to grimace.

'Ok, see you next week,' he whispered hastily and darted towards the back room to take his place in the band. Lexia reappeared before the group as Rebecca found her place besides Angela.

'Right ladies,' she beamed, 'we begin, let's dance!'

Rebecca watched Paul trace the invisible steps towards the practice room and re-join his friends for the drumming practice. Lexia's CD finally kicked into life as she herself took up the lead position and began instructing them in the first section of the sequence, calling out the steps as they followed her choreography of the chosen performance dance.

Angela winked at her over the din as they spun around the floor and drew close to the interlinking steps to take them towards section two. Rebecca felt the blush rise in her face at a speed she wasn't prepared for. Was this all too soon?

Inspector Allen crafted a smile as he sat in his chair, the squeak increasing as he sunk backwards, lacing his hands behind his head and plonking his feet on the edge of the desk.

The office was even more untidy than usual, a fresh stack of memo's from senior management awaiting their arrival, several mouldy mugs gathering dust on the windowsill and a brown plant wilting its leaves randomly across the floor.

'Good work son, good work,' he beamed.

'Thank you Sir,' Sergeant Wellington managed to suppress a wide smile. 'The super will be pleased with that, it's a good result.'

'Um, yes son,' the Inspector agreed. 'The car thefts all swept up in one arrest, sixteen crimes solved at once. The old gasbag's bound to be chuffed.' A low chuckle rumbled across the space between them. 'That'll stick fast on Francis son. No clever solicitor can pull that one from us.'

'Don't forget the mechanic Sir,' Wells prompted.

'Oh I hadn't son, I hadn't,' Inspector Allen pulled his cigarette from behind his ear and flipped it into his mouth with a smirk. 'Accepting bribery with intent to harm, accessory to the car thefts; it's been a good day.' He lit his cigarette, inhaled deeply and closed his eyes in bliss.

'Sir,' Wells mumbled, 'what about Bateman?'

Inspector Allen blew out a perfect ring of white smoke and smiled at it in wonder. Dreamily, he gazed through the haze towards his Sergeant, who coughed loudly as he bit on the stale air floating in his direction.

'Bateman?' Wells prompted, gulping water hurriedly to ease his hacking.

'Get a warrant for his arrest son, we've got enough evidence from the club to hold him for questioning at least,' the Inspector instructed, his eyes following the smoke ring as it dissipated into wisps around the office.

'On what charge Sir?' Wells enquired. 'What am I going to arrest him with?'

'On intent to harm with explosives son,' Inspector Allen mumbled, a long line of whispering smoke soaring towards the ceiling like the trail from an aeroplane. 'Or, whatever the official words are.'

'Right Sir, I'll pull him in,' Wells agreed, 'tomorrow, first light.'

'Marvellous son,' Inspector Allen grinned. 'Bloody marvellous!' He smiled, pinning his burnt cigarette stub between his fingertips and crushing it into a knot. In one fluid movement he swung his feet from the desk, tossed his cigarette into the hidden ashtray in his desk draw and set the fan in motion, the hazy mist scattering thinly across the room like a screen.

'I reckon we've got him Sir, that stuff on Bateman in Francis's office is enough to convict, I'm sure it is,' Sergeant Wellington insisted, busying himself with papers across his desk.

'You may be right son,' Inspector Allen mused, tweaking his moustache and looking into the hazy mist, lost in thought. 'We'll give it a damned good try anyway. At the very least we can quiz him about calling himself Fisher. See if he cracks.'

'Do you think he will Sir, now that we've got Francis banged up?' Wells asked; his round pink face expectant, and his hair curling behind his ears with the day's exhaustion.

'Oh yes son, I reckon so,' the Inspector grinned boyishly. 'I think we're onto a winner now. He may even give us the confession we need to nail them both for attempting to kill our lovely Mrs Houseman.'

'I'm still a bit baffled Sir,' Wells confessed, 'as to why they'd want to kill Mr and Mrs Houseman.'

'That son; is beginning to take shape. We'll have it all cleared up in a jiffy now. Get back onto the records son; Nicholas is his first name, not his last. See what you can drag up about him. According to his brother we should find plenty of people to vouch for his miserable existence, all of it bad news too I shouldn't wonder.'

'Right Sir,' Wells said.

'And another thing,' the Inspector pointed a long finger to the ceiling, 'I want a search of his father's house.'

'Yes Sir, right away Sir,' Wells nodded.

A loud knock sounded at the door and the Inspector almost leapt from his skin. Spraying air freshener liberally around the room he inhaled deeply and nodded at Wells.

'Come in,' Wells called.

The night sky was darkening quicker than she expected and suddenly Rebecca wanted to get home. The afternoon's rain had split the skyline into patches of moody blacks and blues, the shapeless lumps heavy with menacing further downpours waiting to plummet. The green-fingered would be pleased but all Rebecca wanted was to get home as quickly as possible.

Damned silly idea, she thought to herself, quickening her pace along the pavement. A bit of exercise, a brisk walk to the town for a few essentials, the air would do her good, so she thought. Her eyes glanced quickly at the looming black cloud up ahead as she hurried along the road, the chilly breeze whipping around her neckline harshly.

The rush hour traffic was zipping along at a pace, every driver no doubt as keen as her to reach their cosy homes before the next waterfall descended over the dehydrated town.

Splashes from the roadside were slowly spreading up her legs, the hem of her linen summer trousers dampening to the point of clinging to her skin. It had been sunny and bright when she dressed that morning. Only in England could one expect all four seasons in the space of twenty-four hours, she decided gloomily.

Several cars were slowing for the traffic lights a few yards ahead, and as the green light flickered into life they sped away, further puddles exploding by the kerb and stretching towards her ankles as she rushed past.

Sighing, Rebecca wrapped her flimsy summer jacket tighter around her body and clutched at her shopping bags, the wet plastic melting against her trousers and seeping in, cold against her legs. Almost there...

The rain was loud, her hearing almost dominated by the weather as she stooped forwards in a desperate bid to shield the worst of it from her face. She didn't see the car looming up behind her, or hear it approach. The line of traffic at the lights had vanished but a lone car was racing up behind her, its headlights diminished and the darkness of its colouring blending into the wet day like a carbon sketch.

Rebecca pushed aside the ridiculous twinges of someone watching her. Just keep going, she told herself, just get home as quickly as you can.

The car singled her out, the road now otherwise deserted. Rebecca thought she heard something, she turned around, screamed, tried to run, her shopping bags flapping by her sides, her drenched body exhausted and aching as she attempted to run away.

The car was heading straight for her, its headlights bland and lifeless, its driver masked by the pale light behind the tinted window. It was coming too fast, she couldn't get away quickly enough...

Rebecca's legs felt heavy as she sprinted towards the nearest house, flung her head around but she couldn't see, her hair blinding her. Her cries were lost to the rain, her face grey with fright and her eyes wide, petrified.

The car was still driving towards her, the nearest house still several sprints away. She darted behind the gate and ducked beneath the hedge, her entire body now soaked from the damp hedge and the sodden grass.

Her breath was coming in gasps, her body heaving with the effort, her mind circling at a thousand spins a minute. From nowhere she could hear the car's engine building its rage, the driver revving the accelerator as if he were about to... Suddenly she knew it was too late, she would be trapped. She couldn't stay there. Without hesitation she darted to her feet, as the car roared towards her, she sprang towards the gate, her leg clipping the bumper as the car rammed into the front garden and drove straight into the window of the innocent occupants' living room.

The glass smashed; splinters of it spreading out like a fan, catapulted through the air and landing everywhere; fragments by her feet, itchy sparks grazing her face and knotting her hair.

Rebecca stood, paralysed, in the neighbouring garden, holding her breath, her shopping bags torn and spilling their contents messily across the pavement.

A woman stood in the doorway of the house, clutching a baby tightly to her chest, shock painting a frozen expression on her face. Rebecca looked at her speechless, her fingers numbly dialling the emergency services and her voice a victim of the rain. Several people were now peering out of curtains and doorways, lining the street like an audience, grey expressions of fear and shock, a sick excitement bubbling.

Rebecca looked at the car again, the glass scratched over the bonnet and the driver clearly stunned but definitely still alive. He was moving...whoever was behind that wheel was trying to kill her. Rebecca regained her senses. The driver was trying to reverse the car from the wreckage; she could see him, a shape, shifting about in the seat, fiddling with the gear stick, a thunderous sound of shattered glass crunching under the tyres, rubble and debris crashing to the floor as the car disentangled itself from the house, the gaping hole in the poor woman's muddied lounge...the woman holding the baby, fleeing the scene towards the back of the house.

She had to move, now. With a jolt Rebecca began to run, the rain hitting her face as she abandoned her shopping bags; her feet were aching as she pounded the pavement towards home. She could feel the blood plumping in her ears, her heart hammering, her breath short and her mind giddy.

Behind her, the car was still half entangled with the house; white lines scorched across the crunched chassis; glass puncturing the tyres. A squeal of rubber marked the tarmac as it spun towards her and gathered speed, fragments of the remaining windscreen soaring in its wake.

Rebecca heard it approaching her as she rounded the corner. It was after her, who was this maniac?

Fear panted through her lungs, her heart quickening even further to a frightening pace, her hair drenched and matted against her face. She tried to focus but her vision was blurry, tears welling uncontrollably in her eyes. She wiped them away, blending them with the rain as she panted towards the only light she could see. A hotel...

As the car loomed large behind her she ducked behind a telephone box. The car slowed to a crawl a few feet away. Rebecca held her breath, slipped out of sight into a shop doorway and waited.

Eventually she heard the car turnaround, the glass catastrophically spread over the road. Cautiously she peered out of the darkness of the doorway and spotted the car, its headlights still out, crawling down the road back the way it had come. For the first time Rebecca realised she was trembling. She reached for her mobile phone and clumsily dialled a local taxi number.

'Atwood Taxi's' a curt voice announced, its crisp tones making her jump.

'I'm at the Duchess Hotel,' she said, her voice cracking with nerves. 'Please can you come and get me immediately?'

'Yes Madam, we'll be with you in five minutes.'

'Thank you,' she breathed a sigh of relief, 'five minutes.' Putting the phone into her bag she darted the last couple of strides towards the brightness of the hotel and stepped inside, aiming for the ladies toilets, suddenly feeling better that other people were around her. The hotel guests were dressed for dinner, their evening attire in sharp contrast to her exhausted state, but she didn't care. She brushed past them towards the toilets.

Rebecca composed herself, straightened out her knotted hair and dried her face and hands. Looking at her reflection in the mirror she closed her eyes and inhaled deeply. Someone really was trying to kill her...

A moment later she was hovering by the entrance foyer, waiting for her taxi, realising she should have rung one the moment she thought it would rain. The taxi pulled up and she found herself looking at the car and the driver sceptically. It was someone else, a woman driver. Unable to stop herself visibly sighing relief she climbed into the back seat, still noticeably shaking. Trying to ignore the polite chatter of the taxi driver, Rebecca nodded in the relevant places and silently willed the woman to drive faster. She had never wanted to get home quicker. Oh Craig, why aren't you here with me now?

The moment she was inside she locked the doors, slid the deadbolt across and slotted the chain into its tightest position; then she rang the police station and asked to speak to Inspector Allen. It was time she took her family's advice. This was becoming far too dangerous and she was growing much too afraid to handle it alone.

CHAPTER TWELVE – 25TH SEPTEMBER 1964

The lighting is low, sparks of colour streaming, seemingly at random, from a thousand bulbs. I have to narrow my eyes to see properly. The music is faint, the thick glass shielding us from much of it. What I can hear is the clapping, the thunderous applause, see the crowds rise and fall, the fated couple on the floor below bowing to their fans. I curse my father for writing to enter us into this momentous evening of exhaustion and fear. We are listed in the programme now. There is no escape.

This is the Star Championships, London, and I have never felt more afraid. Somehow it is more terrifying than the Winter Gardens in Blackpool. The World Ballroom and World Latin Championships are usually separate events on separate days. Today is different; both championships are being run back to back. It is far more frantic than normal. It occurs to me that Vivanti's premonition of a combined event may come to pass one day.

I look at the panel of judges; the chosen experts of the moment. Eleven suited adjudicators' stood around the edge of the floor in scattered positions, their markings cards at the ready to dash one's hopes in an instant. One decision could cost any one of us our careers, the influence, the power, the indecision, frustration and heartbreak. The worst part is that they actually do know what their marks can do to us.

In the final round each judge marks the couples in order of merit, although we all know it is really their personal preference, without tieing. After all ten dances the judges will mark the order of couples by dance. If we make the semi-finals we'll be one of twelve couples, and then one of six if we reach the final round. They'll use an open marking system for the final. I hate this.

We have to win the first position in each dance to secure the title, an absolute majority of judges. Again, I curse my father. I feel my palms heating up like hot water bottles.

Nervous tension spreads through the room like a fine mist; filtering over us each in turn, making us worry, building lines of anticipation until they are creases of blind panic. It is a wonder we can move our limbs at all.

The glass windows from the dressing rooms are high up, overlooking the stadium. It is far greater than I could ever have imagined; the seating around the sides, rising higher than the floor. This is definitely worse than Blackpool, I think. At least there I know what to expect.

As I look down, my hands pressed up against the glass, I suddenly want to go home. The title is not worth all this hysteria. I feel confident with all the ten dances but suddenly I don't want to dance any of them, not here, not tonight, not now.

When we are down there I imagine we will be like pennies rolling around the base of a bottle, flies trapped in a glass. A cold sweat creeps down my back. I shiver. I interlock my fingers until they go white and stare out at the audience, now hushed and waiting for the next dancers to be subjected to torture.

Michael rips my hands apart, takes one in his and drags me away from the window.

'Don't look,' he says calmly. 'Don't worry,' he kisses me lightly. I take the seat he gently eases me into, my blue ballroom gown lapping around me like a cloak. I smooth out my folding skirts and inspect my finely polished fingernails, the sparkling diamond studs expertly applied earlier that afternoon by the beautician. My hair is spun up into a fancy wrap, piled high above my head, encrusted with silver hoops that catch the light whenever I so much as flick my glance.

Michael looks stunning in his dress suit, the smooth black jacket against the backdrop of his crispy white shirt. His dark hair is glowing in these lights, the shadows playing mischievously at our feet like rainbow jets. He flips out the tail of his jacket and takes the seat next to me, toys with my fingers in his. I afford him a faint smile, appreciate his calmness, feel my stomach undertake several thousand somersaults and close my eyes. I try to block out the noise around us. All I can hear is my own beating heart, above everything else. Whatever happened to me, I used to be so sure of myself at these events. This is not just any event though, even we, the best known names on the list, have never been here before.

The dressing room is fraught with activity. There are people sewing last minute alterations to costumes; their fingers working tirelessly, their frantic energy against the chiming of the ticking clock in the corner. Feathers, sequins, silver boas shimmering in the half-light of the single bulbs placed in rows around the long line of mirrors. Every few minutes the stage director appears at the door, a funnel placed at his mouth, the words echoing around the room like a foghorn. As one couple after another trail away the room lessens with noise, another act to take the bait. The returning couple bring with them a wealth of new excitement, chatter, cheers, and jesting, nervous tension escaping in verbal streams, constant and non-stinting.

I am not sure I can take much more of this. I take in a deep breath, sit silently in my chair and await our call. Michael's fingers are circling my palm, his usual trick to calm me down. I try to give in to him but today I am too highly strung.

'Don't worry,' he whispers. It is astounding that I hear him at all above the din. His voice, however quiet, always reaches me. I look at him gratefully. 'Everything is going to be all right,' he tells me. His voice is so reassuring. I sigh and try to smile at him. If only I had not lost my confidence. I have no idea how he does it. When we were younger it was all so much easier.

Somewhere out there, in one of the reserved front rows, sit my parents, Michael's parents and Vivanti. They will be our harshest critiques. In many ways they are worse than the judges.

I do not even hear the stage director's call. All I see is Michael's face, his unspoken assurances, him leading me by the hand up out of the chair. Suddenly my fear engulfs me and

I feel my feet freeze. I grab my blue stole and fasten its ends to my dress, take the hoop from my dress and link it over my finger but my feet will not budge.

'Come on sweetheart,' Michael says, 'everything's going to be fine,' he whispers. My shoes are midnight blue with silver diamonds down the t-strap, along the edges and stretching down the long heel to the floor. The specialist suede sole provides the perfect blend of slide and grip.

To my right there is a girl, she cannot be any older than fifteen, fluttering in a flamboyant costume that leaves her body basically bare, feathers and lace flopping around her in an unseen breeze.

'She's lost it, the great Joyce Capelli,' the girl mocks me, her voice high pitched and taunting, jibbing at her friend equally loosely attired. 'My God, she's lost it!' There is a mean bitchiness about their cackling that I detest. I feel Michael pulling me behind him. I manage to outstare the girl and she turns away, suddenly silent, a little red-faced.

My feet free themselves finally as we leave the madness of the dressing room behind us and enter the relative peace of the staircase. It is less auspicious than I expect. Large chunks of plaster are plainly visible on the walls as it curves round in a downward spiral. I hold my dress higher than I'd like, try desperately not to let my heels get stuck in the ornate wrought iron steps as we descend.

I feel dizzy, disorientated, my vision blurs as I struggle to retain control on the spiralling stairs. Michael is ahead of me but I have lost all focus. All I see is the mass of black jacket. I aim for it, pray to God I will not trip and fall.

'This way Miss Capelli,' says a voice behind me, an arm extending to my left, the connected torso from somewhere behind my back, in my spherical vision. I pause; close my eyes; take a breath, feel Michael's hand in mine. Thank God we are off the stairs.

When I open my eyes again he is there, looking at me carefully. I see his mouth open and I know what he is saying but I do not hear him tell me everything is going to be ok.

'Three minutes,' the stage director says crisply, returning to his technical gadgets with eagerness. I have not looked at his face and I choose not to now. All I see is the light bursting out in front of us. I can smell the crowds, the raw animal greed of the audience and the heat of the lights ambushing the small wing we stand in. I feel faint.

Michael squeezes my hand as we listen to the judges giving their scores of the last performance. The previous couple have exited the floor, fled through another escape route on the opposite side of the dance floor.

My stomach feels as if it is not even with me. My hands are moist, my heart beating louder than anything else I can hear. The sound in my ears is whishing around endlessly.

'The celebrated Mr Michael Sutton and Miss Joyce Capelli...' the microphone is loud. Even I hear our entrance cue above my own heart. The stage director shoves us on the back.

'Go, you're on,' he shouts into our ears. Michael looks at me, takes my hand, smiles and leads me out through the curtain of light. I try very hard not to squint but I can see nothing. Eventually we reach the edge of the dance floor and he lifts his arm, indicates to me there is a slight step. I mount and we are on the floor. As we walk to the centre I dare not glance around at the audience. The lights are dimming now, the crowd vanishing into darkness and the spotlight hits us with a force.

I have no idea where the judges are standing, nor our parents or Vivanti. All I see now is Michael, his eyes shining out at me, our bodies framed by a sheet of blackness. From nowhere the music floats into life.

A sense of serenity settles. Michael winks at me. I smile. I feel better, oddly happy. As we whirl around the floor I no longer care about the judges, Vivanti or my father. Surely it doesn't really matter does it? I am simply here, dancing with Michael. It feels as if time has stopped. I am not aware of how long we have been dancing. Seconds into our performance I cease to mark my way through our pre-arranged sequence. I sway to his command, float around the room as if we are on air. I could stay here all night.

As the music fades I find myself gathered up in Michael's arms, our final posture of the performance. It is this split second before the chaos breaks loose that I want to remember for the rest of my life.

As the darkness melts away the audience appear in my vision and for the first time since stepping out onto the floor I fully appreciate the sheer mass of them. There must be thousands in the stadium, row after row going higher than I can even see.

'Michael Sutton and Joyce Capelli' the loudspeaker erupts. I almost jump at its sounds. Michael unfolds me, leads me into the curtsey and follows the cue that I seem to have missed completely, to exit the dance floor. We leave on the other side, enter the far wing and stop.

'Well done Miss,' another stagehand is there, shorter than the first and now that the first performance is over I am more relaxed. 'You were marvellous, both of you, Sir, simply magnificent,' he enthuses. His colleague looks bleakly at him as if he is breaking some barrier, stands holding his sound equipment like a police guard.

'Thanks,' Michael shakes his hand, still supporting me with his arm. I smile at the stagehand and we pause to await the scores.

The first score is shown: the crowd are going wild. The second score. The third is slow to emerge. We wait, holding our breath. The fourth, fifth...I have lost all concentration now as the marks are read out. This seems to take an age. Finally the eleventh judge reveals his score. I can't believe it, all top marks. It is unheard of...Michael wraps me up into a hold, picks me up and I scream with enchantment. I had not thought I would be so ecstatic; it's just another competition...isn't it?

'One day darling,' Michael says. 'One day.' Suddenly I can't stop smiling. Maybe we can pull this off, get her back, and escape the fish bowl.

The kindly stagehand is pleased for us, joining in with our delight.

'Well done, I reckon you're gonna win,' he predicts, 'it's this way, back to the dressing room,' he points down a corridor. 'There's another staircase just along there,' he says with a beam.

The night seems endless. We have another nine dances to perform plus the showcase, which will be the Argentine Tango we are so favoured for. We have about ten minutes to change between each dance, as couples are knocked out from the list of entrants, our changing time decreases rapidly. We are down to the last six pairs and our last six dances. Only the winning couple will perform the showcase.

As we take the staircase time after time I feel better, I stop worrying about my heels in the iron steps, the dizziness fades and my stomach half returns to feeling normal.

Unbelievably we have high marks for every dance, the other couples to have made it this far only having achieved two-thirds at most. With the highest score by far our chances are high but we could still be out in a heartbeat.

We are dancing the Ballroom Tango and for the first time I spot Vivanti in the audience, his eyes not on me but our footwork, studying us with hawk-like intent. His presence makes me nervous and I avoid his gaze. Michael notices my concentration dip and he spins me, boldly breaks the sequence, forces me to look at him, to follow him alone, not letting me anticipate his next move or relax into the dance I know so well. I quickly steal a stare at him on my return from the turn. Sometimes he can read me far better than I would like. We make it through the sequence in once piece but I know, deep down, it is only thanks to him.

Only five dances to go, assuming we win and have to do the showcase. The last few marked for judging are the Jive, Samba, Viennese Waltz and Paso Doble.

I hold my breath as we sit with the other couples in the wings, awaiting the final results. The judges are explaining their choices and assessing us each in turn, including those who fell short early on.

They are reading out the position of each couple for each dance. It is taking forever. The first in each dance gets one mark, the second two and so forth. When they've added up all the marks the couple with the lowest aggregate shall be named the winner. I am growing restless and hop from one foot to the other.

'Go and change you two, you're on the showcase,' a stagehand whispers into our ears. That means we've won. I stare at him open-mouthed. 'You can celebrate later,' he hisses at us, 'go; you've got five minutes.'

We run, madly, I take off my shoes and we dart up the stairs. The dressing room is empty, strewn outfits littering the floor, shoes tossed into corners. It is chaos. The other couples are all in the wings waiting to take their bows as they are called out; so we have the room to ourselves at least, in our mad dash. We will be last, the only ones to remain on the floor to perform yet again. We change in haste, Michael zipping up my black figure-hugging dress, it whizzes up like a wasp as I slip into my newest and most favourite shoes. Whilst he laces his shoes I fiddle with a stray strand of hair and apply another coat of lipstick.

Michael stands, ready, waits until I've tossed the red lipstick back into the depths of my bag and draws me close to him. We have about five seconds to spare.

'You do know that I love you,' he says, 'don't you?'

My heart melts. I feel a single tear escaping, he wipes it away carefully so as not to smudge my mascara.

'Yes, I love you too,' I whisper.

'Shall we?' he offers his arm and I take it. We are about to perform our last dance for public demand. I know in my heart that our One Day is very close.

I cannot help but think, as we wait in the wings for the applause to deafen us, that tomorrow night I will find out the truth. Just twenty-four hours and we could be on the verge of being that little family we promised ourselves.

CHAPTER THIRTEEN – MODERN DAY; JUNE

Rebecca opened the boot of her car and stacked the groceries as neatly as she could, wedging the bags so they wouldn't spill on movement. The cloudless sky was a direct contrast from the previous blustery storm-like day and she had opted to drive today, to re-buy the groceries that had ended up strewn across the pavement and were now probably decomposing in the nearest bin. She wished Craig were with her, not for the first time since the terrifying attack.

'I'll get him Mrs Houseman,' DCI Allen had sworn, pacing her hallway the previous evening, his fingers clutching at fistfuls of thin air, his hat slanted on his head and his Sergeant hovering in the wings, faithfully awaiting instruction. They were doing their best, assured her they were making good progress, but she wished he would hurry up.

Closing the boot she blinked, a dart of movement catching her eye. It was probably nothing. Pulling herself together she climbed into the driving seat, withdrew the car park ticket from her purse and held it ready to insert into the machine to lift the barrier. Katherine and Neil were coming to tea later. Eliza and Chris were supposed to be dropping by mid-week; she had offered to have the girls for an hour or two whilst they met up with some friends. Added to that, Tina and Samuel were taking her to bear witness to George's success. Apparently his team were unwavering in their determination to win the football league final match on Saturday. Overall, she knew she would need supplies. It was going to be a busy week. Grateful for small mercies she checked her rear view mirror, glanced and studied her own reflection and attempted a smile. Craig would have wanted her to be brave, to keep going in the face of adversity…for his sake only she had to try. She started the ignition and directed the car towards the barrier, hoping the eggs in the boot wouldn't break.

The traffic was sparse, the Sunday roads quiet and tranquil. She would be home in a moment if she kept to the quiet streets. A dark figure sprang up behind her seat. She almost felt her heart palpitate and momentarily swerved the car towards the oncoming bus, her scream piercing the compacted space in the air.

'The industrial estate,' a low rumbling voice growled, quiet and controlled. She flinched as he produced a knife from his side. 'Nice and easy,' he demanded. Rebecca held her breath as he slipped the knife around her and pressed the blade close to her throat. She drove the car in silence, the blade close to cutting her.

'What do you want?' she whispered. Her voice was hoarse as she glanced in the rear view mirror. The face behind her seat was masked in a black woollen balaclava, two beady dark eyes leering at her, the knife blade sharp, glistening in the sunlight, cold against her skin.

Beads of sweat lined her forehead. Nerves rattled her body and she realised she was trembling.

'Drive,' the voice demanded, twisting the knife at her throat. She wanted to scream but she couldn't open her mouth, the blade turning her into a motionless dummy. She tried to make out who he was. There was something familiar…

'No. That way,' he spat, holding her back in the seat with his other arm. She could barely move as she twisted the car towards the open road heading towards the town centre. Whatever he said she was going to the police station.

She felt the blade sharp against her throat. It felt as if she were already cut, bleeding…feeling faint.

'That way. Over there.' The figure was completely in black, his knife pointing at a road out of town for a second. She inhaled deeply before he swung it back to her. This is it, she thought, this is it…No, the blade was stuck to her again but it didn't slice her.

Rebecca punched her foot down on the accelerator until it wouldn't go any further. Gravity threw him back into the seat with a thump as she churned the car towards the town centre. He slid across the back seat, crashed his head into the side door. She increased speed again and shot through the red lights. Beeps, horns blasted, a swerving fiesta with smoking tyres stranded behind her at the crossroads, twisted in its path.

The police station was less than a mile away. She just had to survive that long. He was still blundering around on the back seat. Jerking the steering wheel she hurtled all over the road, saw him bounce from one side to another like a pinball machine. Her tyres were squealing like a dying pig, lines of scotched rubber streaking the tarmac. He was getting to his feet, attempting to grab her. Quickly she thumped the brakes to the floor. He shot backwards in the seat. Rebecca hit the accelerator flat out, spun the little car away, pushing it to its absolute limits and beyond; an unhealthy protest from the screaming engine as she tore up the road ahead.

'I said that way,' he hissed, his looming darkness once more behind her seat, the knife blade rounding her, back at her throat.

'Never,' she snapped, wrenching the wheel haphazardly across the road but he held on tight. She crossed her hands, spun the car right across the grey tarmac in a blur, steaming towards the roundabout at a rate of lunacy. This time she saw him fly away, land in a heap in the rear passenger foot-well, the knife flew up, landed on the parcel shelf.

The police station was in sight. Her car engine spluttered. She held her breath. It was staggering, lurching pathetically in lumpy hops down the road. Smoke was streaming from the sides of the bonnet. With a loud clonk the engine collapsed. Rebecca screamed, tried to unclip her seat belt. A gloved hand clamped her fingers over the buckle like a vice.

'Now,' he spat at her neck, a nasty grumbling moan. She screamed as he pressed the knife so close she thought she would faint. She could smell blood. 'It's too late for all that drama. I'm going to slice you up until you die,' he whispered hoarsely, his breath in gulps, slowing regaining control. All she could see was the darkness of him capturing her in her seat. She wrestled for the door handle but he twisted her other arm until she thought it would snap. 'Oh no you don't, I've been waiting for this moment. It'll all be mine, all that lovely money. You won't get a penny,' he bellowed over her struggling. 'Not if you're dead.'

From nowhere her car door opened. The rear doors were swung open too. The black figure loosened his grip fractionally. It was enough. She unclipped her seatbelt and leapt from the car, landing in a frightened heap on the gravel of the car park. She had made it to the police station car park.

In her peripheral vision she spotted him, a dark shape whipping across the car park, oblivious to where she had brought him.

'Take it easy now,' a gruff friendly voice was helping her to her feet.

'Sir,' another voice called. She tried to focus. Crash. Smash, breaking glass, a thunderous clonking noise that sounded like an earthquake. Cries, screams, a baby wailing, people shouting...'I'll call an ambulance,' the familiar voice said. Rebecca closed her eyes and took a deep breath.

'Take it easy Mrs Houseman,' Inspector Allen smiled as she looked at him, dazed. 'Come inside.' He helped her to her feet. When she glanced across the car park towards the road she cried. Three cars were piled into the backs of each other, a dark clothed man lying face down in the road. It was him...he was dead. 'Come on Mrs Houseman, let's go inside. My Sergeant will take care of all that,' the Inspector soothed, taking her by the arm and leading her towards the station.

'I'm on to it Sir,' Sergeant Wellington said, nodded at her and marched towards the mess. A sea of uniformed policemen were all around her suddenly, herding the sadistic curious to one side. From somewhere the Sirens could be heard, their intrusive sound booming louder and louder.

'This way,' Inspector Allen was saying, leading her gently by the arm through the doors.

'Ouch,' she pursed her lips, her fingertips feeling the bruises that were turning purple on her arm as she noticed them gathering like a collection.

'Get a medic in here,' the Inspector ordered the desk sergeant. 'This way,' he led her towards the staff canteen. It was lined with square tables, chairs strewn around the room and abandoned meals on the table tops. In her confusion she knew it must have been a meal break, interrupted by tragedy, and death.

'Thank you,' she choked as the Inspector pulled out a chair for her. A round woman wearing a large white apron appeared, plonking a mug of tea in front of her. She managed a smile at the woman who proceeded to clatter together some of the half-eaten plates.

'Mrs Houseman,' the Inspector was smiling softly. 'Are you all right?' Rebecca sipped the hot tea gingerly and nodded, her fingers reaching for her throat. 'This is Daisy,' he indicated a woman in blue medical dress materialising behind her. 'She'll patch you up. Then we'll have a little chat,' he smiled at her, 'thank you Daisy,' he said crisply and marched out the canteen.

'Hello,' Daisy said, 'let's have a look at you. Oh dear, that's nasty but don't you worry we'll sort that out at the hospital. I'm just going to dress the wound until we can take you there, ok?' She was a slight woman with a gentle firmness and emerald eyes that sparkled when she smiled.

'Yes,' Rebecca whispered; her voice crackling and faint. In the background she could hear the police canteen staff clearing up after the rush, water running, plates being loaded into dishwashers, echoing gossip bouncing around the kitchen walls.

'Now this may sting,' Daisy warned, applying a pad of cool cotton wool to her neck. Rebecca winced slightly. 'There, you'll live to see another day,' she smiled brightly. Her hair was auburn, pinched back into a bun at the nape of her neck. 'Hold that there for me dear,' she said, lifting Rebecca's left hand and placing it against the cotton wool. It stung but it was cool, refreshing. Rebecca closed her eyes as Daisy attended to the bruising on her right arm, felt along the bones expertly. 'No breaks, it's a little sprained though. I'll get you a sling, just for a few days.' Rebecca nodded and sat quietly whilst Daisy felt her pulse.

'Thank you,' Rebecca managed to say as Daisy began folding items back into a bag she hadn't even noticed was there. 'They'll give you a proper check up at the hospital,' she smiled, her eyes bright, 'but you'll be ok. Sit here quietly and drink your tea. Take a few deep breaths.' She packed up the rest of her things. 'I'll ask the cook to bring you some biscuits,' she said, 'make sure you eat them. You're in shock and you need the energy.'

Rebecca sat opposite the Inspector. The office was untidy but somehow it didn't surprise her.

'Are you all right Mrs Houseman?' he asked, leaning over the desk with genuine concern. Rebecca felt the bandage the hospital had stretched around her like a necklace.

'Yes, I'm ok,' she told the Inspector with a half-smile, propping her left arm under her right, which was now housed within a sling. The office was hazy, a combination of air freshener and tobacco. Of course, this was Inspector Allen's office... she smiled at the connection, despite the day's events.

'I'm glad,' he flashed a toothy smile and sat back in his chair. It squealed slightly. 'We've discovered quite a lot, haven't we son?' he beamed at his Sergeant who was squashed into his chair behind his own desk in the corner, feverously writing up his notes from the mayhem outside. 'I'm afraid you're in for a bit of a shock,' Inspector Allen said, pursing his lips and fingering his moustache thoughtfully. 'If you'd rather wait until tomorrow...'

'No,' she said quickly, leaning forwards. 'I may as well know now.' She tried to smile. 'I'll never sleep otherwise.' Inspector Allen chuckled lightly.

'That was one of our big clues as it happens, Mrs Houseman.'

'Call me Rebecca, please,' she urged, winced slightly as she moved her arm.

'Rebecca,' the Inspector smiled. 'It was your friend babbling about your dreams that set me on the trail in the first place.' A smile danced satisfaction of knowledge around his lips.

'What are you talking about?' she exclaimed. 'My dreams...but they're just nonsense.'

'Not at all,' Inspector Allen grinned. 'They were the answer to everything. I'm very sorry to tell you that the man who attacked you today was your brother,' he said, resting his elbows on his desk, a blank look on his now impassive face. 'And he's dead.'

'My brother...' Rebecca found her words lost on her tongue. 'But my brother moved abroad...'

'Oh no Rebecca,' Inspector Allen cut in gravely, 'not the brother you grew up with.'

'But I don't understand Inspector...' she wailed. 'How can it be?'

'There's a lot you don't know about your family history Rebecca but I really don't think today is the best time,' the Inspector said quietly, lacing his nicotine-stained fingertips.

'What happened out there today?' Rebecca asked, 'the accident I mean, he was hit wasn't he? By the traffic?'

'Yes, in his attempt to run away he was knocked down and killed outright. It was pretty daring of you Madam, to disobey his instructions and drive here,' the Inspector winked at her and she managed to laugh, a light sound of relief escaping her shocked slender frame.

'You can't hold me down Inspector,' Rebecca smiled. 'At least, not for long anyway.'

'I'm glad to hear it Madam. Now though, you've had a severe shock, now I want you to go home. Is there anyone we can call to be with you?' Inspector Allen looked serious suddenly, more serious than she had ever seen him; even more so than earlier when he had pulled her free from the lunatic in her car.

'Yes Inspector, I have three children. One of them is bound to be free but I assure you I'll be fine...' she insisted, rising from her chair.

'No, you'll have someone with you,' Inspector Allen insisted. 'That's an order,' he grinned sheepishly. Rebecca smiled at him and relented. 'Now, I'll have Sergeant Wellington here drive you home,' he said sternly, 'and wait with her would you son?' he looked at his Sergeant, 'until her family arrive.'

'Yes Sir,' Wells eased himself from his chair slowly.

'But Inspector, that man can't have been my brother.'

'He was Mrs Houseman, and he wanted to stop you from receiving what was rightfully yours. I'll tell you all about it tomorrow.'

'Do you promise?' she asked him, nearing Wells who was hovering expectantly by the now open office door.

'Yes, I promise.' Inspector Allen cast a warm smile as she followed Sergeant Wellington out into the open air.

CHAPTER FOURTEEN – 26TH SEPTEMBER 1964

I take a deep breath. It is 9.50pm, time to go and meet the writer of my note. I must not be late for our 10.30pm meeting.

That cold stab of panic flashes at me in the form of the red ignition light as the engine dies on the sharp left-hand bend of the unfamiliar country lane. It's the usual thing but that panic never ceases to appear. Driving has never come naturally to me, especially in a car that is not my own. Rosa has leant it to me tonight. It is a rare housekeeper who can afford a car of her own, even a 'reliable rust bucket' such as this. My father says we are paying her too much. If I had asked for our car tonight he would have wanted to know where I was going. Worse still he would have called for someone to drive me. I cannot take that chance. This must be secret. I struggle on with the car.

'Treat it like a dance,' Michael had once advised, 'a sequence of steps, actions, to make the car sing.' As yet I fail to comprehend what he means. The engine must be cold, I decide quickly. It's colder than usual for September. I lift my foot off the clutch and within a momentary blink of the eye the engine roars back to life again as I depress the accelerator to continue my journey around the bend.

I'm not looking forward to the evening ahead of me, it's not my cup of tea at all, but at least, I think to myself, I am forewarned. I can handle anything in my quest to find her, or so I tell myself.

The car park is completely packed. I'm going to have to look elsewhere. In the unfamiliar dark streets on the edge of town, I am not confident but it has to be done. I drive on. I notice the hotel as I drive by; it's big and daringly bright like a fluorescent bouncy castle. The roof is lined with ridges that resemble the castle I would have drawn as a small child. In my castle there was always a princess with excessively long hair, always dark. I begin to wonder nervously if I am doing the right thing. All I know, rather all I feel, is that I must take the risk.

There, a free space. I swing the little blue car into the space. Staring back at myself in the rear view mirror I wonder if I am ready to finally face my fears. My small black leather evening bag rests on the passenger seat beside me. In it I remind myself I have my secret emergency card to play at any time I want. With dubious building confidence and a fake smile I exit the car and clutch the bag fiercely. I must be careful about what I clutch inside the bag. The door will not lock, it's an omen I tell myself, and immediately forget it. I'll just twist it a little bit; it's jammed again. It turns and I slip the keys into my bag. I hear a clink as they hit father's gun. Here we go…

The short walk towards the fluorescent castle fills me with dread at each step. My fingers entwine themselves tighter around my bag. I can feel the heat rising up my body like a thermometer.

The door looms ahead of me, its large black hinges only enhancing the brightness of the light behind the glass. As I walk I glance around. I've never been here before. The directions were very clear. Nearby I can see a large building that resembles a town hall, the signs hinting that a very large brand superstore is a couple of miles down the road, one of those new self-service ones that are sweeping the country like a storm.

The light is blinding me now, the doors swinging open as a man ahead of me enters the lit-up castle. There stands the doorman in his uniform of death. A long ebony woollen coat enshrines him like a cloak as he stands tall and menacing staring out into the night, his hat low over his eyes. I wonder briefly if he enjoys his job. He looks miserable. The door looms large before me. I am nearly there.

'Hello Madam,' the doorman says as I arrive nearer to him.

'Hello,' I incline my head, my hat chosen purposefully to conceal much of my face with its white lace veil. That is how I feel at the moment, as if I'm in hiding, all eyes searching for me. In truth nobody is watching me, nobody even realises I am here, but I feel sought all the same.

As he opens the glass door I notice the black hinges grinding. The glass panel is pressed towards his chest and the light floods out like the tunnel from a large torch. The suspension of dust and grime on the floor is visible as I tread over it towards the brick steps that will take me inside. The light is on me now and I don't like it, I don't want to be seen, recognised. I cover my eyes as I move inside. A large fear instantly engulfs me as I take a tentative step further in. At least I can see now, the lights are dimmed once past the initial entrance way. This is worse than the title competition, I think, blocking it from my mind in favour of holding my nerve.

I move towards my right where the events board tells me I must mount two flights of stairs towards room number five. My daughter's age I tell myself, perhaps another omen? She is the reason I am here after all.

The décor is bright, there's a surprise. The walls are a dark cream shade with tinted smoky grey glass frames encasing photos of how the building had looked years before. It's old then, I realise, and wonder if that is significant.

I make my way towards the archway that leads to the staircase. It winds itself around in a spiral to each floor. It reaches up six floors but I am not going that high.

Under the archway there is no escape. The staircase is the only way. I mount the first step, my foot peeking out from the hem of my full-length evening dress. My shoes are new. I bought them last week. Each step seems to increase the temperature within me. I feel my face. It's too hot. I must look flushed and I've only taken two steps. I pause at the landing and take deep breaths. Only one staircase left to climb. What is wrong with me, I'm supposed to be fit.

A man brushes past me, I recognise him faintly. Wasn't he the one who entered this glowing establishment moments before I did? I try to take a closer look from my resting point on the landing. He doesn't acknowledge me. He cannot possibly be here for the same reason I am, can he? Tonight anything is possible. He is gone, too late. Right, I tell myself, let's get it over with.

The second flight of stairs looks down at me as if to say 'what are you waiting there for?' The stairs are partly carpeted in a dull brown shade to compliment the dark cream walls. It's an ugly design. I begin the second spiral round of steps.

The noise from above is beginning to filter down towards me. I can hear a dull drone, as if I'm trapped in a cupboard at a party. It strikes me that nobody would hear me scream right now. I have an urge to scream, to scream loudly and for a long time. Would anybody come running? I decide they wouldn't but do not scream. What would be the point?

My fingers clutch my bag even tighter as I reach the last few steps. I can identify the bag's contents as I hold it. It occurs to me to mind how I hold the bag. I don't want to reveal the contents as an outline to anyone. What would be the point of a visible secret? I'm looking straight ahead at the corridor with doors tunnelled into my vision like a kaleidoscope.

The second landing is warmer than the first. The carpet feels thicker beneath my flimsy shoes. I wobble ever so slightly as I take a few steps towards another events board. It reminds me that I must go to my daughter's age. I head past rooms closed off by soft brown wooden doors. Each door is numbered, odds and evens on each side of the corridor as if it is a residential street. A new sound transcends each door, some of blasting noise, some of people shouting and crying, some of silence. It is the silent ones I dread, they could turn out to be mine.

I glance to my left; room five is the next door. The doors are numbered using gold-plated digits, each one slightly raised to stand proud of the wooden door itself. There it is; the door that may change my life. I stand before it, staring into the golden digits as if they will help me to decide whether or not to open the door. I look at the doorknob. It too is golden. With one hand grabbing my evening bag I move the other one towards the doorknob. A strange magnetic force draws my outstretched hand towards it. I watch my fingers clutching the golden ball as if they have a will of their own. Slowly they turn the knob so the door clicks out of its closed position. There is a gap now and I try to stare through into what lies beyond, still holding the door tight to its frame.

I think of my daughter and wish she knew how much I love her. I couldn't put myself through this roller coaster of emotions for anybody else. The corridor is still. I am alone. The door is still ajar, my hand still fixed in place. I squint through the gap, my eyes adjusting to the narrow viewpoint. There is nobody inside. With a sudden push as if my hand has detached itself from the rest of me, the door is swung open. I stand still, both hands now clasping at my bag again, feeling the gun for confidence. I remain in the corridor looking in. I must look like an outcast at a party. Why do I keep thinking of parties, or rather of not quite being part of the party?

The room is sparse and white. A soft blanket of light falls around the room from the upturned ceiling light. A glow rests over the oval table. It is of the same colour as the door, most likely the same wood. The grain looks bolder on the table. Chairs are neatly stacked around the table. There are two doors to the side; I wonder what is behind them. A bathroom? A bedroom? The later fills me with horror, the former with a possible relief. I could hide there, be of advantage behind a door. I could also be trapped, confined to a limited space. That might not be a good thing. I decide not to take up the advantage.

My feet propel me towards the doorframe. I rest against the frame watching the emptiness ahead of me. Maybe the evening will not go to plan. Maybe I will be alone the entire time. Who knows these answers? Instinctively I look towards the sky but all I see is the roof of the doorframe, the ceiling of the corridor. Nasty blotched tiles held in place by a thick plastic grid like a matrix. There are no answers there.

I move inside the room, the door left wide open. Do I want to close the door? With the door open I can see more, another advantage to me...I decide that advantages are not a good thing tonight. I close the door. There is no knowing who will come, if anybody. An evil streak in me wants whoever comes to go through the same faltering walk along the corridor, to search for the numbers, to hear the silence and be deafened by the fright of it.

I'll sit down. I think I'll sit on the settee. It looks inviting, a soft white fabric, probably rich material only the wealthy and hotels can afford to purchase. I sit on the end of the sofa. It is bouncy; I almost lose myself in the cushions. I decide I'll look for a similar one for the house.

There is a knock at the door and I freeze; my breath static in my throat as I rise from the cushions. I fall sideways on my wobbly heels and drop my bag onto the expanse of white settee cushion. Swiftly I seize at it and close my eyes for a moment. I breathe deeply and open my eyes to see the doorknob turning. It turns slowly. That must have been what it looked like when I turned it. I didn't know what would await me; neither does whoever is turning it now.

The door is slightly ajar now and I move silently to one side. This is one advantage I will allow myself tonight. A foot is all I see at first, a man's shiny shoe. It is patent black and reflects the ceiling light. Then a leg encased by grey pressed trousers. A line has been ironed down the front. So he too has come as if on another mission entirely. At least I am not alone on this score, at least I have done it right so far. I stand and wait. An arm stretches around the door and slowly pushes it further open. He must be looking, searching the room. I can feel his eyes scanning the space before him, just as I did. He cannot see me yet. I am behind the door, well almost. He must have heard me breathe. He pushes it and instantly turns to face me. An immediate full frontal shot was not what I was expecting. My sole advantage did me no favours. Another omen, I wonder.

'Well,' he says, his brown brow rising at one side. 'You're here,' he states the obvious. It annoys me.

'Of course,' I reply curtly. 'What did you expect?' To this he slams the door and strides over towards the window, beyond the dark grained table and the white suite. I haven't ventured that far into the room. Already he is distancing himself from me. Already he has covered more ground, and with ease.

'Well,' he repeats himself. Again, this annoys me. 'Why don't you have a seat?' he inclines his hand at the luxurious white cushions. I shake my head silently. The swish of my hair fills my ears; it reminds me of the ocean. Large pink tinted shells that echo the sound of the waves. I smile faintly. He will not have any more advantages over me, not now.

'You look as I imagined you would.'

I am surprised by this and try not to show it but he notices anyway.

He smiles softly. 'Thank you for coming,' he says quietly and sits on the settee casually, I remain standing.

'Your directions were very clear,' I say. I do not know what will happen next, or what to say to him. He called this meeting. I decide it is down to him to make the first move.

'Good,' he says to me.

I'm beginning to feel as if I'm wasting my time. When will he get around to it? As if he reads my mind he stands and takes a few steps towards me.

'I expect you're wondering what I'll do now aren't you?'

I say nothing.

'I'll tell you,' he says, turning to start what I'll soon realise is a nervous habit of his, pacing the room. 'I'm going to ask you a couple of questions. Then, we'll get the transaction completed. How does that sound to you?' He spins to face me. I am unfazed by this and he looks disappointed.

'Ok,' I say simply. My heart is hammering in my chest and I pray he cannot hear it. I want to appear calm and collected.

'Tell me,' he says, turning again, 'why did you really come tonight?'

'I had to,' I answer, 'I have to know what happened. I want her back.' The room feels small now, close and warm. I glance at the fireplace, the embers of a previous occupant glowing faintly in the grate. I am right beside it. Slowly I move towards him and around him whilst maintaining his glance. It's like a game, a display of control. Nobody wants to lose. I take a stance away from the fireplace and fiddle faintly with my long evening coat that conceals the best part of my dress. My face is feeling flushed again. A small part of me doesn't want him to see me like this, but it is too late. Why do I feel I must impress him?

'Tell me your name,' he speaks at last. With a thud he slams an envelope on the table. It is not cheap paper. It is of the familiar cream shade and the handwriting is carefully crafted across the page, not the hasty scrawl of the previous two, but the writing is familiar all the same. It is addressed to me. Private and confidential it says. I stare at the envelope.

'Tell me yours,' I fire back at him. He smiles playfully. This is ridiculous and we both know it. He knows very well who I am, and why I am about to lie to him.

'All right,' he speaks softly. 'You can call me Bill.'

He is taller than I imagined him to be. Why is it that you can imagine somebody over a phone line or a letter and be so wrong? It's the way they sound usually; tall, short, fat, thin, old, young…the list is endless. I have him all wrong.

'And what pray may I call you for tonight?' he bows ever so slightly as if I am royalty. I ignore his arrogance as best I can and think carefully, slowly. So slowly in fact I must irritate him but he doesn't let it show.

'You can call me Rosa,' I say at last. Tonight I am Rosa then, and he is Bill. We both know that tonight we are not ourselves, despite my suspicion of him wanting me to prove otherwise.

'Rosa,' he repeats, 'what a pretty name.' He speaks in a patronising tone I imagine being used with children by schoolteachers and babysitters. I do not smile at this instead I turn away from him and head towards the window where I stare out into the night sky. The stars are bright tonight. The darkness is large and looming, it covers my face like a blanket and I wonder if I'll ever see the light. I can feel him watching me, as if I might escape, vaporise into nothing before his very eyes. The silence is thick and I almost choke on it. Why doesn't he get on with it?

'OK, do you have the cash?' he speaks suddenly as if he has grown bored of the charade.

I nod my head silently, insistent on staring out at the night sky. Why should I look at him, he holds no intrigue for me, he is just the messenger. I am sure of this now.

'Leave it on the table when you go. Take that with you,' he says indicating the envelope. I can hear him almost stamping his way towards the side doors now. Which one does he open? I forbid myself to turn and look. In one door he goes. He will wait there, I'm sure of this, until he hears me leave room number five. I wait. I do not want to rush this. I must get it right. There will not be a second chance.

I feel numb as I move towards the table and rest my evening bag onto the bold grained surface. In it I can see my reflection; the polish is very good. It has a strong scent of lemon to it like suntan lotion in the shade. I pick up the envelope. It feels like quality paper. I no longer think I recall the handwriting. Was it a trick of the light that made me think I did?

My fingers slowly unzip my bag. They do not feel part of me, that strange magnetic force has taken control again. I do not have much time. I shove the envelope into my bag with measured force. Its corners crumple slightly but I do not care. I glance at the closed door. Safe. I unzip the bag faster and shuffle around the tiny compartment for the rolled-up notes. They are unmarked bank notes totalling five hundred pounds, wrapped around each one carefully and kept together with a beige elastic band. It is exact. I feel the notes between my fingers. The texture is wrong but I do not care. He is not going to waste time worrying about it, I am sure of this.

I wonder what he is doing in the other room, does he wait impatiently or does he just sit and think? What can he possibly be thinking about? I wonder who sent him. The same person who contacted me? Perhaps he, he in the other room waiting for me to leave, perhaps he is the whole thing. It occurs to me that I shall never know but wonder all the same. He in the room beyond may never have seen the one behind all this. He could be as in the dark as I am. Was he instructed to leave the room? It seems odd to me, how else can he be sure I'll actually leave the money? Any moment now I could leave the room, I wouldn't even have to run. I could just walk out, money still in my possession. How does he know I will not do that? How do I know I will not do that?

I look down at the rolled up notes still encased in my gloved fingers. Decision time, what should I do?

My skin crawls at the sound; the sudden beating of my heart makes me jump. Was that a shot I heard? Stuffing the bank notes back into my bag I stare at the door. It is closed, locked even. The door to the room to my daughter's age is still firmly shut. Stupidly I look at the gun in my bag. I haven't touched it. There must be another....

'Bill,' I call. There is no answer. 'Bill,' I call again. Still, silence. Nerves tingle through me like static electricity. I feel as I imagine I would feel suspended from a live wire over a cliff. The power could either pull me back or kill me; it will not be something mediocre; of that I am sure. I walk towards the doors. Which one did he take? 'Bill,' I try one last time. Silence greets me. Both side doors are white with gold handles. Not doorknobs, handles. Why is it that the main door has a knob and these inner doors have handles? Why do I even think of this at this time? Distraction?

My body temperature is rising at an alarming rate consistent with panic, my fingers moist with fear beneath my gloves like humid rain. I'll take the right hand side door I decide with no reasoning whatsoever. I grasp the handle quickly and pull it down. The door is not locked and it opens easily.

There is nobody inside, only bedroom furniture lit up by the impending moonlight. The window by the far wall is open, its net curtain flapping away like a wagging tongue. I walk over to it, peer out into the night, but I see nobody. He is nowhere to be found. With an involuntary shiver I pull the window closed and leave the room.

There is the second door. Perhaps he took that one. Again I wrestle with the uncertainty that may await me on the other side. Slowly I turn the handle and it creaks into life.

This room is darker than the first. I narrow my eyes straining to see a shadow, a movement, any flicker of life. He is not in here either. I decide he must have taken the open window. To be sure I flick the switch with my left hand. No, he is not here. Instead I look at the room. This is no ordinary hotel suite. The space before me is crammed with photographs. They splatter the walls like confetti. Why am I shocked? Nothing should shock me tonight.

There is no furniture, just walls pasted with the present. Photographs are always of the present, you cannot capture the past in an instant, or the future. It occurs to me that I am not supposed to see these. I may have deviated from the plan. Will that matter? Danger lurks in my mind like a stalker in midnight streets. I shudder. It is too bad I decide. It is too late.

The photos are of children, lost children, children in orphanages, foster homes, and hospital wards. Each one is pasted at an angle, not one of them looks back at me in a straight line. A large park seems to be the backdrop, perhaps even a London park. I cannot see much other than the faces, they take up the photograph greedily absorbing all other clues to their location.

There is a newspaper cutting too. It shows me, outside the adoption agency. I look dreadful. It must have been that day soon after her birth. There are other newspaper cuttings too, other children snatched, small columns of text, the grief-stricken parents avoiding the splash I had encountered simply by not being famous. A serial child snatcher...

I have not stepped into the room. I am afraid I will cross some invisible barrier. The ceiling light is low and upturned. A red bulb basks the room with its glow, stretching out like a summer haze. I scan the pictures quickly. She is there. She seems to seek me out as I turn directly towards her. She stares at me and I stare back. Her photograph is recent. Something about her hair strikes me as odd, almost familiar in a way that is strange. It is as if I've seen it the exact second before. The sun is reflective on her hair in the photograph as it drapes down her shoulders beneath a floppy red hat. There is a bold blue blur behind her that is striking against the red of her hat.

I feel my heart begin to race. I clutch at my evening bag tighter, the zip not completely one way or another in my haste to stuff the bank notes back inside. The blue in the photograph is bothering me.

Slowly I raise my right foot, I want to go inside the red room and move tentatively towards the centre. The room is chilly, the air almost damp like early morning rain, a fresh coating crisp and light. My skin is prickled with the chill and I wrap my arms around myself as I take another step towards the back wall from where she is still staring out at me like a spy.

The door to the main suite is still wide open, an invitation to anyone watching. I do not care about the door. Earlier I would have done, but not now. He is still nowhere to be seen, or heard. Why should I care about an open door? It wasn't locked. Nobody said not to come in here.

I study the picture of my baby girl. Something flickers across my mind like a spider across a kitchen floor. The image skittles over me and I strain to see it. It annoys me furiously. I watch the picture of her intently as if it may slip from my vision at any moment. Of course it doesn't, she and I could stare at each other happily forever. It occurs to me that this is the longest period of time we have actually looked at each other. Ironic that she isn't even present for the occasion.

The blueness behind her is still bothering me. I close my eyes and instantly I see it, the sharp blue in blind focus bouncing behind her head as she hops about in the red floppy hat. It is the park. She is happy. It is her birthday. Her adoptive parents have just bought her the floppy hat. She is standing in front of the slide, the large blue slide in the park. That was it, the second when the photograph was taken. Whoever took the photo was there, that day, in the park, when I was…

I open my eyes and there she is. It is almost as if she smiles at me now, as if she knows that I know but I fear it is too late. I snatch the photo from the wall and press it to my heart. I have seen the light. I know she is mine now, indefinite proof, but I still can't reach out and touch her.

CHAPTER FIFTEEN – MODERN DAY; JUNE

Katherine looked at the dead man lying on the cold metal trolley. His body was almost white, drained of life, his face translucently pale. He looked strange, still, those furtive movements gone forever. Thankfully his penetrating eyes were closed now but she still knew it was him. The long cold stares he had treated her to at the doctors' surgery and the football pitch had ingrained his face in her mind. Now, she hoped to forget all about him.

'It's him,' she said quietly. 'It's definitely him,' she confirmed, walking away towards the warmer climate of the relatives room. Behind their retreating footsteps the mortician pulled back the white sheet and pushed the body back into the freezer.

'Thank you,' Inspector Allen said as he opened the door for them to leave the mortuary.

'How did you know I'd seen him?' Katherine asked. Inspector Allen smiled craftily and led the way towards the exit doors.

'Your mother's friend Jean,' he said, pulling his cigarette from behind his ear as they fled the mortuary and reached the open air of the car park. 'You and she talked didn't you, when she took your mother to hospital after the allergic reaction to the envelope?' Inspector Allen lit up his cigarette and puffed out greedily, ignoring the NO SMOKING sign behind them.

'Yes, we did talk then. I'll never be rude about her again,' Katherine managed a light laugh. 'She told you what I'd said about the creepy man who kept popping up at the football game without a child, right?'

'Yes Miss, I interviewed her at your mother's house the other day. She said you were suspicious of him.' He grinned, blew out a long line of white smoke. It collapsed in the air and filtered away on the breeze.

'I was Inspector, yes. I thought he was after me at first. He was watching me at the doctors, I'm sure of it,' Katherine said. 'But I guess he was just trying to get close to mum. I just don't understand why. What did he want? Why did he attack her in her car? It doesn't make any sense.'

'Don't worry Miss Houseman, everything will become clearer tomorrow. I want you to go and see your mother now; can you stay the night with her?' Inspector Allen asked, stubbing his cigarette between his fingertips and casting it in a nearby bin. 'I don't want her to be alone, she's had a shock.'

'I wish I could, but I've got my baby son to feed right through the night. My sister Eliza is staying with her though. I'll go over now, join them for the evening,' Katherine assured him.

'Marvellous, and don't you worry Miss Houseman. I'll have this all cleared up in no time.' Katherine looked at the strange wiry man. He didn't look like anything she had seen on television police dramas, but she had to admit it, he was good.

'Thank you,' she said as they reached her car.

'Oh by the way, you can tell your mother that I've arrested the man behind the stolen car ring, and his mechanic who rigged your mother's brakes, they'll be locked away for a few years to come.' The Inspector grinned quickly and began to walk away.

'What are you talking about?' Katherine called over her car door.

'She'll understand,' Inspector Allen beamed at her as he spun around on his heels to face her. 'I'm about to charge the leader of the car thefts and his accomplice with one of the worse charges they can ever get,' he grinned even wider. 'And I promise you I can make it stick like glue.' Grinning, he turned back towards his car.

'I've no idea who you're talking about Inspector,' Katherine said, bewildered. 'Will she know what you mean?'

'Oh yes Madam, she'll know what I mean. John Francis Miss,' Inspector Allen yelled, already half way back towards his own car, where Sergeant Wellington was waiting. 'He and his friend Bateman, or Fisher as he calls himself these days, are about to be charged with the attempted murder of your mother.'

'But we've never heard of them,' Katherine called.

'They've heard of your mother though,' Inspector Allen said with his hat inclined in his hand. 'Good day Miss, and don't worry, I'm on the case!'

Katherine drove towards her mother's house, her mind whirling. Who were these dubious types who had almost succeed in killing her mum? What did they have against her? What was all that about her car brakes...?

Rebecca ran the hot water until the bath was as deep as she could manage, without dampening her bandaged neck. Dipping her body slowly into the bubbles she laid back, careful to keep her neck above the bubbly surface. The grazes on her right arm were tender and sore. She let it rest against her body, using only her left hand, lightly she washed her face and closed her eyes.

Katherine and Eliza had been full of questions, some of which she didn't know the answers to. Eventually Katherine had gone home to feed little Craig and to fill Neil in with the details; such as they were, sketchy at best. Eliza was in the spare room, making up the bed to stay the night. Later they were going to order a take-away and open the bottle of wine Eliza had put in the fridge to chill. Rebecca was looking forward to it. Spending time with her eldest daughter was neigh impossible since her beautiful granddaughters had come along. They were lovely and she wouldn't want the world to be without them but she missed the times alone with Eliza. The questions had ceased for the moment. The women had exhausted all possible scenarios, none of which were likely to be the real truth.

The dreams, the strange man who had been watching them, some nonsense about her not getting the money that was rightfully hers. Was this what Craig had been trying to warn her about?

The Inspector appeared to have it all in hand, and understand it, which was more than she could claim. If Katherine was right and he was charging two men with attempted murder, and the third now lay dead in the mortuary, then all her fears were over. She could sleep easily in her bed, if Craig and her persistent dreams would let her.

Rebecca closed her eyes and thought about Craig, wondered if he were watching over her. Somebody had been that afternoon, if it wasn't for the Inspector wrenching her car door open at that precise moment…she shivered involuntarily, splashed the hot water over her body and tried to think of pleasanter things.

'Mum,' Eliza was calling through the closed bathroom door. 'I'm going to call the take-away. Be about half hour, is that alright?'

'Yes love,' she sang, 'that'll be perfect.' Bless her sweet Eliza; she was really glad she had her children, especially at times like this. Craig would have been so proud of all of them rallying round. She smiled at his memory. Would he have wanted her to go out with Paul though? Reluctantly she pushed Paul from her mind, he would have to wait. There were more probing questions to answer first, like what was going on?

Perhaps by tomorrow it would all be as clear as crystal. Inspector Allen had promised answers to her questions in the morning.

The car was most definitely a write off. According to Chris she had probably blown up the engine in her little jaunt across town. Neil and Samuel were meeting the insurance assessor, on her behalf, in the morning at the police pound.

Another insurance claim to file then, she heaved a sigh of relief it hadn't turned out to be more serious than a claim file. Craig had bought her that car, it wasn't exactly glamorous but it was another thing in her life that held memories, just like the lounge. The thought of it being crushed generated tears in her eyes. Every scrap of their life together was slowly slipping away. Involuntarily she was being forced to move on.

'Is this your doing love?' she asked the ceiling. 'Are you making me get a new car? I thought you hated decorating.' Rebecca closed her eyes, winced slightly as she moved her arm and smiled. She was going mad. None of this could be Craig's doing. He had never been a subtle man, but she felt sure if the spirit lived on, he was probably safely perched by a lake, fishing. Aside from the family, fishing had always been his idea of heaven.

Maybe it was for the best, after all she would need a new car one day, and she had always wanted to redecorate. It was funny how life turned out. This madman wanted her dead but all he had achieved, if she discounted the bruised arm and the bandage around her neck, was paying for her lounge to be completely overhauled, and getting her a new car – probably.

Despite the string of new possessions, she was thankful that the nightmare was almost over, even if it was still a mystery.

CHAPTER SIXTEEN – 26TH SEPTEMBER 1964

I drive Rosa's car back home at high speed. The roads are empty and I am crying. I hate to admit it, but my father is probably right. The culprit has left me no clue other than the fact that my baby was probably one in a long line of victims.

I take the turn back towards the far side of Atwood, back home, and wonder how the room can be set up like that. I picture Bill carefully arranging the room in the hours before my arrival, hiding down the corridor and watching me enter room number five. I picture him arranging the wall so my little girl shines out, perhaps even estimating my height to position her smiling face in my direct line of vision. I shiver at the thought of such calculated planning and wipe the hot tears from my face in one swipe.

As I park the car and switch off the engine its soft noise falters and dies. I wipe away another stream of tears and close my eyes, try to focus. A flash of light catches my attention and for the first time I notice that the lights are all on inside the house. I sigh. What are they doing up at this time of night? This is odd; they are never up this late. The last thing I want now is to face my parents. I wipe away another tear and prepare to enter the wrath of my father. It is almost midnight when I unlock the front door. Michael comes to the entrance foyer.

'What are you doing here?' I ask, coming in and removing my coat and shoes hastily. 'What's going on?'

I am clutching my evening bag protectively. I remember the letter suddenly and I want to go to my room to read it alone. Maybe there is something more to learn…

'Thank God you're safe,' Michael says. I half smile at him. 'Your father rang, he was worried about you,' Michael explains. Of course, how silly of me to think he may actually forget the date of the summons. I decide I am too weary for this and begin to mount the stairs.

'I'm fine,' I assure Michael, 'but I'm tired, I'll see you tomorrow,' I take the first three steps.

'Oh no you don't young lady,' my father bellows from the marble steps into the large lounge diner. I sigh. Why can this not wait until morning? I ignore him and continue to climb the stairs. I am almost at the top. Michael is still standing at the base of the staircase between my father and me. I see Rosa and my mother join Michael at the foot of the stairs.

'Are you all right Miss Capelli?' Rosa asks.

'Yes I'm fine,' I look at them all, 'I promise. I just want to go to sleep. Goodnight.'

'I said no,' my father bellows and the others leap back towards the door. 'I want to know what's going on,' he demands, his face redder than I've ever seen before. 'You went, didn't you?' he accuses me, 'I told you it was a hoax.' Temporarily he looks smug and suddenly I am angry. How dare he treat me like this; it is his fault anyway, I am sure of it. He was the one who wanted me to murder my child. He never wanted her. The pain of the evening builds in me, transforms itself into a steely knot. I feel my body reddening with poisonous thoughts.

'Do you know what your problem is my girl?' he shouts, his voice echoing around the staircase like a whirlwind, 'um?' I do not answer. Instead I stare at him with sparkling cold eyes; my tears dried up and stained in streaks down my face, black mascara lining their path.

'Leave it love,' my mother rests her fingers lightly on his shoulder but he shrugs her free hurriedly.

'Do you?' he shouts at me again, leaning heavily on the base of the banister.

'Sir, please.' Michael attempts to draw closer but my father spins on him.

'Did you put her up to this?' he yells, his eyes wide at Michael.

'Sir,' Michael tries again but father ignores him, turns back to me where I stand stock still on the stairs. He begins to climb and I do not move. My heart is fluttering but I am used to this, he does not frighten me.

'Sir, please Sir, can't this wait until morning?' Michael calls from the entrance foyer where mother is crying on his shoulder. I see him trying to comfort her.

'Why are you so angry daddy?' I say quietly, my voice dangerously shrill. 'Didn't you want me to know what you did?'

'Leave it love, please,' my mother begins to sob louder than before and Michael pats her on the back.

'You stay out of it.' My father swings his arms in a wild unsteady turn on the stair, almost loses his balance. He has been drinking. I can smell whisky on his breath. 'All of you, I'm handling this,' he assures them, turns back, climbs the step I am on and goes beyond so he is towering above me, blocking my path to the haven of my room.

'You,' he looks down at me, his dark eyes burning with anger and his faint double chin wobbling with rage. 'I warned you, didn't I?' he says smugly. I know it is not a question. I push my bag ahead of me, into his chest to free my path to my room. Instinctively I know it is a mistake. He feels the barrel of the gun in his chest. He rips the bag from my grasp and empties it, the notes fluttering down the stairs like confetti.

'Joyce sweetheart,' Michael calls, 'what's all this?' I hear my mother sobbing louder and louder at the base of the stairs, see her pain and feel Michael's fear behind me.

'How dare you take my gun child,' father roars, then noticing the cash, 'so you didn't leave the money hey? Smartest thing you've done all night,' my father grins nastily, like a man possessed.

'Don't you ever care about anything other than money?' I scream? I reach down to collect my letter from my feet, where it has fallen in his haste to steal my bag, but he tries to take it from me. 'No,' I cry, 'you can't...' I manage to grab it but he tears it from my fist with a force I am not strong enough to resist. I feel my balance compromised. I hang onto it, the tiny shred of cream envelope in my fingers holding my weight. I see it begin to tear, feel my feet lose contact with the stair.

'Joyce!' It is Michael's voice I hear, an anguished cry of helplessness that swirls around me. The staircase is spinning, punctuated with spasms of pain. I do not know what is happening to me. I hear a thump. I feel...

Michael let her mother go, fell to her side on the floor and cradled her face in his hands. No, it couldn't be true. No, Joyce, no...he began to cry, unaware of his own tears until he noticed them spilling onto her evening dress, ripped and torn from the twisted fall down the stairs.

'Joyce sweetheart,' he whispered; his voice hoarse and weak. 'Say something baby...' Emptiness took hold of his body quickly. It took several minutes for him to realise someone was trying to drag him away.

'Come on Mr Sutton,' a female voice was saying, his gaze still fixated on her eyes, wide and staring, beautiful. He felt Rosa take him down the marble steps into the lounge, manoeuvre him deftly into a chair and hand him a glass. He felt her press his fingers around the glass and bring it to his lips. The taste on his tongue was bitter and he closed his eyes in disbelief. What was the point without Joyce?

'Mr Sutton?' Rosa looked at him squarely and he returned her gaze for the first time. 'You stay here,' she instructed, her own grief painted in her eyes. 'Sit here, do not move,' she said. Michael nodded, watched her go across to Joyce's mother. Silently he watched Rosa help the woman step over Joyce and up the stairs, her terrifying screams piercing the silence. It made his head hurt. He sipped at his drink, not even sure what it was, tried not to look at the crumpled body on the floor in the hallway. How could this be happening?

A deathly silence prevailed as Rosa dialled the doctor. Michael sat, frozen, in his chair. From somewhere above his head he could still hear her mother crying, raw pain racking her body uncontrollably. Numbly he saw the doctor hurry into the hallway, watched his face plunge from hope to dread. The doctor looked at him and he returned the frozen stare.

Rosa stood over Joyce, her own body stiff and competent, her emotions bottled up inside as the ambulance took Joyce away. He saw Rosa despatch the doctor upstairs to Joyce's mother and he sat crying silently into his glass.

Eventually the noise upstairs subsided. The doctor left the house in silence, the sound of his car moving further away, crunching down the driveway into the oblivion of the night.

Rosa came down the stairs, her face ashen white, her usually bright eyes pale. She took his glass from him, re-filled it and placed it back into his hand. Michael managed a nod of thanks as she poured a large measure for herself. They sat, two strangers, in the lounge, joined by their love for the woman they would never see again.

'The doctor has given her something to help her sleep,' Roberto Capelli said, his voice almost a whisper. Michael and Rosa stared at him coldly. He walked straight up to Michael, handed him a crumpled piece of cream paper. Michael took it blindly. 'You should have this,' he said. Michael watched Roberto Capelli pour himself a drink and leave the room.

'What does it say?' Rosa asked the moment Roberto had gone. Michael began to read, his own voice sounding hollow and his mind fuzzy.

Dear Miss Capelli

My brother will probably have taken your money and for that I apologise. It was never my idea to ask you for cash. I fully expect to hear tales of his attempts to dramatise the entire affair. My only wish was to send you this letter, to explain to you what happened on that dreadful day and to make amends, if I can, with the simple truth.

This is my hotel you see, so I am able to reserve certain rooms and prepare them as I choose. The photographs are all of children I have taken. A gallery of guilt. It is unnecessary, I know, but if I had not played into my brother's taste for drama he would have refused to attend tonight. My sole purpose was to give you this explanation and I am ashamed to say I am too cowardly to attend myself. So, you see, I needed him. Had I simply left the note on the table you may not have seen it and I am afraid I have only sufficient courage to undertake this once.

I was a desperate woman Miss, I longed for a child. Yours, again I am ashamed to admit, was not the first I had taken, but I made a mistake with you. I just saw her, I fell in love with her and I took her, not knowing she was the daughter of a celebrity. Had I known I would not have risked it, the publicity surrounding the rumours, the scandal of the press; it was just too much to cope with.

I am sorry. Let me assure you I took good care of her whilst she was with me, which was brief. I do not expect she will even remember. The guilt always followed quickly and I always gave the children up. Sometimes I returned them to the hospital. Sometimes I left them in baskets outside the church. I took your daughter to the adoption agency, after I saw the newspaper article I thought you may return there or they may remember and contact you. I am so sorry that did not happen.

I never took another child after yours. Eventually God rewarded me and I did have my own baby, a natural cure you might say, to my problem. I hope you are reunited with her one day Miss. I am convinced she is the girl I see you talking to in the park, and I fully expect her new family would understand if you were to approach them.

You will forgive me not leaving a name, with regret.

Michael put the letter down, noticing the corner of something else in the envelope. He took a large gulp of his drink and looked at Rosa as he pulled the photograph from the torn cream envelope. His hands shook as he looked at the little girl. All he could think was Joyce had been right. The child had his eyes, but she had more than that, she had Joyce's beauty.

The house was oddly quiet. Neither of them knew where Roberto had gone, probably his study.

'She thought it was him,' Michael heard himself say, still transfixed by the picture of his daughter. Rosa nodded in response. 'So it wasn't…after all.'

'No,' Rosa whispered. After a while she asked, 'What will you do now?' Michael looked at her blankly, shook his shoulders resignedly. He had no idea. He couldn't possibly imagine another day without Joyce, how could he dance with a stranger? What would become of him now? 'You could try to get your little girl back,' she suggested.

'You knew all along?' he asked, already knowing the answer somehow, suddenly wishing he had been able to support Joyce better in her hour of need. His love for her and their missing child had consumed him, chipped away at his heart ceaselessly. Joyce had needed him and he had let her down, given into his own silent grief. He didn't blame her for seeking out Rosa for solace.

'Yes, I did try to help her,' Rosa managed a half smile. 'I think she was a good mother, if she had chance to be,' Rosa smiled to herself, sipped at her own drink.

'Yes,' Michael sighed. 'One day...' he whispered, feeling the tears beginning to fall yet again. He pressed the photograph to his heart and closed his eyes.

CHAPTER SEVENTEEN – MODERN DAY; JUNE

Rebecca replaced the receiver, a sad smile on her lips. She had wanted to go to dance that evening, had been secretly looking forward to seeing Paul, to go out with him for that drink he had promised. Having relayed the sorry tale of the attack, fended off his concerns about her injuries with assurances that she was on the mend, and promised him she would explain everything in a few days, she now felt at a loss. How could she explain anyway? The Inspector hadn't yet told her what was going on. In about an hour he was due to enlighten her.

Nervously she made a cup of strong coffee and sat in the kitchen, drumming her free fingers on the table. Her arm was still aching badly and she rested it, sling too, on the table top carefully.

Guiltily she found herself thinking more and more about Paul. Inevitably she would always think of Craig in times of trouble, but now, she wondered, wouldn't he want her to be happy, to have company? The house felt so empty without him. Stupidly she kept expecting him to walk through the door, but gradually she was learning to accept that he wouldn't, and more and more she wanted to believe that he would encourage her to have another relationship. It couldn't ever match up to what she and Craig had shared, but perhaps she could be happy with Paul. He seemed to like her. He was good-looking, smart, reliable, friendly...anyone with any sense would wonder why she was hesitating.

Ok, she decided, in two days she had agreed to meet him, away from the Samba School. She would make a decision then, but not before, casual friends or something a little more intimate? If she opted to give it a go she would have to warn him to take it steady...Something about his whole easy-going personality told her that wouldn't be a problem.

When the doorbell chimed Rebecca jumped. Day-dreaming was a bad sign, she thought, Paul would have to wait. The Inspector's outline, hat in place, was clearly visible through the glass of the door. A mixture of fear, adrenalin and excitement buzzed through her fragile frame as she let him in.

'Good day Mrs Houseman, are you feeling any better?' he enquired, grinning briefly as he removed his hat and, at her invitation, sat on the settee in the lounge.

'A little, thank you,' she said softly. The Sergeant stood by the lounge doorway as she took a seat in the armchair and waited for the Inspector to begin. He coughed slightly, looked at her and surveyed the room briefly. Rebecca held her breath. He was stalling for time. This wasn't going to be nice then, whatever news he had to share with her.

'You were Miss Grey before you married your husband, is that right?' Inspector Allen waited for her to confirm what he already knew. 'Your parents were Mr and Mrs Grey but they adopted you Rebecca,' he said, keeping his voice low and sympathetic. 'I'm sorry but it's true.'

The Inspector watched the colour drain from Rebecca Houseman's face, her eyes widen and her hands fidget. He leant forward on the edge of her new settee, his forest green mackintosh creasing beneath his lanky frame, and his hat crushing by his side. Rebecca stared at him. He was bonkers. This was madness.

'Your parents couldn't have children,' the Inspector continued. 'So they adopted your sister Charlotte, you, and a couple of years later they took on your baby brother Charles too. I'm sorry it had to be me to tell you this. I think your husband probably knew, I'm guessing,' he hesitated, narrowed his moustache with his fingertips, wondering if he should go on. Anything he couldn't back up with solid proof was always a risk, but he had a hunch. The poor woman had a right to know where she came from. 'Your adoptive parents probably told him the truth a long time ago.'

'No, they didn't,' she objected; her words fading as she shook her head, the dizziness threatening to engulf her. She twisted her wedding ring unconsciously around her finger, her thumbs twiddling nervously. 'They can't have…He must have meant something else,' she insisted, tears beginning to caress her face softly. 'They were my mum and dad; they can't have adopted me…'

'Yes, I'm afraid they did. I have the adoption papers,' the Inspector spoke softly, nodding at Sergeant Wellington to produce the folder. Rebecca took it, fingered it lightly and cast it aside on the coffee table.

'Later,' she mumbled, reaching for a tissue from the box on the table and drying her tears. A burst of sun sliced the room in two for a moment before shifting behind a cloud. Rebecca closed her eyes and sighed deeply. This wasn't happening; it couldn't be happening…

'The man who was trying to knife you in your car was your natural brother,' Inspector Allen said quietly. Rebecca felt her fingers lightly touch her bandaged neck as he spoke. 'Your father married, quite a while after your natural mother's death. He had a second family and that man was his second son from that marriage. Your parents' were very wealthy Rebecca. He didn't want you to have any of your rightful inheritance because he had gambling debts, large ones, and he needed every penny he could get. So he decided to kill you.'

'This can't be true,' Rebecca wailed, waving her free arm about, the other still neatly wrapped in the sling. 'It can't be… How did he know about me then, the so-called natural brother?' she grimaced, remembering her hurt arm.

Sergeant Wellington stood as tall as his height would permit, by the doorway as if barring her from fleeing from the truth. The Inspector glanced at him quickly. This wasn't a pleasant task. He had contemplated making Wells tell the poor woman the truth but somehow it didn't feel fair to make him do something he wasn't prepared to do himself.

'I'm afraid it is true,' Inspector Allen said, his voice almost a whisper. 'Your father always intended to find you; we have evidence from his house, and his Will. In it he made provisions for you to be found and to receive your rightful share of his wealth.' Inspector Allen nodded at the folder on the coffee table. 'It's all in there, when you're ready to look at it.'

'So you're saying they gave me up?' her voice pleading him to deny it, her heart beating faster, struggling to swallow a lump of hurt. This tall, rather strange, police Inspector was sitting on her settee, telling her that her entire childhood was a lie, a falsehood, a…It couldn't be true. Rebecca closed her eyes and sighed. So, why then did she believe him?

'No, they didn't, not voluntarily,' Inspector Allen crafted a small smile. 'You were snatched from the hospital Mrs Houseman, when you were just a couple of hours old. Nobody knew who had taken you. They did try to find you but well, things were different then. Your mother searched for you for the rest of her life.'

Rebecca gave up trying to wipe her tears away; they were falling faster than the tissues could contain them.

'It's in the file,' the Inspector said. 'We also found a note at your father's house, from the woman who took you, and a picture of you as a girl. The woman was ill, a serial baby snatcher according to her note. She invited your mother to a hotel suite, to confess, to offer help in retrieving you, I think; at least that's how it reads. She must have felt guilty at taking you. You see, it was your dreams that put me onto it all in the first place…'

'My dreams…?' Rebecca cut in. She had never felt as lost or confused before. She wanted Craig to hold her. She didn't want to hear any of this but she was hooked, something in her had to know, especially now. How could it be that Craig knew all this and she didn't?

'Yes, your friend kept saying you were dreaming about a woman and child in a park. It's in the letter, from the woman who took you, telling your mother she was probably right, that you were the child in the park and the woman you remember talking to you, she was your mother.' Inspector Allen paused; tried to smile at her, to offer some small token of compassion. 'Seems after all her searching she finally found you.'

'What happened to them?' Rebecca asked, 'are they…?'

'Yes,' Inspector Allen nodded gravely. 'I'm sorry. Your mother died shortly after she found you. She was very young, I'm sorry.'

Rebecca collapsed, her wall of tears flooding into the tissues. Inspector Allen wanted to console her but he fidgeted awkwardly, then gradually he moved over to perch on the edge of her armchair, patting her shoulders gently.

'And my Dad?' she sobbed.

'He lived a long life,' the Inspector whispered into Rebecca's hair. 'He died recently. It was probably his death on the news that started you dreaming in the first place.'

'Who was he?' she shot up, her glance directed at the Inspector at close range. 'Craig tried to…' she sobbed, 'tried to say something about the news.'

'Michael Sutton,' he said, nodding again at the file. 'You'll find it all in the folder. 'Your mother was Joyce Capelli.'

'You mean the dance champions…?' Rebecca watched the confirmation in the Inspectors face as he nodded in silence. No, surely not…they were world famous, they couldn't possibly be…

'We've checked with a specialist,' the Inspector said, relocating back to the settee now that Rebecca's tears were under control. 'Apparently hearing anything that you remember from childhood, after the age of 4, is retrievable. Whatever you spoke to your mother about in that park will be the basis of your dreams. Probably all triggered by hearing your father's death on the news, according to our specialist anyway. She'll be happy to talk to you about it,' the Inspector smiled, pulling his chewed pencil from his pocket. The worst of the news was over with now. He felt relieved, gnawed on the pencil harshly. 'If you want to, her details are in the folder too. I've had it all copied for you, so you can keep that,' he pointed to the buff folder on the coffee table. She eyed it sceptically; a pile of secrets burning holes in her past.

'Oh my God,' Rebecca whispered. 'And Craig knew about this,' she spoke more to herself, 'do you know who killed him?' she asked suddenly, her eyes more alert with anticipation. The Inspector nodded glumly. 'Are you going to tell me?' she asked.

'Yes of course. I'll come to that in a moment,' the Inspector said quietly, and waited whilst Rebecca dabbed her eyes with a handkerchief. She tried to smile at him.

'I guess I should say thank you Inspector,' she half smiled. 'Somebody has finally told me the truth.'

'I wish it were somebody else Mrs Houseman, believe me,' Inspector Allen smiled, bit down on his pencil and slotted it back into his pocket. 'There is more to tell you but if you've had enough for one day…'

'No,' Rebecca tried to smile, 'tell me now. I can't do this twice, better to have the worst of it now.' She dabbed her eyes with a fresh tissue and curled a cushion under her arm. 'Besides, I want to know why my Craig…'

'Ok, if you're sure,' the Inspector smiled. 'You're a brave woman Mrs Houseman. This part won't be so bad, I hope.' He nodded at Sergeant Wellington who shuffled across the room and took up the other armchair. 'So, to more recent events,' the Inspector continued. 'Your natural brother, Nicholas Sutton, he was the man who tried to attack you. He was the same man who was behind the attempts on your life throughout, as I said; he wanted the entire estate for himself. The only way to get your share of the inheritance was to have you put out the way.'

Rebecca sighed, flicked her eyelashes and felt guilty for being glad her natural brother was dead. It would explain why she felt there was something familiar about him though, even the look of her Samuel in the eyes of her father on the news broadcast made sense now… Maybe this was the worst part after all; that her own flesh and blood wanted her dead; perhaps the Inspector had it backwards.

'It was Nicholas Sutton who killed your husband Madam. Quite simply Craig Houseman knew too much and Nicholas couldn't afford for him to tell you about it. He was watching you too. I don't think you actually saw him but your daughter Katherine did, she identified the body for me.' Inspector Allen watched Rebecca's face transform into a further expression of shock.

'What? When?' Rebecca exclaimed.

'After he was knocked down by the car, he died. Your friend Jean, again,' the Inspector half smiled, 'she and your daughter had a conversation at the hospital after the little stunt with the fatal gum seal on the envelope. They spoke about your dreams, the man Katherine suspected, one thing led to another...' his voice followed his fingers into an invisible point across the room. 'Jean told me about the man Katherine had mentioned and it all seemed to slot into place. He was watching her when she took her son for his injections at the doctor's, and the same man she saw spying on you at your grandson's football match. He was trying to figure out what you did, where you went, who your family were, how best to get to you.' Inspector Allen waited whilst she digested the news. 'Your daughter was very helpful.'

'But he can't have done all this on his own?' she objected. 'Or did he? You said you were charging two men with attempted...' she found the word lodge in her throat.

'Yes Madam, John Francis, he was the man I told you about behind the stolen cars to order, with the duplicate keys cut by the mechanic. Francis owns a club; it's a dodgy club with an illegal casino hidden behind a wall.' Rebecca stared at him as if he were crazy. It was like something from a spoof film. 'Not anymore though,' Inspector Allen laughed. 'We've burst it open now. Your natural brother, Nicholas Sutton, I'm afraid he was rather fond of the gambling and he owed Francis big time. When his father, I mean, your father Michael Sutton, died, he wanted every scrap of the inheritance to pay back Francis. He's a nasty creature this Francis,' the Inspector grinned quickly. 'Sutton went to him, said he needed help in getting rid of you so he could claim the full inheritance, to pay Francis back. Now Francis, he had some dirt on another club member too, Bateman, calls himself Fisher these days.'

'So these are the men you've arrested?' she enquired, her tears dried, her mascara streaking her face. Inspector Allen smiled at the woman before him. There were very few women he actually respected, admired even, brave, resourceful, intelligent, capable...Admiring the physical woman was quite different from having genuine respect for the real one beneath.

She wasn't unattractive neither, had taken good care of herself…He shook himself out of his trance, he must be getting old, he thought.

'Yes,' he said quickly, jolting back into familiar territory, 'Francis was forcing Bateman to help him, or he'd reveal his criminal history. Nasty business. Jail sentence for explosives.'

'Explosives? So he was…' Rebecca rearranged the cushion beneath her arm and stared in bewilderment at the police Inspector.

'Yes, Bateman sent the explosive parcel, very clever device, no risk until you opened the seal on the parcel itself. It was Francis who bribed the mechanic to rig the brakes on your car but of course we knew that already. I've charged him with accepting bribery and intent to harm. As well as the attempted murder of your good self, Francis is also going down for the car thefts ring. That was not directly related to you of course, it was a side-line he'd had going for quite some time. Just a handy bonus we happened to stumble upon,' Inspector Allen grinned happily, this was his moment, his game and he was winning.

'They'll be safely behind bars for a long time,' Sergeant Wellington added. Rebecca cast him a smile, ashamed to admit she had forgotten he was there, the silent faithful one in the background.

'At Francis' instruction it was Bateman who sent you that satisfaction survey, supposedly from the insurance company. Big mistake there, very obvious it wasn't from the insurance company, they denied sending it, of course. By this time Sutton and, Francis too, greedy for his pay-out, were getting desperate. The poison in the gum seal on the envelope was a fatal dose. You were very lucky.'

'I know Inspector, I have my good friend to thank for that,' Rebecca sighed.

'For more than you know actually,' the Inspector said quietly. Rebecca looked at him strangely. 'Anyway,' he continued, his voice brash and back to full flow. 'I have a little confession to make,' he grinned sheepishly. 'Whilst you were in the hospital I intercepted your post. I'm sorry but it was necessary for your safety. All safe correspondence was duly put through your letterbox. The only incriminating piece was this,' he produced a CD from the deep pockets of his new green coat.

Rebecca watched him remove the disc from the pocket. Craig used to keep the fishing bait in there; she half smiled at the memory.

'What is it?' she asked.

'A hypnotherapy CD; did you order one?' he enquired, predicting her answer.

'No, I didn't,' she said, eyeing the CD the Inspector was handing to her. He looked smug, pleased at his intuition. Hunches were wonderful things, when they turned out to be accurate; sadly that wasn't always the case.

'It's been tampered with I'm afraid, supposed to help you into a deep sleep, but this one's been altered, to make you take an overdose of pills whilst you're asleep.'

'What?' Rebecca fingered the disc tentatively as if it were layered with spikes.

'Yes I'm afraid so, good night's sleep, guaranteed never to wake up.' Inspector Allen held out his hand and she gave it back to him with disgust. 'It's evidence I'm afraid, I've got to hang onto it.'

'Oh, I don't want it Inspector, take it away,' she said, 'believe me.' Rebecca inhaled deeply. 'What about the car that almost hit me?'

'That was Sutton himself Mrs Houseman, Francis was getting edgy; none of their little stunts had worked. It was all very clumsily done; a real professional assassin would have handled it all very differently. The pay-out from your late father's estate was imminent you see, and his instructions to start searching for you were about to commence. Sutton was running out of time. He had to act quickly. I'm not even sure if Francis or Bateman knew about Sutton's own attempts, the car, and the knife attack of course.'

Rebecca shuddered, closed her eyes and took in a deep breath. Thank goodness it was all over. Inspector Allen watched her cautiously, waited patiently whilst she absorbed the latest news.

'Just how big were his debts Inspector, if he was prepared to kill for them?' she asked, her voice composed again, her eyes inquisitive, burning with a concoction of relief, anger and grief.

'Let's just say you're going to be a very wealthy woman Mrs Houseman. I do have a bit of good news for you.' Inspector Allen watched the sun deflect off her hair, a creamy shade of light making her look radiant; despite the swollen arm and bandage that was still protecting her neck. 'Before I tell you that, you must remember that your natural mother and father didn't want to lose you. Your mother spent her entire life looking for you.' Rebecca tried to smile.

'Thank you Inspector, I'm still grappling with the fact that they were who you claim.' Rebecca glanced at the untouched file on her coffee table. When she was alone she would devour the details, but right now she didn't want to see it in stark black and white. Just hearing it was hard enough.

'So, the good news then...' Inspector Allen tried to smile brightly. 'You'll like this.'

'Really? Thank heavens,' she smiled now, a warm genuine smile that lit up her eyes, the colour of dark chocolate.

'You have another brother, the elder son from your father's marriage. Henry Sutton. I'm pleased to tell you he's a model citizen, unlike his younger brother Nicholas. It was far too risky for Nicholas to attempt anything with Henry so he was always safe. I'm going to see him later, if you want, I can ask his permission to give you his details. Perhaps you two can meet, at long last.'

'Yes, thank you, that would be nice,' Rebecca smiled, cut short with a sudden sinking feeling. 'Charlotte and Charles, my...' she paused, 'they'll always be my sister and brother, even if we're not blood relations.' The Inspector looked at her, predicting her question.

'They're in Australia aren't they?' Rebecca nodded. 'They don't know the truth, no, but I can tell them if you prefer?' offered Inspector Allen, his respect for Rebecca persuading him to go beyond the call of duty, even by his overzealous standards.

'No, but thank you; I think I'd better do it. I don't suppose you know who their natural parents were do you?' she asked, 'If they weren't the same as mine?'

'I'm afraid not Mrs Houseman,' the Inspector grinned. 'But they were definitely from different backgrounds to yours. Joyce and Michael only had you. The adoption agency details are in the file though, they'll be able to find out where Charlotte and Charles Grey came from originally.'

'Thank you Inspector,' Rebecca said softly. 'Why did he have to take my Craig though, Inspector?' she whispered, tasting the bitterness of her own tears. It wasn't fair.

'He was desperate.' Inspector Allen offered a sorrowful half smile and rose to leave. 'I'm sorry Mrs Housman, I really am.'

The pub was busy. The two men stood companionably at the bar whilst the barmaid pulled two pints of the establishment's finest, Broadside. Henry handed the money over to the barmaid, waving aside Paul's hand with confident charm.

'Your round next,' he smiled, leading the way towards a table on the far side of the bar. They settled comfortably into the dark wooden furniture. 'Thanks for coming mate,' Henry said, sipping his beer.

'No worries,' Paul smiled, 'you sounded kind of stressed on the phone though, what's up? Is it Nic again?'

'Yeah, 'fraid so. There's no helping him this time though,' Henry said.

'Well, we can try mate, what's the damage?' Paul enquired as a rowdy group trundled through the doors. Henry waited until they were out of earshot at the bar. Despite it being mid-week the place was heaving.

'He's dead,' Henry said. Paul's glass slipped the last inch from his grasp to the table, beer splashing over the sides like a mini tidal wave. 'See, no helping him now,' Henry sighed.

'Oh God mate, I'm sorry,' Paul sipped his beer, unsure what else to say. Nicholas was a drain on Henry in every sense, financially, emotionally, a constant source of tension and stress. Paul couldn't honestly say he was truly upset that Nicholas Sutton was dead.

'It's all right, he had it coming to him,' Henry reasoned. 'I'm glad father didn't live to witness this. He was always so disappointed, I think that was the worst part really, father wanted him to do so well and he just threw it all away.' Henry let out a sigh, sipped his beer as if it would comfort him. 'And mum, God bless her, she was blind to Nic's faults all along. Thank goodness neither of them lived to see his sticky end.'

'Yeah but; even so...' Paul stammered.

'You wait until I tell you mate, it's a long story.' Henry rested his glass down and looked at his friend. Paul was going to be his rock at this time and he knew he shouldn't lean on him too heavily but right now he felt he needed to talk about it, just to tell someone else, finally. To admit he had a half-sister.

'I've got all night mate, if you want to talk about it that is?' Paul listened as Henry told him about the police Inspector's visit that afternoon, the messy end his brother had met under the cars outside the police station, his grisly attempts to kill the poor innocent woman who was their half-sister, how she was now suffering from some pretty nasty injuries. 'Oh my God mate, I never knew your dad had another child, before you two I mean.'

'Neither did we,' Henry admitted, 'until last year. Dad was getting pretty ill; the doctors said they couldn't do much more for him; it was just a matter of time. I guess he wanted us to know, before....'

'So, did your mum know?' Paul lowered his voice, conscious that Henry may not have even considered that possibility yet. Henry nodded.

'Yeah, apparently she knew all along, even assisted dad in trying to trace her at one point,' Henry half smiled, 'poor dad though, they never found her. He left instructions and money to fund another search for her. I think he really missed mum's help, you know, after she died.'

'Do you know who she is?' Paul asked, sipping his beer, his curiosity aroused.

'No, not exactly, they can't tell me; data protection or some rubbish like that. I've given the police permission to give my details to her though. I'm hoping she'll ring. It would be nice to meet her, see if we've got anything in common,' Henry managed a light laugh. 'What with both mum and dad gone now, and Nic,' Henry sipped his beer to stop himself from sighing.

'What did you say her injuries were?' Paul put his glass down with slight force.

'Poor woman has a bandage around her neck but thank God it's just a flesh wound. Nothing else really, bit bruised so they've put her arm in a sling but it's not broken or anything...' Henry's words faltered. Paul was staring at him as if he were crackers. 'What?'

'I think I know her,' Paul whispered. 'She's lovely...' Could it possibly be her, his Rebecca? Surely not...it couldn't really be that small a world that he had fallen for his best friend's half-sister, could it?

SPOTLIGHT EXPRESS – THE INDUSTRY'S CHOICE
1st October 1964
CAPELLI DANCES INTO DEATH

The famous female part of the Sutton and Capelli world titled dance champions has died after a fatal fall. The tragedy occurred late last month at her home in Suffolk. Her partner, Michael Sutton, is said to be devastated and understandably does not wish to comment on the future of his dancing career.

A private funeral service was conducted yesterday close to the family home, and the body laid to rest, the headstone reading: *Joyce Capelli, 1st May 1942 – 26th September1964; the brightest flower dancing in the breeze, cut down in her prime.*

The family requests that no flowers should be sent but all donations greatly appreciated, to the Suffolk Adoption Agency, situated in Atwood; further details by request to the editor.

A spokesman for the family reports that the death of Joyce Capelli was an accident. The family are deeply shocked and plans for the future are, as yet, uncertain. It is unclear where Miss Capelli had been the evening of her death, but her fall was at her home and is not being treated as suspicious.

The scandalous columns in the newspapers that plagued her over a secret child have now been officially put to rest at the family's request. '*Spotlight Express* wishes to offer its apologies for any distress such a story may have caused Miss Capelli or her family in the past, and assures readers that the story has now been dropped indefinitely.'

'It is simply awful, so very sad,' Michael Sutton's father Timothy says, 'she was so bright, so alive, such a lovely girl. We will miss her terribly, Michael especially so.'

During her short career Joyce Capelli, with Michael Sutton, was the brightest star in the dancing profession. Having achieved top medal status in every dance they were the reigning regional champions year after year, undertook performances by request to delight private parties, and were sincerely loved by all in the industry. Only the day before the tragedy they had been crowned the winners at the Star Championship contest in London. The world has truly lost one of its brightest and most talented dancers.

JULY 1970

SPOTLIGHT EXPRESS – THE INDUSTRY'S CHOICE 15th July 1970
SUTTON TO QUIT DANCING

The famous dancer Michael Sutton announces today his intention to quit professional dancing in favour of marriage to his fiancé, Patricia Ashley, and their plans to raise a family immediately.

Sutton, most famous for early success with Joyce Capelli, who died following a fatal fall at her home in 1964, has since partnered a string of female dancers but never equalled his early success and fame.

'It is time to retire,' Sutton claims, 'I have been fortunate enough to find Patricia and we wish now for an ordinary life, away from the cameras and lights,' he chuckles, 'and the press!'

It was rumoured that Sutton's first and only true love was Joyce Capelli herself and he admits the pair were lovers until her untimely death. Sutton's mother says 'Michael was devastated at losing Joyce. His heart simply wasn't in dancing after that dreadful day. We are so pleased he has found happiness again with Patricia and completely understand his decision to quit dancing professionally.' When asked if he had made a decision about a new career Marie Sutton said, 'I think he has something in mind, but he has forbidden me to tell you.'

One thing is clear though; it would appear that his love for Miss Ashley will rob the world of another talented dancer.

The private ceremony is arranged for next month, and the newlyweds plan to honeymoon in the Caribbean.

CHAPTER NINETEEN – MODERN DAY; JULY

Rebecca had never seen Jean so quiet, not even after the police interview, her fears when she had rushed her to the hospital, her own divorce, her mother's death…whatever the problem was, it was deeply emotional for Jean.

Rebecca stirred the teapot with a spoon and poured out two cups.

'I can't wait for our holiday,' she enthused. 'After everything that's been going on lately I really want to get away. You were right; it'll do us both the power of good.'

'That's just it though dear,' Jean moaned. 'I'm no longer sure you'll want to go with me,' she eyed the teacup Rebecca put in front of her. 'Not when I tell you that…Oh God Becca love, I didn't know, I swear I didn't know.' Hot tears began to spill down Jean's face like a torrent.

'Whatever's wrong?' Rebecca patted her friend on the shoulder. 'It can't be that bad…'

'Oh it is Becca dear, it's dreadful!' wailed Jean hysterically.

'Now come on, we've been friends forever, you can tell me anything. You know that.' Rebecca watched Jean try to compose herself, the shade of the kitchen spreading over the table. She couldn't take too much more bad news, prayed it wasn't as bad as Jean was making out.

Jean needed a nice man, Rebecca decided, one who could console her, treat her little outbursts with the right delicate balance of compassion and understanding, equalled with a measure of strength to quell the hysteria, before it erupted.

'It's just that the Police were round again today,' Jean sobbed into her cup, gripping it between her hands as if it were a crystal ball. 'They came to tell me…' she cried bitterly into her cup.

'Oh Jean, come on, it'll be all right,' Rebecca soothed.

'They came to tell me that…' she wiped a tear aside harshly, 'that it was my mother who…' more sobs threatened to erupt.

'Whatever it is Jean, we'll still be good friends,' Rebecca encouraged. 'It can't be all that bad.'

'That my mother was the one who stole you from the hospital,' Jean wailed; her screeches piercing as she flopped down on the table, her bouncy platinum blonde hair splayed out like a fan.

Rebecca held her breath. Of course, Duchess Hotel, it was in the file the Inspector had given her. It was where her mother had gone to meet the woman who had taken her… The hotel had belonged to Jean's mother forever. She had only sold it to pay for nursing care a few short years before she died. That would explain her mother taking Jean to grow up in Cumbria, far away from her baby-snatching turf… It all fitted, that must have been what the Inspector had wanted to quiz Jean about. It was what he meant the other day, his odd comment about her having more to thank Jean for… Rebecca wondered fleetingly if the Inspector would have linked it up if Jean hadn't reverted to her maiden name of Duchess after her divorce.

'I didn't know Becca love; I swear I didn't know you were one of them,' Jean was crying, thumping her fists in anguish on the table.

'Oh Jean dear,' Rebecca rose, wrapped her free arm around her friend's shoulders. 'It's ok, it was all long ago.'

'You forgive me?' sobbed Jean into Rebecca's cotton sleeve.

'Of course dear, it wasn't your fault, any of it,' Rebecca soothed. 'Come on now. Let's have a cup of tea. You said yourself your poor mother was just desperate to have a child. Come on now,' she insisted charitably. Whatever she felt now she would bottle it up, deal with it later, when Jean had gone. It wasn't Jean's fault.

'You'll still go on holiday with me?' Jean cried, drying her tears and wiping her mascara across her face.

'Of course dear,' Rebecca smiled as brightly as she could, 'of course I will. I'm looking forward to it,' she insisted.

'You're such a wonderful friend,' Jean tried to smile, sipping her tea with slight composure now.

'I'm a wonderful friend,' Rebecca laughed, 'that's backwards, you saved my life, now shall we call it quits?' she beamed. Jean managed to smile brighter and the two women opened the holiday brochures, making great progress with the packing list.

Rebecca flicked off the bedside light. Since the Inspector's revelation she had slept every night, lovely dreamless sleep, despite her bruised arm. Everything was finally resolved, even George's team were through to the final in their football league. His little voice had proudly informed her over the phone line that evening that they were going to win.

According to Neil, Paul's help had been invaluable and the new business was up and running with the newly recruited receptionist proving to be an asset. He had opted for experience over qualifications, and his gamble was paying off.

Little Craig's daddy was going to make a success of the business, which would mean a lavish wedding to enjoy later in the summer. Samuel had been honoured when Katherine had asked him to give her away at the ceremony. The family were coping much better than she had expected without Craig, missing him but making him proud too, just getting on with life and sticking together. She had a lot to be thankful for, even after the secrets of her ancestry were laid bare.

Rebecca smiled, curled down beneath the covers a little further. Life was improving every day. Inspector Allen had put her in contact with the solicitor handling Michael Sutton's last Will and Testament. The inheritance would be paid out to her, as his rightful heir, equally with his other remaining son, Henry Sutton. He had seemed a nice man when she had met him briefly at the solicitor's office. They had agreed to keep in touch. After all, he could tell her about her father. With a tinge of sadness she knew she would never really know him, not having met, but Henry could at least give her some of the background. He could even tell her the warm sentiments Michael Sutton had apparently told him about Joyce Capelli, her mother, the woman who had died trying to find her.

Rebecca felt tired; her entire world had been turned upside down around her, and twisted up again in a new formation. Instead of feeling disorientated she somehow felt quite stable, more solid than before, even without Craig to support her.

The town centre Samba performance was in three weeks. With any luck she would be fit and well by then. Surprising herself she found she was actually looking forward to it. The background, the history, it was all quite fascinating. It was a new lease of life and she loved it, the movements, the excitement of the drums made the entire dance a new experience.

If anything was going to keep her awake tonight then it would be nerves; tomorrow she would meet up with Paul. That last unanswered question; was she ready for a new relationship, or not?

A blanket of black mourners lined the church path as the coffin was lowered into the ground. Henry Sutton stood by the pallbearers, his eyes downcast and his face slightly pale. Rebecca watched him uncomfortably, knowing full well he hadn't attached any blame on her for her brother's death. It was an accident, a tragic accident, brought on by Nicholas himself, fuelled by his greed, his uncontrollable lust for gambling and his desperate need to re-pay John Francis, to avoid whatever terrible punishment Francis would inevitably inflict on him.

Rebecca tried hard not to look at the coffin with disdain. It housed the man who had murdered her husband, who had inflicted cold fear into her very soul, and frightened her beyond description. Vowing to push it from her mind she glanced up into the sky, praying for faith, hope, direction, anything that would ease some of the hatred she felt for the dead man.

The greying sky was threatening more rain, and she shivered, remembering the day Nicholas had tried to run her down. As the vicar concluded his reading the mourners started to dwindle. Rebecca hesitated, should she say something to Henry? Wouldn't it be decent to say a few words? Maybe now wasn't the time…she glanced again, yes, she wasn't mistaken. It was Paul, standing next to Henry.

'Rebecca,' Henry saw her, came to her side. She choked on her words as Paul joined them. 'Thank you for coming,' Henry smiled, kissed her on the cheek. 'Paul tells me you've met already.'

'Hi,' Paul smiled at her. She attempted to smile, nod and breathe steadily. How, why…?

'It's a small world isn't it?' Henry chuckled. 'You'll come back to the house won't you? Please,' he took her hands in his. 'Bring your friend,' he smiled over her shoulder at Jean who had come to collect her. 'She looks like a bubbly character,' Henry observed.

'Oh yes,' Rebecca laughed, more at ease, 'she is, definitely.'

'Hello,' Jean sang, reaching Rebecca's side, 'I'm parked on the yellows dear, are they strict around here?' her hair bouncing liberally over her bright yellow blouse. Rebecca smiled. It was highly unlikely that Jean would even consider dulling down her dress colour, even to pick her up from a funeral. 'Oh yes, that reminds me, we must sort out a taxi to take us to the airport next week Becca dear…'

'No, I don't think they're too strict when it's a funeral,' Henry answered her question, extending his hand. 'Hi, I'm Henry Sutton. And err, here's a thought, why don't I take you both to the airport? Paul can pick you up,' he smiled at the ladies brightly, pressing Jean's hand in his. Paul nodded at Henry's suggestion, his eyes locking into Rebecca's, making her feel giddy. 'But right now, you can follow me, back to the house. Come on,' Henry smiled briefly at Rebecca, took Jean's arm and happily began to lead her away towards the cars.

'Shall we?' Paul offered his arm to Rebecca. The sling had been abandoned, her neck bandages gone too, but she still felt slightly protective. 'Henry's a nice chap,' Paul smiled, 'I've known him ages. Your friend could do a lot worse,' he laughed.

'They've only just met,' Rebecca exclaimed with a light giggle as they followed Henry and Jean across the bumpy grass towards the road.

'Yeah, I know,' Paul grinned, 'but it's the first time I've ever seen Henry voluntarily pair off with any woman. Between you and me,' he lowered his head towards hers, his smile making her feel warmer inside, 'I reckon his brother's death will be a new beginning for him. He's sort of,' he paused, 'freer now, less restrained.'

'Good for him,' Rebecca smiled. 'We had better weather for the performance, didn't we? You were excellent by the way,' she tapped his arm softly. The town's samba performance had been a huge success.

'Thanks, gee, so were you. I'd never have known you were quite new to it, Lexia is right, you are a natural,' Paul smiled at her hand on his arm.

'Well I have inherited natural ability,' she giggled. Her body had ached a little afterwards, but she knew she was now a firm member of Lexia's little group. The thrill of the crowd's applause was the best thing to have happened since Craig's death. Until now, maybe…

'Oh yes, of course, I'd forgotten that,' Paul teased. They were approaching the road. Rebecca smiled at the sight of Henry, clearly quite spellbound by Jean, chatting happily by the cars.

'I've err, made a decision,' she whispered. Paul kept his gaze steady, ahead, his body freezing slightly. 'It'll have to be slow though,' she sensed him stiffen, 'to begin with. I'm still grieving you understand, but…'

Paul stopped, held her before him, his arms gently on her shoulders, 'I'm positive Craig would have wanted me to move on with my life,' she smiled, her eyes sparkling with hope. 'So ok, but…'

Paul drew her closer to him, wrapped her into his chest. Suddenly it didn't feel so daunting, breathing in his musky aftershave, his arms holding her safely, his warmth encapsulating her against the chilly breeze.

'I'll be on my best behaviour then,' he whispered into her hair with a smile, the alluring scent of her coconut conditioner making him tingle with excitement. 'At least to begin with…'

MIЯRORS
DANCE

Latin American - Salsa - Ballroom - Argentine Tango
Wedding Choreography - Freestyle - Street Dance - Rock 'n' Roll

MIRRORS DANCE offers professional training for beginners
through to professional examinations, offering weekly
classes and private lessons

"We're devoted to making your dancing experience the best
ever. Whatever your schedule or your personal dancing
goals, dance a little or dance a lot, this is the place to have
the most fun doing it!"
- Founder, Trudina Youngs, Fellow Hons IDTA

The fun starts with your very first lesson... start dancing!

* Warning - Dancing is highly addictive + dangerously good
for your social life.

www.mirrorsdance.com

Also by the same author:

Distant Shadows

One shot in the dark and everything changes.

When Richard Burkett shoots his victim in 1935, and gets away with it, he doesn't expect to be caught over seventy years later.

Zoe Peterson is shocked to find two police detectives – one being the captivating DC James Clark – interviewing her grandparents about an unsolved murder.

Simultaneously Cathy and Stephen endure emotional turmoil in 1957. The revelation of her father's identity frightens Cathy.

Zoe is concerned about her father and her ex won't accept her ditching him; until James plants his size twelve's into her life. Will finding the dying criminal and earning her grandparents' gratitude be enough to win her heart?

In 1957 the shadows are stalking Cathy, until breaking point catapults her into Stephen's arms and the awful secret is revealed.

A chance comment reminds James that the identity of the victim is more important than that of the murderer...